Fear Death by Water

A HARRY BROCK MYSTERY

Fear Death by Water

Kinley Roby

FIVE STAR
A part of Gale, Cengage Learning

GALE
CENGAGE Learning

Detroit • New York • San Francisco • New Haven, Conn • Waterville, Maine • London

Set in 11 pt. Plantin.

Printed on permanent paper.

LIBRARY OF CONGRESS CATALOGING-IN-PUBLICATION DATA

Roby, Kinley E.
Fear death by water : a Harry Brock mystery / Kinley Roby. —
1st ed.
p. cm.
ISBN-13: 978-1-59414-644-2 (alk. paper)
ISBN-10: 1-59414-644-6 (alk. paper)
1. Brock, Harry (Fictitious character)—Fiction. 2. Private investigators—Florida—Fiction. 3. Gulf Coast (Fla.)—Fiction.
I. Title.
PS3618.O3385F43 2008
813'.6—dc22 2008027477

Published in 2008 in conjunction with Tekno Books and Ed Gorman.

Printed in the United States of America
2 3 4 5 6 7 12 11 10 09 08

Fear Death by Water

1

Usually, somebody in the village was watching the young trash, but it was like trying to keep track of weasels in a woodpile. They were here, they were there, and then they were gone.

On this particular May morning Bobby Scrubbs and Fannon Jones, two skinny Hook kids with sun-bleached hair and ragged, black shorts hanging off their butts, sneaked off unnoticed to Old Beetle's Boat Dock where they lifted a skiff while Beetle was snoring in his hammock and were now poling up the north shore of the Okalatchee River as fast as they could, hoping to make it into the mangroves before somebody nailed them.

On the bottom of the skiff lay an old single shot twelve-gauge shotgun and a ten-foot bamboo pole with a running noose of clothesline rope tied to the pole's thin end. Stowed in their pockets were half a dozen shotgun shells, loaded with buckshot. They were supposed to be in school and not on the river at all, but with the coming of spring the adventurers had cast off with their winter clothes the guidance of *should* and *shouldn't.*

As Southwest Florida rivers go, the Okalatchee wasn't big or particularly dangerous. But it was a hundred and fifty yards wide at Old Beetle's dock and a mile inland from a shallow Avola Bay, which quickly widened into the Gulf. Twice a day a strong tide surged east around the point of the Hook, creating a dangerous chop when a southwest wind was pushing it. It was an unusual year when the river didn't drown somebody from the Hook. It's only fair to say, however, that most of the victims died after falling out of a boat while under the influence.

Even so, the river was not the best place for children. It was home to some big alligators and in recent years also a few reticulated pythons that had gotten large from eating things. A year ago, one measuring twenty feet had been shot near the river. More recently, a crabber coming in from the bay saw what he thought was an even bigger one tangling with a fourteen foot gator not more than half a mile from the Hook marina. According to the man's wife, he hadn't slept well since.

It was a burning desire to capture or kill one of the big snakes that had the boys poling like demons toward the mangrove swamp. Before starting on their escapade, they had spit on their hands and vowed to lasso or shoot one of those suckers. When they slid into the green shadows of the trees without being caught, they gave a victory yell. Then, noticing for the first time the crowding in of the dark trees, the stillness of the black water, and the heavy silence that had swallowed their shouts, their courage slipped a little.

Bobby recovered first. "Let's find us a snake," he said with more enthusiasm than he felt. He dropped his pole beside the shotgun and ran to the front of the skiff. "You pole and I'll keep us off the roots," he said.

Fannon broke free from whatever had him standing like a post. "Here we come," he said and shoved his pole into the muck.

Wild as they were, this was the first time they had ever poled a boat into a mangrove swamp, and the deeper they went into it, the thicker the trees grew, the darker it got, and the more the arching roots of the red mangroves looked like the legs of giant spiders getting ready to run at them.

"This ain't the best place I was ever in," Fannon said, more to break the silence than anything else.

"Just keep poling," Bobby answered, not liking how he was feeling.

He had stumbled on the unhappy thought that under this tangle of low branches and dense leaves, a python might now be hunting them instead of the other way round. As he struggled to force the bow through a narrow place in the channel, he wondered what he and Fannon were going to do if twenty feet of snake dropped into the skiff.

Then, pushing aside a branch, Bobby saw it. "Oh, shit," he groaned in a breaking voice.

"What is it?" Fannon asked as if he didn't really want to know.

"Stop poling," Bobby shouted and came scrambling back toward his companion, looking as if he was going to be sick.

"What did you see?" Fannon asked, his knees beginning to shake.

"A woman, and the crabs are on her."

Then he was sick.

2

At the same time Bobby Scrubbs was vomiting over the side of the skiff and Fannon Jones was poling backwards towards open water as fast as the Devil would let him, Harry Brock and Colleen McGraw were sitting on their heels in the shade of a big willow on the east bank of the Okalatchee two miles east of the Hook. They were studying a small and very dead mangrove snapper Colleen had just dipped out of the river with a short handled net. The fish, eight or nine inches long, had a nasty red and white sore on its side and more infection on its ventral fin.

It was hot and both of them were sweating from wading through brush and heavy woods for the past half hour to reach the river.

"That mess is caused by *Pfiesteria piscicida,*" Colleen said, pointing at the sore. "Don't touch it."

She was a slim, brown haired woman, divorced, in her early forties, and although she didn't look it, sitting on her boot heels on the riverbank with her hair tied back in a ponytail, Director of The Pickett Library at Southwest Coast University.

"And, basically, what the Stoneman Douglas Alliance is trying to do, Mr. Brock," she continued, "is to stop this infection from spreading and keep the river from dying. But before we can do those things, we have to convince a lot of people that it's sick. That's what the poster is all about."

She was referring to the poster she had shown Harry before they set out for the river. The poster, which Harry had already seen in various places along the coast during the past month, was a flame-red rectangle with a yellow slash of color running from the top left to the bottom right of the picture, carrying the name OKALATCHEE in blue letters. A black dagger, dripping with blood and labeled POLLUTION, was driven into the center of the yellow slash. On the red portions of the poster were the name THE STONEMAN DOUGLAS ALLIANCE, printed in large white letters, and an urgent appeal for help to save the river.

"Despite what you see in this net, some people don't want to believe the evidence," Colleen continued, "and some people are just downright angry with us for making it public."

"Who's doing the science for you?"

"Joyce Fields. She's a senior ichthyologist with the Florida Fish and Wildlife Conservation Commission. Her work identifying pathogens in the river and giving us leads to their sources is fueling our drive to be heard."

Harry saw her shoulders slump. "What is it?" he asked.

"Nobody's seen her for almost two weeks."

"Hasn't her family filed . . . ?"

"No. I don't think she's got any family, at least not around here. Bob Walker, her chief assistant in the commission, says she does this sort of thing every so often and not to worry."

"Strange behavior for a person in her position."

"That's what I think, and I wish she hadn't run off just when I was beginning to get a grasp of what was causing all this damage. We're more or less frozen in place until she gets back."

Harry looked at the fish again, then into her very green eyes and became intensely aware that, even dressed in a faded blue work shirt, khaki pants, leather boots, and a Red Sox cap that had seen better days, Colleen McGraw was a very attractive woman. Crouched beside her, he could smell her sweat and her perfume. It was a combination that worked for him. With an effort, he wrenched his eyes back to the fish.

She told him some more about how the infection got into the fish, and then she dumped the fish back into the water and stood up. Harry rose with her and scrambled up the bank after her. At the top, she turned to wait for him. Harry reached her a little short of breath. She was not, and he promised himself he would start jogging again. He was deeply tanned, of medium height, solidly built with short, graying hair. He pulled off his hat and mopped his face with his sleeve, gaining time to steady his breathing.

"Hot," he said and started to say he didn't see how hiring a private investigator could help her or the Alliance when something zipped past his head, scattering bits of leaves and twigs. The slam of a high-powered rifle told him what it was. He grabbed Colleen around the waist, and threw her and himself over a fallen cabbage palm and hit the ground face down.

The second bullet banged through a six inch mahogany tree a little to their right with a sound like a wet slap. By then Harry was trying to cover Colleen with his body and wishing he was thinner, while at the same time spitting dirt and pine spills.

"Which one of us is the son-of-a-bitch trying to kill?" she grunted, scraping leaf mold off her face.

As she spoke a three-foot, spiny-tailed iguana shot around the log and flattened itself in a clump of cord grass with a loud hiss, eyeing them suspiciously.

"A fellow traveler," she said, gaining points with Harry.

Before he could reply, the top of the log exploded, spraying them with dirt, bark, ants, and bits of resurrection fern. The heavy WHAM of the rifle arrived a quarter of a second later.

"I don't think it's the iguana," Harry said and rolled onto his side, yanking his 9mm out of its shoulder holster. "Stay here."

He wriggled around the end of the log and crawled on his knees and elbows through a stand of black stopper bushes, trying to see the river. Colleen shimmied up beside him.

"I thought I told you to stay put."

"I don't speak Spanish and the green guy back there is an illegal from Mexico."

Harry laughed. "Stay very flat," he said and squirmed further ahead until he could see the river through the leaves. Colleen stuck with him.

"There he is," she hissed.

A big man, dressed in a black T-shirt and trousers, with a shaved head and wrap-around sunglasses was standing in the steering well of a low end crab boat. He held a scoped rifle in his right hand and was scanning their section of shore through binoculars. The boat was wallowing in the current about fifty yards from them, its engine throttled down, holding it against the thrust of the incoming tide.

"Did you see him when we were on the bank?" Harry asked, disgusted that he hadn't been more observant.

"No, but can we discuss whether or not to shoot him?" Colleen asked in a charged whisper.

"I wasn't planning to."

"Why not?" she asked.

He couldn't tell whether she was surprised or disappointed. "Because he wasn't trying to kill us."

Colleen watched as Harry dug a fifteen-round clip out of his side pack, popped the shorter clip out of his CZ and pushed in its replacement. Spreading his legs for extra stability, he shoved the barrel through the bushes, aimed at the boat's waterline, and began turning the hull into a sieve, the sound of his shooting echoing back and forth across the river like a cannonade.

The man in the boat dropped from sight as if he'd been bludgeoned.

"Oh-oh," Colleen said, but a few seconds later, the crab boat's engine roared into full throttle, lifting the boat's prow and sending it churning toward the Hook.

Harry stopped firing, but they stayed hidden until the boat disappeared around a bend. Then they stood up and began knocking the dirt off their clothes.

"That was kind of fun," Colleen said. "Only you got to do all the shooting. What makes you think he wasn't trying to kill us?"

"His rifle had a scope on it. Even in an unsteady boat, at that distance it's hard to see how he could have missed us, unless he was doing it on purpose."

3

"What's the use of shooting the boat?" Sergeant Frank Hodges of the Tequesta County Sheriff's Department demanded incredulously, scowling at Harry as if he'd failed a mental test.

Hodges was broad and thick and red-faced, and his shirtfront looked like a spinnaker in a stiff wind.

Colleen laughed. "Harry thinks the man was sending a message without trying to kill us, but it felt real enough to me."

Colleen, Harry, Sergeant Hodges, and Captain Jim Snyder were crowded into Snyder's cement block office with its death row green walls and gray metal furniture. All that was lacking was a drain in the center of the brown tile floor. Colleen had been reluctant to come with Harry to the Tequesta County Sheriff's Department to make a report, but now Harry saw that she was enjoying herself, and made another revision in his view of librarians.

"Even if Harry's right, Dr. McGraw, it's still a felony," Captain Jim Snyder said solemnly.

He was tall and thin with hair so pale it was almost white. His ears were big, and his everyday expression was one of earnest interest. He had come to Avola from a farm in eastern Tennessee where his father had divided his time, not very successfully, between preaching and farming. The ancient adage that miller's beast and parson's child prosper seldom and often run wild didn't fit Jim Snyder. But his adjustment to the outside world had been slow, painful, and in Harry's view, incomplete.

For one thing, he still held to the view that most people did the best they could and were basically honest.

"Did you ever see this man before?" he asked Harry.

"No, but he needs a boat yard."

"That depends on your shooting," Jim said, kicking his chair back from the desk with a look of discontent.

News of violence disconcerted him.

"It was good," Colleen said, grinning at Harry. "I wish I could have done some of it."

Jim looked startled by the comment, but managed to say that he would send a couple of deputies to the Hook. "There are one or two places out there where the man could get that hull plugged without answering a lot of questions."

Hodges snorted with amusement at the understatement. "It don't make no sense that he should be shooting at you, Harry," he complained. "You tell anyone you was going out there?"

"No, I didn't tell anyone but Tucker LaBeau."

"That leaves you, Dr. McGraw," Jim said, his ears turning red. "Could the shooter have been coming after you?" Harry suppressed his amusement. Jim was shy of women, and his ears gave him away.

Colleen smiled and leaned toward him, tightening her shirt across her generous breasts, and held her hands toward him palms up. Harry watched Snyder try not to look and fail.

"Captain," she said with a smile, "I think half the County would shoot me if they could."

Hodges laughed loudly, and Jim, his face blazing, glowered at him. He had often told Harry that Hodges had been sent to him as a test of his Christian forbearance. And just as often, Hodges had said that the Captain was never meant to be a policeman, that he should have stayed in the mountains, married a woman with a big ass for winter warmth, and, like his daddy, preached on Sundays and given over the rest of his time to running a still, farming, and hunting coons.

The assessment had intrigued Harry, because a long time ago when Jim was still a deputy, Tucker LaBeau had said much the same thing without making any reference to the wife's physical endowments. Harry was undecided. He thought Jim was one of the best C.I.D. officers in the state.

"You mean because of your work with the Stoneman Douglas Alliance?" Jim finally managed to ask Colleen, his ears shining.

"Yes."

"What are your people doing that causes so much strong feeling? I probably ought to know but . . ."

"Don't apologize, Captain. A year or so ago the Alliance began devoting time and money to the preservation of the Okalatchee River and trying to change the way some people use it. That's when the trouble started."

"What's wrong with the river?" Hodges demanded loudly. "The last time I looked, it was still running into the Gulf."

He grinned all around but there were no answering smiles.

"Frank," Jim began, his voice rising, but Colleen cut him off.

"The Sergeant's not the only one who doesn't know that the Okalatchee is on the point of collapse. Its fish are already dying, and it's only a matter of time—and I mean a very little time—before people will be affected—in fact, it may be happening already." She paused and shot a cold look at Hodges and Jim. "So the time is past when being ignorant about the calamity engulfing this river is funny."

Hodges stared at the floor and shifted uncomfortably in his chair. Harry almost felt sorry for him.

"Dr. McGraw, I surely don't think it's funny," Jim said, "and I'm sure Frank doesn't either." He bent a ferocious look on his sergeant.

"No, no," Hodges sputtered, shaking his head. "I don't think it's funny."

Harry stepped in to ease the strain. "The Alliance has trod on a lot of big toes, most of them in the Southwest Florida Development Association. Even so, when Dr. McGraw first talked to me about feeling threatened, I thought she had exaggerated the problem, but after this morning I've changed my mind."

"Tell me about the Association," Jim said, showing more interest.

Colleen leaned forward in her chair again.

"It's basically a group of big farmers, realtors, and developers who don't want anyone interfering with the way they've been using the river and their plans for the land along its banks. In addition, there is a scattering of mining people, fishermen, and property rights activists who have joined them. I'm guessing the shooter belongs to one of those last-named groups."

"Aside from shooting at you, what kind of trouble have these people been giving you?" Jim asked.

"I've had some threatening calls, e-mails, and a couple of semi-literate letters. . . ."

"Do you still have the e-mails and the letters?" Jim asked.

"Yes, and three of the calls on an answering tape."

"You don't have to answer this," Jim said, "but how is Harry supposed to help?"

"If the Alliance is going to fight its opponents effectively, I've got to know why the Association is creating all this unpleasantness. Also, I want it known we're ready to fight back."

Apparently forgetting it was an attractive woman he was talking to, Jim pulled himself back to his desk and said with a worried shake of his head, "I don't think this is the right time to crank up the confrontation with these people, especially when you don't know who's chivvying you."

"The Captain's right," Hodges said earnestly. "Why not let us track down this shooter, wring him out, and nail whoever put him up to it?"

"Unless Harry wants the job, this could all be moot," Colleen replied, turning to him with a quizzical expression.

Harry met her gaze and found he didn't have to think about it. "I'll do what I can, but Jim may be right. Hiring me may only cause you more trouble."

She waved a hand dismissing his concern and said, "Now, if I can persuade the St. John's River Coalition to come in on this with us, I'd be one happy woman. But I'm sure the Captain will help," she added quickly, giving Jim a dazzling smile.

"He'll do it," Hodges put in earnestly. "And so will I."

4

Harry lived on Bartram's Hammock, a low, densely wooded island, separated from County Road 19 by Puc Puggy Creek on the west and bordered on its other three sides by the Stickpen Preserve, a twelve thousand acre bald cypress swamp. His only neighbor on the hammock was an old farmer named Tucker LaBeau, who lived alone with a dog, a mule, a rooster, and a flock of hens.

Some years earlier, Tucker had deeded his farm to the state in exchange for the right to live on the Hammock for the rest of his life. The state claimed the house and land Harry had been leasing in an action against a convicted felon, then asked Harry to stay in the house as the Hammock's unofficial game warden.

Harry gladly stayed, fully aware of the irony of the arrangement. Twenty-five years earlier, he had been a game warden in western Maine. That career vanished when he tried to stop a man from jacking a deer. The man responded by trying to shoot him. Harry shot and killed him. There was a fierce public outcry over the death. In the ensuing trial Harry was cleared of the murder charge brought against him. But his wife left him, taking their two children with her. Harry became a private investigator and moved to Florida.

The same afternoon that he and Colleen McGraw had talked to Jim Snyder, Harry had turned off the highway and was crossing the hump-backed bridge across Puc Puggy Creek when his phone rang. He pulled to a stop and answered it.

"The Captain thinks you might want to get over here," Frank Hodges said. "It looks like we've found that Fields woman."

"Where's *here?*"

"The Hook. Old Beetle's Boat Dock. She had some identification in a pocket. And that's a good thing because you can't tell much from the face, and the fingers are mostly gone. The crabs have been working her pretty good. You talk about stink. . . ."

"Has anyone called Colleen McGraw?" Harry asked quickly.

"I ain't."

"Thanks, Frank, I'm on my way."

He dialed Colleen's number. "I've got some bad news. They've found Joyce Fields."

"She's dead."

"Yes. I'm sorry."

"Was she murdered?"

"I don't know yet. She was found in the water." For his own sake as much as hers, he left out the part about the crabs and the smell.

"If she was murdered, I'll never forgive myself."

"You're way ahead of yourself," Harry said, wondering why people confronted with a death so often felt responsible or angry or both. "It could have been an accident. And believe me on this, even if it wasn't, it's not your fault, and there's nothing you could have done. They found her at the Hook. I'm going out there now. As soon as I have more information, I'll call you."

He paused. He had the sense that she had stopped listening to him and was following her own thoughts. "Colleen," he said sharply.

"Yes, sorry, what?"

"Don't go near the river alone. All right?"

"Yes. God, Harry, I feel awful."

"Have you got anyone you can be with?"

The line was silent for a moment. Then she said she had although Harry didn't know whether or not she was telling the truth.

"I'll call as soon as I can."

"Okay."

By the time Harry reached Beetle's Dock, it was well past noon. A small crowd, made up mostly of women, preschoolers, and old men, was gathered in the boat yard, kept off the dock by a bored deputy, sweating in the sun. At the outer end of the dock a woman in light orange coveralls and white surgical gloves was working over something laid out on the dock.

Two Crime Scene officers were making notes. Snyder and Hodges were standing under a chicki hut, talking with a heavy, bald man Harry assumed was Old Beetle although he didn't look to be more than forty. Behind them on a bench two boys sat leaned forward with their elbows on their knees, looking thoroughly wretched.

I'll bet they found her, Harry thought, feeling sorry for them, then spoke to the deputy and was waved up the stairs. He walked past the hut and continued along the dock between a double row of dented and scraped aluminum rental boats, stacked bottoms up to shed the rain. It was too early for the daily downpours of summer, but May had already brought a couple of heavy thunderstorms that had doused the lights in the county.

"Hi, Kathleen," Harry said when he reached the blonde woman.

"Hello, Harry," she answered, zipping up the body bag. "I hear somebody tried to pop you this morning."

The stench surging up from the bag made Harry jump back before he lost whatever was left of his breakfast.

The M.E. stood up and looked at Harry with a broad grin.

Kathleen Towers was short and slender. Her blue eyes were bright with intelligence, and she was obviously enjoying Harry's discomfort.

"I see they missed," she added, pulling off her cap and shaking loose her thick hair.

"I don't think I was the target, but it got my attention." He glanced at the bag. "What about Joyce Fields?"

"So that's who it is. I'll know more after I get her to the lab, but my guess is she went into the water after she was shot. Small hole going in. I'd say a forty-five. A hole in her back big enough to put your fist in. Probably blew her heart to pieces. What's your interest?"

"Colleen McGraw, Chairperson of the Stoneman Douglas Alliance, has hired me to find out who's been harassing them. Looks like they've got more trouble than they realized."

Kathleen peeled off her gloves. "What's Field's connection?"

"She's been working the river, giving the Alliance the scientific punch it needs to make some things happen."

"I don't know McGraw, but I've heard of the Alliance. They've been kicking up a stink about the crap being dumped into this river."

"That's right. How long has Fields been in the water?"

"Eight or ten days."

"Any other damage besides the gunshot wound and what the crabs have done?"

"I didn't see any, but I'll look closer later." One of the CS officers called her name. "Got to go," she said.

"A nasty business," Jim said without preamble when Harry stepped under the chicki roof. "This here is John Dee Rudd. He owns the place."

Harry shook hands with the big, shaggy-headed man and asked him about Old Beetle.

"My grandfather," Rudd answered as if he was tired of

answering the question. "It's been called Old Beetle's Boat Yard for sixty years. I saw no reason to change it."

The heavy voice had a trace of belligerence in it that Harry recognized as the Hook's way of fending off outsiders.

"Sounds like a good name to me," he said. "Those the kids who found Dr. Fields?"

"That's them," Judd answered, looking back at the malefactors sitting on the bench. "If their Daddies don't whop 'em, I will. Outlaws, the pair of 'em."

When he looked back at Harry there was a flash of teeth through the beard. Harry saw that the boys weren't in much danger from Judd, despite his growl.

"You mind if I talk to them while you and Mr. Judd finish your business?" Harry asked Jim.

"No, but Sergeant Hodges has already talked with them. I won't keep Mr. Judd much longer."

"My name's Harry Brock," he said to the boys, upending a crab pot and sitting down in front of them. "What's your names?"

"Bobby Scrubbs," the shorter one said.

"Fannon Jones."

To Harry they both looked scared and half sick. "Could you drink a Coke?" he asked them. They nodded.

There was a cold drink machine beside the door to Judd's bait shop, and Harry came back to the boys and passed them the sweating cans.

They said, "Thanks," together.

"I hear you were hunting snakes," Harry said.

They nodded and stared at their Cokes.

"Did you see any?"

They shook their heads.

"I guess you're in some trouble."

They exchanged worried glances and nodded.

"Well, don't worry too much about it. Your pictures are going to be in the *The Avola Banner.* When you found Dr. Fields, you did something good. People are going to say some good things about you. Do you know who Dr. Fields was?"

They shook their heads and brightened up a little but not much.

"She was a scientist working for the Florida Fish and Wildlife Conservation Commission and was trying to find out why some of the fish in the river are getting sick."

"We've seen some of that," Bobby burst out.

"Pa says they're dickheads," Fannon said with sudden belligerence.

"You're not talking about the fish," Harry responded in a neutral voice.

"Those people from Tallahassee," Bobby put in.

"Do a lot of people think Dr. Fields was a dickhead?"

"A lot of people in the Hook do," Fannon insisted.

"What do you think?" Harry asked.

"I don't like the way the fish are dying," Bobby said.

Fannon shrugged and drank some Coke. Harry allowed himself a moment to feel depressed over the sneering dismissal of the dead ichthyologist then pushed past the feeling, reminding himself of where he was.

"Did you see anything else or anybody beside Dr. Fields in there?"

"No," Bobby said, "just trees and water and. . . ."

His voice trailed off.

"That's okay," Harry told him and got up. "Thanks for talking with me. Cheer up, you two. You're going to be heroes."

"Tell that to Pa," Fannon replied.

Walking away from them, Harry suspected that with the pragmatism of youth they saw the shotgun and the skiff outweighing any claims to fame they might have garnered by finding a dead woman.

Jim and Hodges were waiting to talk to Harry. Judd had retreated to his bait shop.

"We're going to have to wait for the M.E. to finish her autopsy before we've got the official cause of death," Jim said, "but she was murdered."

"There'll be a new star in the east if she tells us Fields was drowned and shot after she was already dead," Hodges put in with a laugh.

Jim sighed heavily. "Frank, take those kids home, tell their parents what happened, say the boys made an important contribution to our work, and say we thank them. Then warn them that the media is going to be after them. You know what to say about that."

"Indeed, I do," Hodges said, trying to look solemn.

Hodges collected the boys and left.

"Did you get anything from Judd?" Harry asked Jim.

Snyder stretched and shook his head. "He claims that nobody fitting the perp's description has visited his dock today, and he hasn't seen a boat fitting the description go down river."

"How likely do you think that is?"

"Not very. There can't be more than a dozen boats like that on this stretch of the river. And I'll bet Judd knows every one of them."

"Then he's not giving out any real information until he finds out what's going on and where his interests lie."

"That would be my reading. When are you going to tell me that the shooting this morning is probably connected to Dr. Fields' death?"

"It would be a good guess," Harry answered. "But I'm puzzled."

"About what?"

"If he's already killed one person, why did he spare McGraw and me?"

5

They were interrupted by angry voices. A heavily muscled man in a white T-shirt and dungarees was climbing onto the dock, and the deputy trying to hold him back was being bounced around.

"I'd better give Pollack a hand," Jim said.

Harry went with him. Kathleen had left, but two of her crew were still bagging equipment and preparing to load Fields' body into their van. They dropped what they were doing and ran to help Pollock. But by the time Jim and Harry reached the knot of struggling men, the three men were getting the worst of it, and men from the small crowd that had gathered were moving toward the melee.

"Hold it right there," Jim shouted.

He waded into the fray, shoving his people out of the way as he advanced. Harry stayed with him. The man at the center of all the attention pulled back a large fist to punch the new arrival and found himself looking into the muzzle of a .45. He rethought the punch. The men behind him backed away.

"Good," Jim said into the sudden quiet. "Let's all settle down."

Harry had his CZ half drawn, planning to lay the barrel across the man's head if he popped Jim. He slid the gun into its holster.

"What's your name?" Jim asked.

The man was still breathing heavily, but his anger was obviously burning off. For the time being, the crowd behind him had decided to watch.

"Derwood Jones," he said in a loud, harsh voice. "And I want to talk to that son-of-a-bitch Harry Brock, who told my boy he was a hero."

"That would be me," Harry said.

"We all praised the boys for telling Judd what they'd found," Jim said firmly. "Did you speak with Sergeant Hodges? I hope he told you the same thing."

"He may have tried, but my shotgun was taken without my permission, and one of Judd's boats. That's stealing in my book. I don't tolerate stealing or anyone coming between me and my son. I intend to make that clear."

As Jones talked, Harry had a chance to look at him more closely. He probably weighed two twenty-five and was mostly bulging muscle. His face was broad and red, his hair, light and thin. His eyes were set close together under a sloping brow. A steroid-popping bomb, Harry thought and instantly felt sorry for Fannon.

"This is what's going to happen," Jim said, the gun still pointed at Jones' head. "You and I and Mr. Brock here are going up to that chicki hut in front of Judd's bait shop and have a short talk. Depending on how that goes, you're either going to jail for assaulting police officers or going home under your own recognizance. Do you understand me, Mr. Jones?"

"Sure," Jones said with a sullen scowl.

Jim stepped back, easing the hammer on his revolver. The officers behind Jim divided, and he and Harry with Jones following went up the steps to the dock. The officers went back to what they had been doing, and the crowd began breaking up.

Jim kept the conversation brief, telling Jones what they had asked his son and what they had told him. When it was over, they all shook hands.

"There's just one more thing, Mr. Jones," Jim said. "If I hear that you've hurt that boy, you're going to be sorry. There's a lot of law I can call on if I have to."

Jones had done well up to that point, but being told what he couldn't do regarding Fannon set him off.

"Ain't that just how it goes?" he snarled, puffing up like a big toad. "You try to bring up your kids to fear God and do right, and here comes the goddamned government, messing into your business. It's just like this river, and that dead woman from Gainesville. If you'd all just leave us and the river alone, we'd get on with our lives and do what we need to do to live, and there wouldn't be no trouble."

With that he turned and stamped off the dock, shouting as he went, "Judd, I'll come by on Saturday and make good on the rental for that skiff the boy took."

"Do you think he believes what he calls *government* is the cause of all his troubles?" Jim asked quietly as they watched Jones leave.

"Probably," Harry replied, "but here's another question: How did Jones know the woman in that body bag came from Gainesville?"

Harry and Tucker LaBeau were sitting on Tucker's kitchen stoop and had been talking about Joyce Fields' death and Harry and Colleen McGraw's being shot at. Harry had just finished describing the run-in with Derwood Jones and had wondered aloud how Jones knew there was a woman in M.E.'s body bag.

"The same way he knew who you are," Tucker said, leaning back in his rocker and drinking from his mug. "Fifteen minutes after those kids told Judd what they'd found, most of the adults in the Hook knew it. Then, when you and Jim and the M.E. and the Crime Scene crews arrived, they soon all knew that too."

Harry tried some of the tea without dying. Now, the two men

sat looking into a wood of tall live oaks, cabbage palms, hickory, loblolly pines, and figs, filled with deep shadows and shot through with long bars of afternoon sun. The under story was made up mostly of red maple, persimmon, and saw palmetto. The lianas and vines and twisting ropes of roots from strangler figs gave the jungle a powerful presence, and the sound of cicadas and locusts buzzing and fiddling in the trees added to the scene a sense of vibrant energy.

Harry had once wondered how Tucker, who was somewhere in his eighties and might have weighed a hundred and thirty pounds soaking wet, kept his farm from being swallowed by the encroaching forest. But after knowing the old farmer a while, he saw that his seven-ten work schedule was the answer. Not that the old man ever seemed to be hurrying, and as often as not Harry would find him where he was sitting now, rocking and drinking tea while the breeze rattled the fronds in the cabbage palms and lifted his fringe of white hair like dandelion fluff.

"Where's the staff?" Harry asked, noticing that, as was usually the case, once he stepped into Tucker's yard, the world and its demands seemed to lose their power to command his thoughts.

"Let's go find out," Tucker said, jumping to his feet and putting on his straw hat.

He was dressed in a white shirt without a collar and faded denim bib overalls that gave him the look of a very lively scarecrow. Harry gratefully put down his mug and followed.

They had reached the barn when Tucker said, "Speaking of the devil."

A tall, black mule, wearing a straw hat, and a very wet and muddy big blue tick hound with a bedraggled blue bandanna tied around his neck were trotting up the yard toward them.

"Sanchez has been in the creek," Harry said.

"Summer is officially here," Tucker replied.

Sanchez gave Harry a grin of welcome and then shook himself

vigorously, spraying everybody. Oh, Brother! pushed his nose into Harry's chest and waggled his ears in greeting.

"Why didn't you have a swim?" Harry asked him, patting his glossy neck.

The mule threw up his head and looked at Harry as if he had been insulted.

"Oh, Brother! has more brains than to swim in Puc Puggy Creek with Benjamin still visiting his lady friends," Tucker observed. "Back in April, I reminded Sanchez to put off his first swim of the year until Benjamin had gone back into the Stick-pen. And only last night I heard him rumbling out there like a giant tomcat."

"So did I, but I haven't seen him this year," Harry said.

"All fourteen feet of him," Tucker added with an appreciative chuckle. "And still growing. I'd give odds that he weighs half a ton now. Sanchez would make a nice snack for Benjamin while he's between bouts of lovemaking. But Sanchez hears what he wants to. It's what comes of his having learned English as a second language. When he doesn't want to hear, he pretends he only speaks Spanish."

"Have you noticed how the number of alligators coming out of the nests along the Creek has been dropping?" Harry asked.

"Yes, and from what I hear and read, it's happening all over the Okalatchee River basin," Tucker said, shaking his head sadly.

"And frogs with five legs and two sets of sex organs," Harry added sourly. "Neither of which work."

"The toe bone's undoubtedly connected to the foot bone," Tucker replied cryptically.

"I've got to talk to some people in the Hook about Joyce Fields' death," Harry said, changing the subject. "How do I do it without getting shot at?"

"Very carefully," Tucker said, leading them back around the barn and toward a group of beehives placed in a gentle curve under a stand of holly trees.

As they approached the hives the humming of the bees grew louder, and workers began zipping past Harry. Oh, Brother! and Sanchez drifted away in the direction of the house. Harry wished he was going with them. But Tucker went on talking and advancing steadily toward the hives.

"This is close enough for me," Harry said.

"I'll just check this fourth hive, to see if the new queen is all right."

Standing in a cloud of bees buzzing around him like tiny fighter planes, Tucker lifted a super off the stack and peered into the brood hive.

"She's doing fine," he said, and, unscathed, he replaced the super and walked back to where Harry was standing, trying to look like a tree. "Don't worry," Tucker said. "Those bees are too full of honey to care what either of us does. Flowers are coming into bloom, and as far as they're concerned, all's right with the world."

"Back to the Hook," Harry said, glad to put some distance between himself and the hives.

"For a long time, the brightest young people from the Hook have been growing up and moving away. You follow me?"

"It's a struggle but, yes."

"All right, a doublewide is a luxury home, and new pickups either belong to service people or are stolen. But almost nobody steals while *in* the Hook, and if they do, they have a fire—if you see what I mean."

"Okay," Harry said.

"And they look out for one another."

"Do you know Derwood Jones?"

"I knew his grandfather a little, but, of course, that was a long time ago. However, family traits seem to recur. If you've got business with the young Jones, I'd stay between him the door. *Derwood* was the grandfather's name, and he would rather fight than eat."

"I've met the young Derwood. I do not want to fight with him. In fact, it wouldn't be a fight at all."

Tucker had walked Harry to the road. Now he shook hands with him as he always did.

"You don't need advice on how to do your job, but in going to work for McGraw and the Alliance, you're walking into the middle of a squabble that's going to grow into a brawl. The Hook will be dead set against whatever the Alliance wants to do to the river. Keep that in mind, Harry. I don't want you to end up floating in the mangroves."

"It's that bad?"

"Worse. For a long time the developers, farmers, fishermen, private property advocates, and so on have had things pretty much their own way. They've had time to develop the conviction that what they want is what God intended them to have; and as Joyce Fields has proven, there's nothing more dangerous than greedy self-righteousness with a gun in its hands."

"I'll keep that in mind," Harry said and went off down the white sand road toward home, thinking he might have made a mistake in going to work for Colleen McGraw.

6

On his way home Colleen called him.

"I know it's short notice, Harry, but I've called a meeting of the Alliance Board at my place at eight tonight for all those who can make it. Joyce's death has left us twisting in the wind. Come if you can. The sooner you get to know us, the better, or maybe it's the worse."

She left him an address and directions.

Colleen lived in Wildewood, a golfing and tennis association a mile and a half east of Route 75 off the Goodnight Road, which fifteen years earlier had been home to raccoons, opossums, a small herd of deer, and an old, cranky, one-eyed bobcat. "And," Harry told the security guard at the gate, continuing his thought as he was being checked in, "back then the name didn't have an *e* in it."

The security guard looked at him as if he was in need of counseling.

The houses, Harry admitted reluctantly, were set attractively among trees and shrubs, more or less native to the region. Although the light was fading as he walked up the path to her house, he noticed that Colleen had gone in seriously for xeriscaping and gave her extra points.

"Well, you make six," Colleen said in a resigned voice, leading Harry down the steps into a sunken living room with white walls and a floor of large, red Mexican tiles. Two men and two women holding drinks stopped talking while she introduced him.

"This is Elaine Porter," Colleen said, holding his arm. "She's our treasurer and the scourge of my existence."

The tall, dark haired woman in a black designer dress regarded him bleakly through thick glasses and said, "It looks as though we hired you two weeks too late."

"If you're referring to Joyce Fields' death," Harry said, not liking her cold scrutiny, "it might not have made any difference."

"Then why are we wasting the money?" Porter asked huffily and pulled herself up another inch.

Harry thought that if she had been wearing a toga, she would have flipped a corner of it at him as she threw it over her shoulder.

"Joshua Bates," Colleen said quickly, pulling Harry away before he could reply. "Joshua is our vice president. He's also our legal brains and our liaison with Tallahassee. Josh put us and Dr. Fields together."

Bates, dressed in a rumpled gray suit, was twenty-five pounds overweight, had the face of a worried child, and a baldpate that shone as if it had been polished.

"That was her bad luck," he said, shaking Harry's hand vigorously and trying to look chagrined. "Never mind Elaine. I'm relieved you're aboard."

"Arlen Gott," a much larger man in his fifties said in a South Carolina drawl as he pushed forward. "I'm secretary of this outfit although I can barely write my name. And this here's Cora Wingate. She owns The Spice Islands Gallery in Avola, and I'm obliged by a love of truth to abandon chivalry and say it would never have occurred to me to call a woman this good looking *Cora.*"

He scowled down on Harry through a bristly, red beard and

eyebrows, but his eyes and a vagrant smile belied the gruffness. Harry still withheld judgment. There was a quality in the big man Harry couldn't define, and it made him uneasy. Cora Wingate was, Harry guessed, in her early forties with short brown hair and an arresting figure. She was dressed in dark blue slacks and a cream-colored jersey. She blushed slightly at Gott's introduction and gave him a good-natured push that failed to budge him.

"Mr. Brock," she said in an accent deeper and further south by at least two states than Gott's, "Professor Gott is an historian of repute and a very successful teacher. You may safely disregard his remarks about being barely literate. But, I regret to say, he is disgustingly rich, which can be terribly seductive, and a shameless flatterer. In his vicinity, unchaperoned ladies like me are not entirely safe."

She gave Harry a smile that transformed her face into a thing of beauty, and there was a moment when Harry thought he had passed dying and gone straight to heaven. Also, he wanted to sit down beside her and listen to her say *disregard* as long as her voice held out. Inspired by that smile, he told her it was a risk borne by all beautiful women and not only when near Mr. Gott, bringing out that smile again, which he had been fishing for.

"Arlen," she said, taking Harry's arm, "would you get this poor, thirsty man a drink?"

Arlen went off grumbling.

Cora turned to Harry, still smiling, and whispered in a way that made him feel several years younger, "Come over to the divan with me. We'll sit down, and you will say for me, 'Park the car in the yard,' and then I'll ask you to say, 'Bar Harbor.' "

"Nope," Colleen McGraw said, grasping Harry by his free arm and pulling him away, "he's mine. We've got to get this meeting started."

"The story of my life," Cora said, giving Harry an enchanting smile.

Arlen returned in time to pass Harry a whisky and soda strong enough to walk on. Harry paused, drank some of it, and when he'd caught his breath, said so to the departing Gott.

Over his shoulder, Gott replied, "If you're going to dance with Cora, you'll need it."

Harry was further disconcerted to find himself sitting next to Elaine Porter, who was still able to look down on him.

With everyone sitting somewhere, Colleen said, "You've all met Harry and know why he's here. Elaine said we were two weeks late in hiring him. Modestly enough, Harry doubts he could have saved Joyce. Perhaps not, but I'd feel better if he could have been trying."

"What, exactly, would Mr. Brock have been looking for?" Cora Wingate asked with apparent innocence.

Harry stifled a grin. Maybe Gott was right about her and behind those china blue eyes was an unladylike mind.

"Cora, stifle it," Joshua Bates said impatiently.

"It's a good question," Harry put in. "At the moment, as Dr. McGraw told Captain Snyder, it could have been half the county."

"What will you do?" Arlen Gott asked.

Elaine Porter turned to Arlen. "It's obvious," she said, *"Chercher l'argent."*

"Oh, my *dear,*" Cora said to Elaine, "isn't that clever. We didn't need Mr. Brock after all."

Elaine glowered but made no response. Gott was grinning appreciatively. Bates rolled his eyes. Colleen looked at Harry and shrugged.

"It's a good place to begin," Harry responded, feeling somehow responsible.

Cora was the only one who laughed. It was a good laugh.

Harry liked it.

"Moving on," Colleen said firmly, "I've had a letter." She waved a sheet of paper at her listeners and went on speaking. "We know Joyce was leader of her group and that Bob Walker, her assistant, is now acting leader. I talked to Walker this afternoon, and he told me that Joyce had not involved him in her work with us, that it was, as he put it, extra-departmental, and he had no interest in pursuing it. He was fairly nasty, actually, and we can forget getting any help from him."

She was interrupted by Gott's swearing and a clamor of concern from the others.

"I know. I know," Colleen said, "it's a loss, but things may not be entirely stranded. This letter," as she fluttered the paper again, "is from Joyce's lab assistant, Marcia Graham. Did Joyce mention her to any of you?"

A chorus of denials and a "Get on with it," from Elaine Porter let Colleen continue.

"I'll make it brief. Marcia has written to say she has copies of all of Joyce's notes as well as her reports. She's willing to help us."

"Why?" Cora asked.

"Probably because she's in the middle of her dissertation, and she needs to continue the research in order to complete it."

"Where is funding coming from?" Bates inquired.

"The University of Florida. She's a doctoral candidate at the Gainesville campus. The bad part is that Bob Walker has told her he will not replace Joyce as her offsite supervisor. She says that's a problem but one she can probably solve through the Chair of her academic department."

"Does she say why Walker's being difficult?" Elaine Porter demanded.

"No, but she mentions that he and Joyce have quarreled in the past over the role the Conservation Commission should play in water management issues."

"A kid," Gott rumbled dismissively.

"She's thirty-five," Colleen snapped. "She taught biology for ten years in the Tampa system before going back to school."

Harry started to say he wanted to talk to her, but something stopped him. "Has she had any experience at field work?" he asked instead.

"Good question," Elaine said, surprising Harry.

Colleen's shoulders slumped. "No, but she has done most of the lab analysis for Joyce and, as I said, she has Joyce's notes."

"But if Marcia Graham can finish the work Joyce left her, that might be enough for us to go ahead with," Joshua Bates said hopefully.

"Why not recruit another biologist?" Cora asked. "However good Ms. Graham is, she's not going to lend a lot of credibility to our endeavor."

Harry thought attaching a new senior scientist to the Alliance was a good idea.

"Where's the money coming from for that?" Gott protested. "Fields worked for nothing."

"I've asked Marcia to come down for a visit," Colleen said. "She's agreed to meet with us and give us a detailed report on what she has done and has left to do. After we've heard what she has to say, we can make up our minds what we should do. And one other thing. I'm still working on the St. John's River Coalition. Don't give up hope."

The meeting ended without Harry's saying more than goodnight to Cora and the others. He was on his way out when Colleen asked him quietly to stay.

"Can I get you another drink?" she asked when the others had left.

"No, thanks," he replied, thinking she looked worn out.

"Then I'll drink alone," she said from the sideboard and

poured herself a hefty scotch with a dribble of water.

She came back to where he was standing and waved him into a chair. For a moment she rummaged in her file that was still beside the sofa and passed him a folded piece of paper.

"I found this in the mail box when I got home today."

Harry opened it. The words were made of letters that had been cut out of a magazine and were of various sizes and colors: "FIELD IS DEAD. LEARN FROM IT."

"Was it in an envelope?" Harry asked.

Colleen dropped into a chair facing Harry and shook her head. "The other stuff hasn't really gotten to me. This one has."

"It's nasty," Harry said. "And I think it should be read as a direct threat. With your permission, I'll let Snyder look at it."

"For all the good it will do," she said in a defeated voice.

Harry felt a deepening concern for her. "You might want to think about pulling the Alliance off this Okalatchee project," he said.

"Is that what you think I should do?" She frowned at him over her glass.

"Not necessarily, but as the person who sent you that note says, Joyce Fields is dead."

She took another swallow of her drink.

"Here's what I think," Colleen said. "We can't say for certain why Joyce was killed. It may have had nothing to do with her work for the Alliance. We have no proof that whoever wrote the note is her killer or knows who is. Finally, the man who shot at us may have no connection with either Joyce's death or the note. How am I doing?"

She gave Harry a shaky smile.

"Not bad," he answered, returning her smile, "but the weakness of your argument is that you might have said the opposite with equal conviction."

"Then my version has a fifty percent chance of being right," she responded, her smile widening.

"That's right, but would you walk under a ladder if there was a fifty percent chance that you'd be killed?"

Her smile held. "But we don't really know what the odds are that someone will try to kill me."

"Where does that leave us?"

"Exhausted," she answered and stood up.

"One more thing," he said. "Are you sure these attacks are not coming from someone with a more personal issue with you?"

"Are you asking am I involved in a love affair that's gone really bad?"

"Yes."

She paused. "That's kind of flattering, Harry, but no, I'm not being stalked. And I'm not quitting. Are you?"

"No," he said. "I just want to be sure you understand what you're getting into."

She slipped her arm through his and walked him to the door.

"Give Jim the letter," she said. "I'll be interested to hear what he makes of it. Will you ask him to call me?"

Driving home, Harry thought of a number of things he had heard and seen during the evening. The note caused him the most concern, but he found himself coming back several times to Colleen's using Snyder's first name and asking that he call her. Harry's nose felt a little out of joint, but he consoled himself with memories of Cora Wingate.

7

The next morning Harry decided to clear his desk and give himself some breathing room. He had three small cases in hand, an insurance fraud investigation; a peek and squeak for a County Commissioner, who was worried his wife was having an affair and even more worried that his political enemies would find out and spill the beans; and a ridiculous job involving a newspaper thief in Piney Woods, a small condominium association in East Avola, north of Rattlesnake Trace.

The president of the association had pestered Sheriff Robert Fisher about the thefts until Fisher called Harry and said he needed a favor. Harry groaned out loud but took the job because his work was difficult enough without having Fisher mad at him.

Paperwork on all three cases had been accumulating, and Harry finished his breakfast determined to chain himself to his desk until he was caught up. Then he remembered talking with Tucker about Benjamin, the alligator, and told himself if he didn't see him soon, he wouldn't get a look at him until next year.

Easily convincing himself that now was the time to do it, he hurriedly gathered his hat and shoulder sack and stepped out of the house just as a huge, molten sun was rising beyond the swamp and setting Puc Puggy Creek on fire. Harry watched the morning break with familiar stirrings of awe and delight. Over time, he had grown more and more attached to the ceremonies of nature. He seldom missed a sunrise.

Flights of herons, ibis, and egrets were stringing themselves out along the Creek and spreading across the marsh. A new breeze began swaying the willows on the Creek's edge and whispering in the big live oaks on his lawn. All around him the locusts and cicadas were tuning up while the frog chorus that had kept the night company slowly faded into silence. The fact that he enjoyed such events in solitude was a concern to his friends. His ex-wife Katherine had accused him at Christmas of turning into a hermit.

Minna, their eleven-year-old daughter, brushed aside his denials and said, "Harry, you're getting as bad as Mr. LaBeau, talking to Oh, Brother! and Sanchez as if they were people. One of these times when we visit I expect to find a bear living with you."

Even somber Jesse, now fifteen, and deeply distracted by the pain and burdens of adolescence, laughed at his sister's prediction and voiced agreement.

When the sun had cleared the fringe of trees at the eastern side of the marsh, Harry set off up the road in search of Benjamin. He knew where all the breeding female alligators along this side of the Hammock had their nesting sites and thought it was likely that if the big alligator was still in the Puc Puggy, he would be courting one of them.

The road ran along the creek for all of its three miles, and Harry had gone half a mile beyond Tucker's place when he found Benjamin in a wide eddy of the creek, swimming slowly around a big female that Harry had watched grow up. Benjamin was swimming with most of his enormous head, tail, and barrel-like body above the surface of the water, making his best impression. Harry thought he had grown at least a foot in the past year and agreed with Tucker that the huge gator now weighed about twelve hundred pounds.

Harry eased himself off the road and found a place to sit down where he could watch the two animals, both of which ignored him. Harry was pleased with his good luck. It was a rare treat to watch such a courting ritual. The thing that impressed him most was the gentleness of the proceedings. While Benjamin circled her, the female lay quietly in the water, apparently indifferent to his attentions.

For his part, the big alligator swam slowly, making scarcely any wake, and gradually drew closer to her until his nose was gently touching her right side. Moving his head along her body until he reached her shoulders, he then lifted his head and very carefully slid himself onto her shoulders, pressing her under the water.

He held her there for a moment then released her. As soon as she surfaced, he began swimming very slowly around her again, but this time with his snout caressing her side, her head and jaws, and then down her other side until he had come back to his starting place. Now Benjamin moved forward very slowly until his hips were even with hers. Again he waited. A moment later they sank deeper into the water and began mating.

When it was over, the female slid gently away from Benjamin, to float quietly beside him. Harry sat watching them until she swam away. When she was gone, Benjamin sank slowly under the surface until only his eyes and nostrils were visible. The lover becoming the hunter again.

Harry got up, knocked the dirt and leaves off his clothes, and stood for a moment watching the lovely scene of water and willows and tall rushes swaying in the soft wind and wondering whether or not some silent, insidious corruption was at work in the Okalatchee watershed and through its dark chemistry would eventually destroy the capacity of these great animals to produce healthy offspring. With a sigh he stepped back into the road and headed home.

When he came to Tucker's farm, Sanchez and Oh, Brother! were waiting for him. While he scratched Sanchez's back and then patted Oh, Brother!'s neck and was nuzzled in return, he told them about Benjamin. Harry admitted they liked being talked to, but he flip-flopped on the issue of how much they understood. He tried to believe that Sanchez's grin and Oh, Brother!'s waggling his ears had no particular meaning but wasn't always successful.

As they led him to where Tucker was turning over one of his compost piles, he mentioned his concern about the alligators' declining birth rate. Sanchez stopped grinning and Oh, Brother! pricked up his ears and regarded Harry steadily as if he was disturbed. Harry insisted it was his imagination, but, nevertheless, he was sorry he had said anything about his worries.

"Your escorts look as if they'd lost their last nickel," Tucker said with a frown, straightening up from his labor. "Something bad happened to you?"

"No," Harry said, shaking the old farmer's hand, "I was just telling them about seeing Benjamin mate with one of his girlfriends and happened to mentioned something about the way the hatch rate was falling off."

"That accounts for it," Tucker said with obvious relief. "They're inclined to worry too much about that sort of thing although Oh, Brother! takes it harder than Sanchez. That's the mule genes kicking in, excuse the pun. Now Sanchez, being a hound, is inclined to think there can't be too much wrong with the world as long as his nose and digestion are in good working order."

"Are you about done here?" Harry asked, trying not to look at Oh, Brother! and Sanchez, to see how they were taking

Tucker's remarks.

"Yes," Tucker said, waving his hand at the newly turned pile of blackening leaves, grass, and whatever else Tucker thought would rot down to earth. "What do you want to talk about?"

"I went to a meeting last night. I want to run some things past you."

"While you're doing that, there's something I want to show you. Let's walk out to the citrus grove."

Their walk took them past the henhouse where a big Plymouth Rock rooster was scratching in the run and gurgling to his hens, who were conducting their own search for grubs while keeping one eye on their lord and master. The rooster saw Harry and Tucker and welcomed them by racing around the run, scattering his flock, and came to a stop in front of Tucker and Harry, then, standing on tiptoe, crowed lustily.

"Longstreet seems to be in top form," Harry said, grinning down at the heavy bird.

"Yes, but I suspect Bonnie and Clyde will be calling one of these days."

"Those two gray foxes have been quiet for a long time," Harry remarked.

"Biding their time. By the way, we had a bear through here last night."

"Did it do any damage?" Harry asked.

"No. Sanchez ran him off, but it's a bad sign. The increased development east of us is pushing the big animals this way. Remember the female panther that moved in a few years back?"

Harry said he did. Thinking about the panther triggered another memory. "Remember Weissmuller?" he asked.

Weissmuller was an enormous dog that, several years earlier, had been killing deer on the Hammock until Tucker trapped and tamed him. He had also been harassing the panther Tucker mentioned.

"I do, and I miss him," Tucker replied. "So do Sanchez and Oh, Brother! They did a lot of the work in recalling Weissmuller to the life he had lost, but in the end, as you remember, we couldn't keep him out of the woods. I'm sorry Guy Bridges shot him, but that's his job. You'd know something about that."

"Unfortunately," Harry said, wincing at the memories that surfaced, memories that the passage of time had not made more bearable.

"Are you thinking about Maine again?" Tucker asked as they moved on toward the orchard.

"Yes," Harry said, trying to throw off the gloom brought on by the recollections.

"If you hadn't shot Justin Stone, he would surely have killed you," Tucker said gently.

"Yes," Harry agreed, "and Jennifer would have divorced me and I would have lost Sarah and Clive, even if the shooting hadn't happened, but it gave her the excuse she was looking for."

Tucker dropped a hand on his companion's shoulder. "Guilt is the gift that goes on giving, Harry. But you've heard me on that subject before."

Harry managed a weak laugh. "What are we doing out here in this orchard?" He looked around at the trees, took a deep breath and added, "But doesn't it smell good?"

"It does. Earth and sun and citrus trees make a heady combination. Remember what it was like six weeks ago when most of the trees were in bloom?"

"Yes, and it looks as if the fruit is setting on well," Harry answered, pulling down some of the branches to examine the tiny buds of fruit.

"This is what I wanted you to see. If things go all right, which they almost never do in an orchard, it should be the best harvest I've had. But the ten months it will take these oranges to ripen is a long time. Now tell me what's on your mind."

Tucker led them to a split oak bench, set in the shade of one of the trees, with an angled view of the orchard and the shifting play of shadow and sunlight in the trees.

"One of my favorite spots on the place," Tucker said with a sigh of satisfaction as he settled onto the bench, "but never mind that. I want to hear what you've got to say."

Harry gave a quick summary of the meeting at Colleen McGraw's house and ended with the note Colleen had received.

"I've been keeping in mind what you said about the extent of the resistance there would be to what the Alliance is trying to do, but what I can't tell at this point is whether what I'm seeing is part of that resistance or actions motivated by something more personal."

"What does Colleen say?"

"She denies that any personal involvement has gone sour or that she is being stalked."

"Do you believe her?"

Harry wanted to say, yes, but he couldn't. "I don't know, at least not yet."

Tucker nodded and pointed to a blue-gray gnatcatcher, not much larger than a hummingbird that had landed on a branch a few feet from them and begun searching for aphids. They watched the bird for a few moments. Tucker broke their silence.

"It will not come as a surprise to you if I say people don't always act in their own best interest."

Harry waited for the application. He had become used to Tucker's roundabout way of thinking his way into a problem.

"Unless I've badly misunderstood the situation, the effort to clean up the Okalatchee River is going to be an example of what I'm talking about."

"You've got to do better than that," Harry replied.

"All right. Take Derwood Jones as an example. He is going to oppose every effort to impose speed restrictions on any part of that river where he drives his boat."

"Even if someone can show him that speeding over grass beds will kill or seriously injure manatees during that period of the year when they are in the river?" Harry asked with a marked lack of sympathy for Jones' position.

"That's right. Do you know why?"

"He's stupid?"

"Oversimplification. He's ignorant. He may or may not be stupid. But the level of his intelligence is not the issue. It's about control. How much control would you say he has over his life?"

"Very little."

"Right. He's dirt poor. He has a family, an old car, a beaten up boat his father left him, and a house that needs painting and a new roof. He fishes for a living, and every year there are fewer fish to catch."

"You don't know that his house needs a new roof," Harry said worriedly.

He was accustomed to Tucker's knowing more than he expected him to know, but his knowing Jones' house needed a new roof was too much.

"No, but if it's not that, it's something else. Everything else is true because it's true of almost every man in the Hook. Now, when people he doesn't know and doesn't like because they're strangers come along and tell him the manatees have to be protected and tell him they are recommending that the state impose a no wake rule on a part of the river he has to pass through every day of his working life, what does he say?"

"That everybody cares more about the welfare of the manatee than they do about him."

"That's it."

"And then there'll be the private property pitch."

"That too," Tucker agreed.

"Silly me," Harry said, "I thought talking to you would make me feel better."

8

Harry parked his Land Rover in the Visitor Parking area of Cora Wingate's high-rise condominium in the Silver Sands section of Avola. He had decided to begin his investigation for the Alliance by talking to all its members. Since he had met Cora at Colleen McGraw's house, she had been slipping in and out of his mind in a very pleasing way, and he was not happy about having to ask her questions she would not want to answer and was likely to consider impertinent.

On the whole, Harry did not find thinking about women a happy experience, mostly because he now had so few of them in his life to think about, and several of those were *ex* this and that, including two wives. Even in his cheerful moods he regarded his record with women as dismal. So it was with a strong sense of *déjà vu* that he admitted wanting Cora Wingate to like him. Well, perhaps something more than *like* him. But he had agreed to help Colleen, and if in doing it he offended Cora, then that was the price he paid for making a living by prying into other people's business. She would have forgotten him by now anyway.

He got out of the Rover, locked it, and tried to put himself into a more positive mood but failed because he recalled with a sharp sense of loss that he had never locked his old LR, which he had driven until two years ago when the motor mounts rusted through and dropped the engine onto a street in downtown Avola, to the merriment of everyone who saw it happen. Then he cheered up a bit, remembering that the dealer gave him a hundred and fifty dollars and a fancier horn not to trade it in, and Harry sadly committed the *Flying Dutchman,* Tucker's name for his transportation, to the recycle yard on Grackle Street.

Cora lived on the 20th floor, and Harry was lifted to it in a brass and Brazil wood elevator that, except for a quiet sigh as the doors closed and opened, rose in heavenly silence. Cora greeted him with a smile of welcome when he stepped into her private lobby. She was dressed in a pale orange and white dress that looked to Harry like an abstract painting. Its braided cord belt enhanced her figure.

Greetings over, she led him into the apartment.

"I'm not accustomed to being questioned by private detectives," she said, "so you must forgive me if I'm a little nervous."

Because of what looked to him like mischief twitching the corners of her mouth as she spoke, Harry doubted she was nervous, and he thought he detected in her voice some of the flirtation that had appealed so strongly to him at Colleen McGraw's house. He hadn't been mistaken about her. She was definitely a very attractive and interesting woman.

She waved him into a lemon yellow chair in a wide, bright room with white walls mounted with large, boldly colored paintings, all of which, Harry noted, had the unmistakable presence of originals.

"It's not nearly as bad as a visit from the IRS," he told her and won a smile. "Are the paintings from your gallery?" he asked.

"Some are. Some Holly, my woman Friday, found, and the rest I've picked up for myself while on buying trips. Perhaps later we can look at them together."

"I'd like that."

"Good," she said. "Sharing my paintings gives me a lot of

pleasure. Let me fetch us some iced tea."

While she was gone, Harry got up and walked toward the wall of glass opening on the shimmering blue and green Gulf. Turning around, he saw another glass wall sixty or seventy feet away and beyond it a perfectly flat landscape that appeared to extend all the way to the Everglades.

"Do you like the views?" she inquired, returning with a wicker and glass tea tray inset with butterflies.

"Yes," he replied, returning to his chair, "but do you ever feel disconnected from the world up here?"

She gave a throaty laugh. "I'm inclined to feel separated from the world wherever I am. What about you, Mr. Brock. Do you feel the same way on your Hammock?"

"Call me Harry," he replied, deciding to take her question seriously. "Sometimes, I do get a little lost in the Hammock," he admitted. "At least for me, the immersion can become addictive."

She passed him his tea.

"Interesting," she said. "I confess that I find my eagle's roost a sanctuary which I leave reluctantly and return to gratefully, and call me Cora, unless you find it too ugly. Arlen says the name reminds him of a crow cawing."

"That seems harsh," Harry protested while wondering about her relationship with Gott.

"Don't be embarrassed," she said with a weak laugh. "When I was a little girl, the boys used to chase me at recess, shouting, 'Caw! Caw! Caw!' I hated my name. Then, later, I became resigned to it."

She paused, apparently remembering. Based on her expression, Harry thought it was not a happy experience. Then she rallied. Her smile came back and she said, "Let's get started. Do I have to sit under a bright light?"

"When I introduce the bamboo splinters. I'm trying to learn

as much as I can about everyone associated with Colleen."

"And Joyce Fields?"

"Yes. Why are you in the Alliance?"

"I don't have many skills, but I do have a little money, and through my gallery I'm in contact with a lot of rich people, many of whom have a passionate interest in preserving the area. I thought I could introduce Colleen, whom I greatly admire, to those who are in a position to support what she's doing."

"Do you think the Alliance is doing anything worthwhile?"

She seemed uneasy with the question. "I hope so. Arlen and the others think it is."

"What led you to the group?"

"Arlen Gott. He's a cousin. I've known him all my life. I went at his invitation and stayed. I like the people. They all do things."

"Is there a Mr. Wingate?"

"There was," she responded in a suddenly cold voice, "but I prefer not to go there."

Strike one, Harry thought. Be careful.

"Why do you think Joyce Fields was murdered?" he asked.

"Because she was gathering information that would strengthen the case for intervention by the state and federal agencies in the management of the Okalatchee."

Harry was impressed by her response. "How sure are you that was why she died?" he asked, pressing her.

Cora crossed her legs and looked past Harry toward the Gulf.

"Not entirely," she said when she was ready. "This is not a confession, but I didn't like Dr. Fields. That doesn't mean I wanted her dead. She was cold and, I think, extremely calculating. She was also as finely finished as a polished steel ball. I tried to be friendly, but she always presented me with the same cold, impermeable surface."

"Did Arlen find her as hard to approach?"

"What makes you think Arlen made any effort to *approach* her or that I would know if he had?" she demanded.

"You said you've known Arlen all your life. I thought you might know if there was anything between them."

"Do you mean were they lovers?" she asked with a sharp laugh.

Harry shrugged but watched her very closely. She was doing a good job of concealing it, but she was angry.

"You would have to have known Dr. Fields to realize how ridiculous the idea is."

"Colleen tells me she was a very beautiful woman."

"Yes," Cora said flatly, "but I don't think she cared one way or the other."

"I have a friend who said of another beautiful woman that she was burdened by beauty."

"Yeats," Cora said, looking at Harry in a new way.

Harry nodded. "I take it you mean Dr. Fields was not burdened by hers."

"No. She did not use it as a part of her capital assets, not at least as far as I am aware. Where is all this going, Harry?"

"How did she and Colleen get along?"

"Very well."

"What do you think of Colleen?"

"We share a common interest."

"The river?"

"No. Books."

Harry looked around without seeing a book or magazine marring any glistening surface.

"She doesn't allow them in here," Cora said with a whimsical grin.

"Who doesn't?" Harry asked in surprise.

"Estelle, my cleaning woman. Come on, I'll show you."

The library was large with a west-facing wall of glass. The

remaining three walls were covered with floor to ceiling shelves, stuffed with books. Two magazine racks sat back to back in the near center of the room, flanked by a huge globe in a mahogany frame. Three leather chairs with reading lamps and ottomans were arranged on a large, alizarin and cream carpet.

"They are prisoners of this room," Cora said.

"No entertainment center in sight. Is it hidden behind a section of the book shelves?" Harry asked, wondering but also half teasing.

"I've never found one," Cora replied with a straight face.

"Why?" Harry asked, astonished by the room and what it told him about her.

"I was an unattractive child," she answered in a matter-of-fact voice. "Reading became my refuge and later my passion." She paused and then said with an obvious effort at lightness, "I have never been burdened by beauty."

Her ironic tone did not fool Harry.

"I think you and Joyce Fields also had something in common," he told her.

"What?" she demanded.

"You're beautiful and don't seem to know it."

"If that's supposed to be a joke, it's not funny."

"It's not a joke. You're a beautiful woman, and when you smile, it just gets better."

"If you're not serious, you're being extremely cruel," she said. "If you are, you should have your eyes checked."

"I'm very serious, and my eyesight is excellent."

They had turned to face one another, and she was looking at him with a disturbingly vulnerable expression that made Harry think he had gone too far. He wanted to put his arms around her, and the impulse alarmed him because he thought it was entirely out of line.

Then things slid further out of line.

"Harry," she said, "are we finished with the Q & As?"

"Yes," he said, still thinking about what he wanted to do.

"Good," she said and stepping forward threw her arms around his neck and kissed him on the mouth.

Suspending all thought, Harry put his arms around her and kissed back, becoming more and more aware of what was pressed against him. Without much luck, he tried to make his stomach smaller.

When they finished kissing, which wasn't right away, Cora leaned back in his arms while still maintaining physical contact and said a little huskily, "Telling a woman she's beautiful is a good thing to do, Harry. Look what it got you. I hope you wanted it, and if you didn't, don't tell me."

"You're safe," he answered, trying to slow his breathing.

He fervently hoped he wasn't going to have a seizure and spoil this, but at the rate his heart was beating, it seemed a possibility. She moved against him a little and smiled.

"I thought I was," she said. "Let me know when you're tired of standing."

He said he was good for a while yet.

"Very gallant," she replied, "but I think we can be more comfortable."

Before Harry noticed whether or not the bed was comfortable, they had made a shambles of the pillow arrangement. The quilt didn't fare too well either, being quickly kicked onto the floor. Then the blanket went. When things quieted down, they were left sprawled across one another, naked and unmoving like victims of a double homicide.

After a long time, Cora managed to lift her face out of the rumpled sheets, strands of wet hair plastered to her forehead. "God, Harry," she gasped, "think what we'd be like with practice."

Harry, on his back, arms flung wide, eyes still closed, tried to laugh and only managed a choking sound. "The mind boggles," he croaked.

A resurrection of sorts gradually took place, and they crawled out of bed looking like characters in a Stanley Spencer painting, emerging from their graves, stunned to find themselves in the world again.

"How about some lunch?" Cora asked while they were dressing, struggling to keep from laughing.

"I'm grateful for the offer," Harry replied, sitting on the side of the bed, pulling on his stockings, "because I'm starving, and I lack the strength to leave."

She gave a snort of laughter and took him by the arm. "Come on, let's look at some pictures. Then you can help me with the salad."

They shared a roasted walnut and pear salad and a bottle of better wine than Harry ever bought. The power of speech having been restored, they ate and talked as easily as if they had been wrecking beds for a long time.

"What can you tell me about Elaine Porter?" Harry asked when they had leaned back from their plates and were dawdling over the last of the wine.

"A couple of things," Cora said. "I don't like her, so what I say is biased. She's a snob and a hypocrite. Aside from that, there's not much I can tell you, except I wouldn't trust her as far as I can throw a bale of cotton."

Harry grinned. "How much time have you spent on the old plantation?"

"About as much as you."

"Why don't you trust her?"

"She's got more money than a Gulf Emirate, but she will wiggle harder than a pole dancer to keep from picking up a lunch check for twenty dollars."

"Okay, that leaves Josh Bates. Anything I should know about there?"

"Honest as the day is long and a lot smarter than he looks."

"You trust him."

"I do. He's preparing our suit against the state."

When it came time for Harry to leave, Cora walked him to the door.

"This is the awkward part," she said, her color rising slightly, "but I'll try not to make it worse than it has to be. For your information, if you make it, I'll take your call."

"I'll make it," Harry said and reached for her.

Considering where they'd been, their goodbye kiss was remarkably chaste.

9

Still thinking about Cora, Harry drove into the shade of the big live oak on the front corner of his lawn and was stepping out of the Rover when his phone rang.

"Harry, it's Sarah."

After the divorce, Jennifer had not allowed them to call him Dad or Father or any name suggesting their relationship to him. It had been more than a year since he last called her, and in that conversation she had been so hostile that he decided to let her call him.

"Hello, Sarah," he said and waited, expecting the worst because something had to be very wrong.

"Harry," she said again in the same cold voice, "I need to talk to you. There is no reason why you should want to talk to me, but . . ."

Her voice trailed off into silence.

"Sarah," he said, forcing some conviction into his voice, "I'm more than willing to talk to you. What is it?"

"God, this is hard," she said as if she was speaking to someone else. "All right, here goes. I want to come to Avola. I'll stay in a hotel. . . ."

He was so surprised that for a moment he couldn't speak. She broke violently into his silence. "Okay," she blurted. "Forget it. I never should have. . . ."

"Sarah," he said, finding his tongue. "Of course you can

come, and you will stay with me. It would be wonderful to see you."

"I doubt that," she said with no trace of humor.

And, in truth, he might have been stretching it. She was in her thirties now, and had been angry with him for twenty-six years. He had not seen her for ten years. Although he remembered the child with love and affection, he hardly knew the woman. True, her anger and her brother Clive's anger had more to do with their mother than with him, but knowing that didn't lessen the pain it had caused him.

"The offer stands," he said.

There was a moment's pause before she said, "All right, with the understanding that I may decide to move to a hotel."

"Of course. When can you come?"

"I haven't said anything about this to David. I'll have to do that, and he's not going like it. My husband doesn't like much of anything I do lately."

"Do you want to talk about anything now? I can call you back."

That made her laugh a little. "I can pay for the call, Harry. No, it can wait until I'm with you." She paused. Then, before she hung up, she said as if the words were being wrung out of her, "Thank you."

Harry suddenly found himself self-conscious about his bachelor house. He put new sheets and pillowslips on the guest room bed, bought half a dozen new towels and facecloths, hung a new shower curtain in the upstairs bathroom, and laid in enough boxes of tissues and stacks of toilet paper to withstand a siege. He bought toothpaste, shampoo, and even bubble bath, remembering how much she had loved it as a child.

He devoted hours to cleaning the house and groaning over scars, scrapes, and stains on the walls, the humps in the dining room floor, chips in the dishes, the family of squeaking bats in the attic, and worried that she would be disturbed by the gopher tortoise living under the lanai, who occasionally plodded around under there at night, bumping his shell on the cross timbers.

On the evening after Sarah's call, he took Cora to the Harborside and with the candlelight and the wine as a support group confessed his worries about the upcoming visit. She laughed cruelly at his preparations and tried to keep her face straight when he said it was going to be like having a stranger in the house only she wasn't.

"Just remember not to walk around in your birthday suit and everything will be all right," she said, patting his hand, her eyes shining with amusement.

"It's not a laughing matter," he said, a little shocked by her levity.

"Of course it isn't, Harry," she said with a smile and waved away the waiter. "Let's have dessert at my place."

Sarah was arriving in three days, and when he wasn't cleaning and buying things, he talked to people connected with the Okalatchee and the Stoneman Douglas Alliance. The first was John Dee Rudd, the owner of Old Beetle's Boat Dock in the Hook.

"I'll talk to you, but you're wasting your time," Rudd said, scratching his chin through his beard and shifting a little in his folding chair.

He and Harry were sitting in Rudd's chicki hut, the wind rattling the dry palm fronds over their heads. Beyond the dock the river was flashing with a small chop from the making tide, and an osprey hovered above the leading edge of the flow, searching for fish, its wings flickering in the morning sun.

Harry got things going by asking how Rudd was getting along with Bobby Scrubbs and Fannon Jones. Rudd grinned. "I think they're walking the straight and narrow," he said and added more seriously, "but I worry a little about young Jones. Derwood can get drastic sometimes."

"Is the boy all right?"

"So far. Whatever that Captain Snyder said to Derwood stuck. The trouble is he resents that kind of interference, and when he decides to do something about it, I'm worried he'll go for Snyder through Fannon. Or Marjory."

"That's his wife?"

"Yes. There's some rough history there."

Harry wasn't surprised to hear it. He let Rudd go on talking about it for a while before asking if he knew Dr. Fields.

"I knew who she was and saw her now and then with her nets and bottles and so on. She buzzed around here like a goddamned deer fly."

"Around your dock?"

"No. The river."

"Did you ever talk to her?"

"I sold her some gas once. She told me she'd been seeing big tarpon rolling in the Bend. I said they always gathered up there, but it was hard to get them to strike anything."

"So the conversation was civil."

"That's right. You know, she told me tarpon can breathe air, and when they're young they have to at intervals. I asked her if that was why big tarpon roll, and she thought it was likely, but she wasn't certain they had to. I learned something there. She was finding out some interesting things, and that part of what she was doing I approved of. What I didn't like was her politics."

"What do you mean?"

"She was trying to persuade the state to make changes in the way the Okalatchee is being used."

"Because of what she was discovering about the health of the river?"

"That's right. I'm a property rights man. If I own a piece of land, what I do with it is nobody's goddamned business but mine."

Harry wanted to ask if that including poisoning the river, but he knew he would get nowhere with that argument and made no response. Rudd wasn't ready to let it go.

"All we're asking for here is that our interests get as much attention as whatever the scientists say has to be done to protect the sea grass, the mosquito fish, the manatee, or whatever the hell it is today, tomorrow, and the next day—because it's always something." He paused and then added, "People are more important than fish when it comes to deciding what happens to this river."

Harry listened and nodded, thinking how easy it would be to dismiss what Judd was saying, to point out that if the scientists said the river was dying, it probably was, and something was going to have to be done about it. Without admitting that, the so-called stakeholder argument was really a thinly veiled effort on the part of those with personal and economic interests to perpetuate destructive practices and to keep from having to modify them. It was, however, he thought with a sinking heart, as Tucker had said, "In the face of ignorance, even the gods fail."

"Was there anyone else around here who knew Dr. Fields at all?"

Rudd shook his head, still scowling over his thoughts.

"How about Colleen McGraw? Do you know her?"

A couple of men, probably customers, clumped onto the dock. Rudd pushed to his feet. "I've never seen her, but she's head of that Alliance that's been making trouble. What are they but a bunch of rich do-gooders with nothing better to do with their time? They even filed a complaint against my dock, and I had somebody from the EPA sniffing around, looking to see how much oil and gas spillage there was. There's no damned escaping them."

Harry put out his hand. "Thanks for your time, Mr. Rudd. I appreciate it."

"Some of the people out here are a lot more radical about this subject than I am," the big man said, holding onto Harry's hand and regarding him seriously as he spoke. "Your people need to know that and trim their sails to suit the wind."

"I think they do know," Harry replied.

One of them was already dead.

Harry left the Hook and drove to Joshua Bates' office in downtown Avola. It was only a thirty-minute drive, but it took him from a third world to a first world setting. Josh was a partner in the law firm of Pierson, Osgood, Goodlette, Hirshhorn, and Bates on Bigelow Avenue. Pierson, *et al.* occupied the third floor of the brown glass building, and Bates' office was air conditioned to a meat locker chill, but it boasted a full wall view of the Gulf four blocks to the west.

"This isn't too shabby," Harry said to Bates, "and when you die, they can just stand you up in closet to freeze and wait for global warming, science, or the resurrection to revive you."

Bates, who seemed to be having trouble shifting his attention from whatever he had been thinking about to Harry, made a bad job of being amused.

"We all wear suits," Bates said, making an effort, and asked Harry to sit down.

Harry was wearing shorts, and the leather chair felt like a block of ice.

"I'm worried about Colleen," Bates said with a frown, leaning toward Harry from his matching black chair.

Harry had noticed that the lawyer's gleaming black desk was swept clean of paper, and he wondered where Bates worked. He thought of asking him and changed his mind. He wouldn't think that was funny either.

"Why?" Harry asked.

"Hasn't she told you?" Bates demanded impatiently. "She's had threatening letters."

"I think I've seen everything she's been sent," he said. "I've seen, I think, two letters. Are there more?"

"She won't say. But if she won't be forthcoming with you, the situation is worse than I thought."

"It's not pleasant for her getting that kind of mail," Harry told him, "but I don't think she's in any immediate danger. Has there been anything other than the letters?"

"For Christ's sake, Brock, you were with her when someone tried to shoot her. Have you forgotten?"

Bates had gone in an instant from being nervous and distracted to red-faced and angry.

"I told all of you the other night that I didn't think that was a serious attempt on either her life or mine. And remember, the message might have been intended for me."

Bates settled back and blew out his breath. "Sorry," he said. "I really don't want anything to happen to her."

"Is there anyone you know who might want to harm her?"

"No," Bates said quickly and then looked away from Harry. "The Alliance is making enemies by pressing ahead with water quality issues in the Okalatchee."

"Who's the most worked up?"

Bates jumped to his feet and began pacing. "We're off the record here. No attribution. Nothing."

"Okay, unless you're going to tell me about a crime that's been committed or is about to be committed."

Bates gave a snort of disgust and continued pacing. "The people who don't like us have the deepest pockets in Southwest Florida. They have whole law firms working for them. They bankroll dozens of election campaigns for lawmakers, judges, state and county officials, including sheriffs."

"Who are they?" Harry asked quietly.

"The Southwest Florida Development Association is the umbrella group for most of them," Bates said, glaring at Harry. "The big three are agriculture, realtors, and developers. The SFDA is represented by Frederick Klugson Associates, one of the biggest litigation firms on the East Coast."

"If I was going to talk to a person in the Association, who would it be?"

"You could try Adelaide Slocum. She's CEO of Blue Skies Realty and President of the SFDA's Board of Directors. That's if you can get an appointment."

It turned out to be a matter of making a phone call.

Adelaide Slocum was a large woman with abundant silver hair. Even Harry knew that her dark blue pants suit had not come from Marshall's. She exchanged greetings with him and broke into a wide grin. "You're a long way from home," she said, obviously pleased and letting her own Maine accent out a little.

"Nowadays, I get there on County Road Nineteen," he replied, laying it on a little.

"It sounds like the Richardson Lakes to me," she said, coming around her desk to shake his hand, which left him knowing his hand had been shaken. "Twenty years of swinging a golf club and standing in reception lines," she added, noting his quizzical look.

"Rangeley is close enough," he said, admiringly. "What about you?"

"Portland, and don't ask me when. Oh, my God," she burst out, grasping his upper arms, her hazel eyes wide. "Now I remember. About twenty years ago. Parmachenee Lake. The murder trial in South Paris. That's you, isn't it? Warden Harry Brock."

"Twenty-five, actually, and I've had better years."

"I can believe it. Sit down. My God. That was a nasty business."

"Going through it once was enough," he said, feeling a little less liking for her.

"Of course. I'm sorry. I shouldn't have mentioned it. But it felt as if I knew you. That was probably the accent. There aren't that many real people down here, and I got carried away."

"Great save," Harry responded when she released her grip on him. "I'm glad we had this talk first because later on you may not feel so warm and fuzzy about me."

She laughed. "You're working for the Stoneman Douglas Alliance. The ichthyologist Joyce Fields, who was sharing her research with you, has been murdered, and you and Colleen McGraw were shot at. I didn't have to be a member of Mensa to know you'd be coming to see me."

"Impressive," Harry said.

She shrugged off the compliment. "In the end, you're only as good as your information."

"Who in the SFDA is angry enough with the Alliance to start killing people?" he asked in a friendly voice.

"I fervently hope the answer is nobody," Slocum said calmly. "For sure, the Alliance has raised hackles the whole length of the river, and true enough, the Association is not pleased with everything they're doing. But, Harry, we're neither stupid nor evil. We know the Okalatchee is in trouble. Where we and the Alliance part ways is over what to do about it. That and their efforts to bring the St. John's River Coalition into the argument."

"You make it sound so reasonable," Harry responded. "But someone is threatening Colleen McGraw's life, and if I have my way, somebody's going to jail for it."

Slocum looked hard at him and said, "It's not us. How would we benefit from killing Joyce Fields or harming Colleen? In the end, it would only strengthen the Alliance, give it more influence in Tallahassee, pour bad publicity all over us, and weaken our ability to achieve our goals."

"Which are?"

She shrugged. "Simple. We want what we think is best for Florida."

Harry suddenly thought of Auden's horse rubbing his arse on a tree while Icarus was falling and the tortured man screamed. Harry weighed those images against the awful blandness of Slocum's response and wondered if the parallel was real.

"We might not agree on what that is," he answered.

10

Sarah arrived on time, and Harry was waiting for her. She came through the gate wearing a tailored black suit, a severely plain white blouse, and carrying a large black leather bag and a black coat. Uncharitably, Harry wondered if she had joined a Puritan sect. But that nervous response was lost in his realization that with her long black hair and chiseled features she looked exactly like her mother at that age, and, also like Jennifer, she walked as if she was marching onto a stage.

"Hi," she said when she reached him and thrust out her hand. She did not smile, and her large, brown eyes regarded him with what Harry read as a marked distrust.

Harry took her hand. Its coldness came as a shock, and he wondered if she was frightened. He found that possibility disturbing and wondered if he had made a mistake in urging her to come and if both of them would regret it.

"I'm glad you're here," he said, trying to reassure her.

"That's good," she replied.

Harry noted with grim resignation the chill in her words and the fact she had not said she was glad to be here.

While they waited with the crowd at the carousel, Harry kept stealing looks at her and recalling his long campaign to persuade her mother to marry him, making, he thought bitterly, the first major mistake of his life. Then her luggage came, and, dividing it between them, they went out into the warm, moist night.

Before they reached the parking lot, she stopped to shed her jacket.

"It was forty-two in Minneapolis when I left," she said.

"A couple of nights last January," he responded, desperately trying for a light note, "it dropped into the forties here."

She didn't laugh and said something about the late spring they had had and the ways it had complicated life in the city. That got them to the I-75 access ramp.

As he turned onto it, Harry said, "Is your mother okay?"

"Why would you ask that?" Sarah demanded.

"I guess I could give you an answer," he replied, suppressing his anger, "but you and I have some history to get past before we can even begin talking about why I say or do anything. But I'd like to get to where we can have that conversation. How about you?"

Sarah dropped her head back against the seat and stared at the roof. Harry thought she looked wasted and wondered if he should go straight into Avola and put her in a hotel. But she surprised him.

"Well, I'm here," she said at last, seeming to have made up her mind about something. "My being here can't make much sense to you. Not given what you call our *history.*" She hesitated, then continued, "I think I'd say lack of history."

"That too," he replied. "I take it it's not because of your mother."

"It may be."

The comment surprised him. "Meaning?"

Sarah turned her head away and said in a cold voice, "There are times when I think everything I do is because of her."

Harry decided not to pursue it, and except for yes and no, she said nothing more until they crossed the bridge to the Hammock, and she looked out at the moonlight falling in pale, slanting bars on the white sand road and the Creek.

"You really do live in the woods," she said, and when they stopped in front of the house, she sat looking at it for a moment after he switched off the engine and said, "Peaceful."

After getting settled in her room, she came back downstairs to the kitchen where Harry was making their supper and said she had opened her window for a breath of fresh air and was surprised by all the sounds.

Harry checked the grouper filets in the broiler and took her out onto the lanai. He stood beside her for a few moments, trying to recapture the feelings he experienced the first night he heard what she was listening to.

"Mostly, its colony frogs," he told her. "Each colony has is its own sound, and all the males in the colony sing the colony song. That way, their females don't get confused and wander next door. Then there's the southern bullfrogs, called pig frogs because of their grunting calls. They carry the bass. The locusts and crickets are the strings, but I don't know a quarter of the peeping, stridulating, and whooping creatures serenading us. You may find it hard to sleep at first."

Sarah turned to Harry to say something just as a muffled rumbling like distant thunder or a long roll of jungle drums made her catch her breath.

"What is that?" she asked a bit uneasily, peering through the screen toward the glitter on the Creek from where the sound seemed to be coming.

"That's Benjamin," Harry said with a laugh.

"I thought you lived out here alone except for Tucker LaBeau."

"Benjamin is a big male alligator. He's telling all the females where he is, in case they're interested. He does that somewhat the way a cat purrs. If you could see him, you'd see the water around him being vibrated into little ripples."

The sound died away, and Sarah said, her voice a bit less

tight, "You live in a zoo."

"A zoo without bars. Come on, the grouper's done."

"I don't remember wine with dinner!" Sarah said as she sat down.

"You were what, seven, the last time we ate dinner together?"

"Parmachenee Lake," Sarah said. "It seems in another world."

"I used to think that. Then I found out it's still this one."

They ate and talked about what she remembered of Maine until Sarah pushed her plate back with a comfortable groan.

"I didn't know how hungry I was. I was hoping the heat would curb my appetite."

"You look pretty trim to me," Harry said truthfully.

"Thanks, but the war is never won."

"The price of beauty."

"Well thank you, Harry," she responded with a trace of a smile, then lost it and said, "If it's all right with you, I want to explain why I'm here."

Her delivery was stiff enough to make Harry think that what was coming had been rehearsed and that she still wasn't altogether happy with it.

"All right," he observed, pouring the coffee.

"I'm leaving my husband, and I'm one and a half months pregnant."

Harry sat down a little quicker than he intended. "You've got my attention."

She nodded. "I'm also being a terrible coward. You're the first person I've told."

"That you're leaving David or that you're pregnant?"

"Both."

"Okay."

He forced himself to sound calm, but he wasn't. He was scared enough to want to jump up and run. She was looking at him with those burning brown eyes, waiting for something from him, and so far all he had been able to say was okay. Then she gave him a reprieve.

"The divorce part started with David's mother and father," she said. "They're about your and Mom's age, and after thirty-five years of marriage, they've decided to call it quits—at least Wallace has. He's moved out, leaving Helen the house."

"Was their separation hard on David?"

"Yes. It's taken them two years to reach this point, and the cost has been high for all four of us. Helen is a good woman, but she's hell on wheels to live with."

"But David doesn't see it that way?" Harry almost gasped with relief to find himself still able to think.

"Worse than that! As soon as David and I recognized what was happening, he and I began fighting about it. He won't hear a word of criticism against Helen, and he blames his father for everything. When I defend his father, David gets red in the face and begins shouting at me."

"Is that why you haven't told him you're pregnant?"

"At first I was waiting for us to stop fighting long enough to talk about it. About the time I got it figured out that we weren't fighting about Helen and Wallace's problems but about ours, I thought, if things are this bad, maybe it's the wrong time to be having a baby."

Harry felt his stomach lurch. She couldn't be thinking of . . .

"That really scared me, Harry. You see, I'd come to realize that in our marriage I was Wallace and he was Helen. David has never been able to see that. He's like his mother. If he's not in every corner of my life, he's not happy, and when he is there, he never stops making suggestions about how I could improve."

Harry laughed. "What does Jennifer say?"

"She sides with David. The few times I've tried to defend Wallace in her presence, she's become furious with me."

"And?" Harry asked.

"And it all began coming apart," she said grimly, dropping her gaze.

"What did?" he asked, puzzled.

"All our lives since Mom left you, Harry," she said in a tight voice, "Clive and I have believed that you destroyed our family. That you ruined Mom's life. That because of you, Clive and I grew up without a father. Mom never let us forget what you did."

She stopped talking and stared at the table.

Harry knew something of the sort was coming, but hearing it from Sarah hit him hard, and he had to get past the flaring anger it produced before he trusted himself to speak.

"How much do you know about what happened between your mother and me?" he asked when he felt he was in control of his emotions.

"Only what she told us, which was that it was a miracle the man you shot hadn't killed you, and that with a wife and two small children you had no right to put yourself in danger the way you did." She paused to look with a hard face at Harry and added, "She said over and over that you put your stupid pride before your responsibility to love and protect us."

"That's quite an indictment," Harry said. "How much of it do you believe?"

"Until recently I've had no reason not to believe all of it."

"What's changed?" he asked.

"One day when we began arguing, I suddenly wondered if she'd been as unfair to you as she was being to Wallace. I couldn't get it out of my head."

Harry wondered if after all the years that had passed there was any point in saying more. But he found he couldn't leave it as it was. There were things he needed to say.

"You want to hear what you call 'my side' of it?"

She was now sitting rigidly erect, her eyes dark with emotions

Harry couldn't name, but she was obviously in pain.

She folded her hands and dropped her head, as if what she was about to say shamed her. "Yes. It's one of the reasons I'm here."

"All right," he said. "I don't know how much you remember, but at Parmachenee Lake we had no near neighbors. Your mother was accustomed to living with a lot of people around her, and she had nothing in common with the few people who lived on the lake. You had no decent school. The winter went on forever, and I was gone most days and often Sundays. She was too proud to say so, but I think she was afraid a lot of the time."

Sarah finally raised her head, her face, pale and strained. "I know all that, but it's not how I remember it. I thought the lake and the woods were magical places. Clive and I spent whole days outdoors. I remember swimming and watching the moose wade into the lake to eat lily pads. We snowshoed and went on winter picnics, and you pulled us on a toboggan and built huge fires. I remember going into the woods to cut our Christmas trees. It was a wonderful place for a child."

It was Harry's first glimpse of how she had experienced her childhood, and he felt tears of gratitude stinging his eyes, but he fought them back.

"I'm glad at least some of your memories of that time are happy ones," he said.

"They're all happy, except for the times you and Jennifer quarreled."

Harry let that pass. He had more to say. "Your mother was wrong about why I went after Justin Stone. Pride had nothing to do with it. Justin told the men in the village he was going to shoot a deer in his orchard. The hunting season had closed. I tried to stop him. I knew that if I had to arrest him, he would go to jail. He and his family were wretchedly poor, and with Justin in jail, they would have suffered. But I was too late. The deer was down. He had forced a confrontation."

Harry paused, remembering the snow filled orchard, the darkening sky, the bitter cold, and the big, rawboned man standing up from the dead deer with a rifle in his hands.

"Is that all?" Sarah asked quietly.

"Almost. I found him where he said he'd be, in his orchard. He had shot the deer and was cleaning it when I got there. I called to him. He stood up and shot at me. I shouted twice, but he fired again and clipped my shoulder. I got off a shot, intending to hit him in the right hip and knock him down. The bullet struck bone and broke up. A piece of it went through his heart and killed him. I was tried for murder and acquitted, but my career as a warden was over. Your mother stayed through the trial and left as soon as she heard the verdict. Do you remember any of it?"

"A little. I remember the creaky, old room, the smell of woolen clothes, all the people, and the sound of the steam knocking in the radiators. Clive doesn't remember anything about Maine. I'm the only one."

"And your mother."

"Yes."

There was a long silence. Harry broke it by asking if hearing what he had said was any help.

"Did Mom ask you to stay away from Stone?" Sarah had relaxed a little but not much.

"Yes, several times. We quarreled about it."

"Then why did you insist on going?"

"You're not a child, Sarah. I had taken an oath to enforce the law."

She was quiet for a moment and then asked, "Have you killed any other men?"

"One. And I don't want to talk about that."

"But you have shot others?"

"Yes."

"Thank you for being so frank and so patient," she said in a formal voice. "I appreciate it." She paused, preserving her distance, and added, "I'm going to have to think about what you've told me."

"Take your time," he said, regretting her reserve but willing to give her whatever space she needed.

11

At the end of the week, having met Tucker, Oh, Brother!, and Sanchez and been shown Benjamin, Sarah told Harry it was time she rented a car, did some shopping, and started getting a tan. For the latter she wanted a beach. She had too much company on his lawn.

On her first foray into the sun, Bonnie and Clyde had chased a rabbit across the lawn where she was lying on a blanket and across her back, and on the next day she was wakened from a nap by four cold, wet raccoon noses poking under her bathing suit in search of pockets. It was Harry's fault. He had taken to carrying goldfish in his shirt pocket when he was working outside and letting the cubs climb over him to find them.

"I'm cutting you loose, Father," she said when she returned to the Hammock with a rented, red Chrysler convertible and several fat shopping bags.

He thought with pleasure that her calling him *Father* might be the first sign of a softening in her attitude toward him. Maybe, he hoped, she would find she enjoyed being his daughter. He also wanted very much to know what influence, if any, his description of his and Jennifer's breakup was having on her thinking about her marriage and her pregnancy, but he was determined to let her be the one to broach the subject.

"Okay," Harry responded. "Three rules: sunglasses, at least number thirty sun block, and a note telling me when you're going to be late."

"Oh, heavy dad stuff," she said with a grin as she crossed the lanai.

"I've had two short stints of fathering," he replied. "I was pretty good at it."

She dropped her bags on a chair and sat down beside him on the swing. "I keep forgetting you remarried. I've got two half brothers and a half sister, haven't I?"

"That's right. And you're old enough to be the mother of two of them."

"Ouch. Is that tied to my telling you I might terminate this pregnancy?"

"Absolutely not. It's a reminder of how long I've been without you."

"You know, I think I like you even if you are pretty weird."

"I'm not weird," Harry protested.

"Oh, no! I mean, you're a private eye, living on an island in a swamp, who takes his company to meet a giant alligator named Benjamin? How strange is that? I'm not even mentioning the grinning dog and the mule with a straw hat."

"Interesting, wouldn't you say?"

"Yes, especially Mr. LaBeau. He's the first person I've ever met who talks with bees and has a bear visiting him on a regular basis."

"They're not too happy about the bear."

"That would be Tucker, Sanchez, and Oh, Brother!"

"That's right."

She laughed and gathered up her stuff, then paused. "Would I have liked Katherine?" she asked, blushing and failing to keep her voice steady.

"Yes," he answered, "and she would have liked you. Without pushing anything, there's no reason for you not to know her."

She nodded and got to her feet.

"You know," she said on her way into the house, "you may

have gained a permanent, live-in daughter."

That, he told himself, was better than a stick in the eye.

Then he remembered Cora Wingate and lost some of the smile. How was he supposed to explain her to Sarah? His first impulse was to lie by saying nothing. That lived in his mind for a nanosecond before being fried. He was going to have to tell her, and he would, but not just yet. He got up and called Jim Snyder.

"I'm twisted tighter than a pig's tail," Jim said and sounded it. "Can you come in here to talk? Maybe that way I can do five things at once, but I doubt it."

The Sheriff's Department's parking area was sizzling with heat and cicadas. Harry cracked the windows on the Rover, thinking he never had to do that with the old Rover. The wind blew freely through its tattered canvas.

"Frank is out in East Avola dealing with a rolled over cattle truck," Snyder said as Harry came through his office door. "The good news is that none of the yearling bull calves in the truck were hurt, but they all got loose when the truck went over. Did you ever try to catch a big bull calf?"

"No. What do you do with it when you do catch it?"

Snyder was taking papers from on a stack on his right, signing them, and placing them on a stack on his left.

"We'll ask Frank when he gets back, if he gets back," Jim said with a grin. "He's got a dozen of them busting through fences and running over gardens. Of course, we may have to visit him in the Avola Community Hospital."

"I've had a talk with Adelaide Slocum," Harry said, dropping onto one of Snyder's folding metal chairs.

Jim tossed his pen onto the desk and leaned back. "Not everybody gets to see her."

"That's what I hear. She said the SFDA had nothing to gain

and a lot to lose by killing Fields and threatening Colleen."

"Did you believe her?"

"I believed her when she said bad publicity would lessen their ability to carry out their agenda."

"Which is?"

"Whatever's best for Florida."

"Said the spider to the fly."

"Yes. I think that's about it. She didn't say it was wrong to kill Fields or harass Colleen."

Jim suddenly began to shift uncomfortably in his seat, his ears growing pink. He picked up his pen and dropped it, picked it up again and, gripping it like a piece of the True Cross, he faced Harry and said, "You're going to find this out, and I'd rather you heard it from me. The thing is, what it is is, well . . ."

He stuck, his ears red as a locust's eye.

"Jim," Harry said, intervening, "spit it out before it chokes you."

"I'm seeing Colleen McGraw."

"You're dating her."

"Well . . ."

"Jim."

"Yes. We've had dinner a couple of times. Seen a movie. Talked on the phone. So I guess . . ."

For a moment, Harry felt slightly annoyed. He had seen her first and . . . He heard himself and stopped. Of all the selfish . . . And what about Cora?

"That's good news, Jim," he said, rallying. "She's a really nice person. Congratulations."

"It's nothing serious! We're just . . ."

"Jim, it's wonderful."

A slow smile spread across Snyder's long face. "Yes, it is," he said.

★ ★ ★ ★ ★

With Sarah tooling around Avola in her red convertible, Harry returned to work. But before he did that, he called Cora.

"I was congratulating myself on having become involved with a man too old to have living parents, and in my weakened condition, I forgot your children. How many are there? Do you keep them in a shoe? Is having tea with your ex-wives part of the package?"

To this quasi-humorous riposte, he had replied that, smartass stuff aside, he wanted her to meet Sarah.

"I haven't seen much of her. I don't think I've really absorbed it yet."

"Are you and I going to get together anytime soon?" she asked.

"I see good things coming out of this," Harry said, pushing the positive line.

"And the referent for *this* is?"

"Getting together, you and Sarah meeting."

"Harry, she's your daughter. We can't have a threesome."

"Jesus, Cora."

As soon as he finished talking with Cora, he went to see Elaine Porter in old Avola at her office in Portland Square, which, if it had been larger, might have been called Avola's financial district. She was an accountant with Ely Sprouse Associates.

"Do you specialize in tax law or something like that?" Harry asked her, pretending not to be slightly awed by the grandeur of the offices, decorated with dark wood, thick carpets, individually lighted paintings, and a crystal chandelier in the waiting area where Porter came to rescue him from the *Forbes* and other financial magazines.

"I navigate the shark infested waters of estate planning," Porter said, looking down at Harry with a straight face.

"Must be profitable," he responded.

She twitched the lapels on her stunning lavender suit and said, "It's a living. Come with me."

Porter had a corner office with a treetop view north and east.

"A perfect place to paint," Harry said approvingly, thinking somewhat guiltily that he had all but abandoned his own painting.

"Perhaps I should set up an easel by that north window wall," Porter replied. "Sell my work to The Spice Islands Gallery."

The shot was not so much across his bow as through it, but he maintained composure. "There could be a living in it, but, of course, you already have one."

Porter smiled, and Harry wondered a little uneasily how much she knew about him and Cora. They sat down on two upholstered mahogany fireside chairs, which, Harry noted, were either originals or astonishingly good copies.

"If I'd known I was going to have to spend time talking with people in these trashy surroundings," he said, settling back in the chair, "I don't think I would have taken the job."

Porter chuckled and folded her hands across her stomach. "What, exactly, is your job?" she inquired.

"That's a good question. Here's another. Have you had any threats against your person or your professional life in the past year?"

"Aside from the occasional phone call with no one there when I answer, I don't think I have had anything even resembling a threat."

"Why not?"

She looked at him sharply. "I've wondered the same thing myself. But, as far as I know, no one on the Board but Colleen has experienced any unpleasantness." She paused, sat up, and pulled her jacket a little more tightly around her and then said,

"I wasn't joking the other night when I said, 'Look for the money.' "

"I know. You haven't forgotten Dr. Fields?"

"No, Mr. Brock, I haven't."

"Call me Harry. Do you think there's a connection between Fields' death and the trouble Colleen is experiencing?"

"Not necessarily, Harry. Please call me Elaine." She inclined her head in a slightly mocking bow.

Harry was getting to like her. He liked her mind, and he was even a little flattered that she was taking the trouble to amuse herself at his expense. "Is that a maybe?"

She smiled and then became more serious. "It's more an 'I don't know,' and it bothers me that I don't because on the face of it, it's a no-brainer. Somebody has a list and has crossed off Fields. McGraw is next. But something's not right. All that shooting from the boat, for example. I'm inclined to agree with you about that. But if the man was missing on purpose, what does it mean? Was killing Fields a mistake? 'Oops! I hit her. Sorry.' "

"What do you mean when you say, 'Follow the money'?"

"Nothing very profound. Who benefits financially from having Fields and possibly Colleen dead?"

"I've talked with Adelaide Slocum. There's certainly money enough there. But she claims the Association loses big time if members or associates of the Alliance start dying. Should I believe her?"

"Adelaide knows as well as anyone that truth is contextual. What she tells you will be true within carefully calculated parameters."

"Which means what?"

"Don't believe anything she says."

"That's my thought, too. But she has a point. I don't think killing the opposition would be the first thing a group as much in the public eye as the Association would think of."

"Oh, I think killing the opposition, more or less metaphorically speaking, is just what they would think of, but I agree that doing it with guns is a little obvious. Besides the costs can't become a tax write-off, whereas the work of lawyers, equally fatal when done well, is a legitimate deduction."

"Good point. Is there any reason you can think of why anyone on the Alliance Board would want Colleen dead?"

He hoped the quick change of focus might shake something loose, but Porter was unperturbed.

"We are a remarkably bland lot. Even Venus de Wingate is probably incapable of doing anyone any real harm, except, possibly, by unintentionally inflicting on her partner a variety of crib death."

Harry experienced a crisis of allegiance but laughed anyway because he couldn't really stop himself.

That left Arlen Gott.

Harry found him in his office on the Southwest Florida University campus, newly located east of I-75 on several hundred acres of reclaimed maleluca swamp. After a heavy shower, wading birds flocked to the faculty parking lot to feast on frogs and half drowned worms. It was dry and baking hot when Harry stepped out of the Rover and looked around for the Hagg Building. It had not moved. It was still beside the library.

Professor Gott's book-lined burrow on the J-3 level was a letdown after the opulence of Elaine Porter's office. Gott was hunched over his desk like Quasimodo, marking papers. As soon as he saw Harry, he swept them aside and heaved himself onto his feet.

"Come in, Brock," he said with a theatrical wave. "I am stranded on an island of student essays, allegedly written on the background of the Gadsden Purchase. I cannot think why I made such a ridiculous assignment. What brings you to this remote corner of learning?"

"I'm talking with all the members of the Alliance Board, hoping for a better understanding of why Colleen McGraw is being threatened," Harry said, sitting down gingerly on the battered wooden chair indicated by Gott's gesture where students usually sprawled.

Gott sank back into his own relatively upscale desk chair and asked what Harry had learned so far.

"That Elaine Porter and Cora Wingate are not best friends. Other than that, not much. Maybe you can tell me something useful."

"Don't be surprised if I can't," Gott said, scratching around in his russet beard as if he was looking for something.

"Who, outside of someone opposing the aims of the Alliance, might have reason to harass her, possibly even want her dead?"

Gott shook his head. "I can't think of a soul. Colleen lives what used to be called an exemplary life. Her work at the library brings her nothing but praise. No one in the Alliance has any reason to hate her. Even our opposites in the Association don't, so far as I know, think ill of her. I suppose she could be harboring a dark and dangerous secret, but I doubt it."

"So do I," Harry said, recalling Snyder's confession that he was "seeing" Colleen. She seemed to Harry exactly the sort of woman one would *see*.

"However," Gott said darkly, "along the oxbows and in settlements like the Hook some people's first inclination is to reach for a gun or a can of kerosene when they're angry. She may have attracted the attention of one of them. It does look as if Joyce Fields did."

"It's tempting to think so," Harry replied, "and that's what bothers me."

"Too tempting?" Gott asked.

"Too easy," Harry said, thinking of Derwood Jones.

"Something like it happens in history research all the time. *Post hoc, ergo, propter hoc.*"

Harry laughed. "It's one of Tucker LaBeau's favorite examples of feeble thinking: After the fact; therefore because of it."

"The troublesome part, as your friend probably knows," Gott said, having another dig in his beard, "is that sometimes it's true."

12

Harry got home to find Sarah crumpled on the couch, weeping.

"What's wrong?" he asked, sitting down beside her and resting a hand on her shoulder.

"Oh, God, Harry," she said, pushing herself off the cushions, "I'm sorry. I didn't want you to see this, but I couldn't seem to stop."

Her face was wet with tears, and she needed to blow her nose. Harry went into the kitchen and came back with a box of tissues. Still trying to apologize, she wiped her eyes and blew her nose and made a stab at pulling herself together. It occurred to Harry that she had not been indulged very much when it came to expressing her pain. She began apologizing again.

"It's okay, Sarah," he said quietly. "What's wrong?"

She halted in mid-sentence and shot him a startled look, took a deep breath, let it go, and said in a tight voice, "Jennifer called."

She sat very straight, staring at the crumpled tissues in her hands. Harry waited.

"And?" he asked finally.

"She's angry with me."

"About what?"

"David told her where I was."

"She didn't know?"

"No. There was no point in telling her. She wouldn't . . . doesn't understand. She's furious."

"Because you came here."

"That and because I've left David."

"Then you've made the decision?"

"Not yet. But I'm sick of living Jennifer's and David's emotional lives."

She blew her nose again, giving Harry time to think. They had not really talked about her situation since the first night she was here. Perhaps the time had come.

"How much will your being pregnant influence what you're going to do?" he asked.

She scowled at him. "Am I going to get a talk about my responsibilities to the unborn?"

"I hope not," he said. "I'm just trying to find out what your thinking is."

But running under the words was the question of how he felt about her terminating her pregnancy.

"My experience tells me that means giving you information that will be used against me later."

"No wonder you were crying. It won't happen here. But I can't be much use to you if I don't know what you want to do or what you think your options are."

And what were his? What was he entitled to say, if anything? Was he even entitled to an opinion? Well, he seemed to be acquiring one.

She sat a little straighter and regarded him suspiciously. "This is a test, and you'd better not flunk it."

Harry laughed despite himself. "I've been warned," he said.

She relaxed a little. "This is how I see it. If I go back to David and have this baby, my life will remain what it has been with the added complication of a child. If I leave David, I will not only lose the structure he has provided in my life, but I will also alienate my mother because she has decided David is the reliable, responsible person you weren't. She also needs the comfort and stability having me married gives her."

"And your pregnancy?"

"On my own, it's very tough for me to see how I could continue it."

"I'm not saying this is what you should do, but could you live with your mother, have the baby, and go on working?"

She shook her head. "I can't live with Jennifer."

"How much pressure are you feeling to make the choice?"

"It depends."

"If it's any help, you're welcome to stay here as long as you want. And I mean right through having your child and beyond."

"Is that what you want?"

"Probably, but what I want most is whatever you decide is right for you."

She gave him a pained look and said, "I thought coming here was going to make things easier."

A little after seven the next morning, Frank Hodges called Harry to say that Joshua Bates and his wife had been shot and killed, apparently in their sleep.

"Burglary?" Harry asked, knowing what the answer would be but wanting it out of the way.

"It doesn't look like one."

"Who found them?"

"Here's the bad part. It was Anna, their ten-year-old daughter. The kid said she got worried when she woke and didn't hear her mother making breakfast. The Captain wanted you to know. We'll be back in the office in a couple of hours. I've got to go."

Sarah came into the kitchen wearing a forest green robe with a towel around her head and bringing with her the smell of soap and shampoo. The night before, after their rocky start, she and Harry had settled into a long talk, and Harry was grateful for it. He went to bed feeling that he could finally say he had begun to know this long absent daughter.

"Who calls you at this ungodly hour?" she asked, slumping into a chair.

"Bringers of bad news," he said. "What do you want for breakfast?"

"Whatever's going. What kind of bad news?" She loosened the towel and began drying her hair.

"Eggs and bacon?" he asked, putting off answering the question.

"Fine," she answered and waited for him to go on.

Harry decided he couldn't keep her shielded from what his work involved. If he expected her to be open and honest with him, he would have to be the same with her. "Okay, before you came, the Stoneman Douglas Alliance, a conservation group, hired me to find out who was sending their president threatening letters."

Harry skipped over the part about being shot at. "Frank Hodges, a sergeant in the Tequesta County Sheriff's Department, just called to tell me that last night Joshua Bates, the Alliance attorney, and his wife were shot to death in their sleep."

Sarah had stopped rubbing her hair to listen. "That's awful, Harry," she said in a shocked voice. "Did you know them?"

"I knew him slightly."

"Did they have any children?"

"A daughter, ten. She found them this morning. The killer must have been using a silencer on his gun. She had heard nothing. It probably saved her life."

"My God," Sarah said in a choked voice. "How can you stand encountering this sort of thing all the time?"

"Something like this shooting is very rare," he replied. "In fact, I don't encounter death all that often. But it's true that over time I've learned to accept it as something that happens. It no longer shocks me the way it does you."

He stopped speaking and let Sarah absorb what he had said.

"Except on television or in a picture," she said very quietly, "I don't think I've ever seen a dead person, and no one I know has died." She stood up, clutching her towel. "Excuse me," she said. "I'll get dressed."

Harry watched her go and thought sadly, *Well, that's that. She'll be on a plane tomorrow.* He got up and without much enthusiasm began making breakfast.

But before he was finished, Sarah was back in the kitchen, wearing black jeans and a striped tank top.

"If you can do this, so can I," she said briskly, striding toward the stove. "I heard you say something about bacon and eggs."

"You'd better make some fresh coffee," he said with a grin.

"That's next." With the bacon sizzling and the egg water heating, she stood beside Harry, fists on her hips, and said, "I don't think much of your job, Harry, but you're not the shit Jennifer says you are."

Harry was thoroughly pleased by her comment. Now, if he could just persuade her to have the baby.

Two hours later Sarah called to him from the lanai. "Sanchez is outside and seems to want something, but I can't figure out what it is."

Harry had been on the phone with Colleen and then Jim Snyder, who confirmed what Hodges had said and expressed his dismay over what had happened.

"It's tough not to jump to the conclusion that whoever killed Fields killed Bates. But where's the proof? I have to tell you, Harry, I hate this case already."

Harry had just hung up when Sarah called him. Feeling adventurous, she had been lying on a blanket on the lawn again, fallen asleep, and wakened to find the big hound sitting beside her, grinning.

"It made me feel really funny," she said, "sort of as though I should strike up a conversation."

"He and Oh, Brother! have that effect on people," Harry told her. "He's probably got a message from Tucker in his bandana. What color is he wearing today?"

"It's orange," she said, following Harry out of the house.

"He has a different color every day."

"Tucker goes to all that trouble?"

"Oh, no. Sanchez picks it out himself. He won't wear it otherwise."

"Come on, Harry."

"Honor bright."

Sanchez grinned at Harry and gave him a push in the crotch with his nose. Sarah laughed.

"When he does it to you," Harry said with a grin, "you'll know you've been promoted to honorary dog."

"I can't wait," she said and then blushed a deep red.

"Tucker wants us to come over for lunch," Harry said, reading the note and pretending not to notice. "Do you want to go?"

"Sounds great," Sarah replied.

Half an hour later Hodges called again and told Harry that a Sheriff's Department Marine Patrol on the Okalatchee had found the crab boat he had shot full of holes. It had been abandoned at a private dock on the river a little west of where Harry had shot at it. The owner of the dock had been away and came home to find the craft sunk under his boatlift. They also found a rifle in the boat. There was no reason to think the owner had any connections to the shooter, but the deputies who found the boat were questioning the owner anyway.

Harry made a note of the man's name and address.

★ ★ ★ ★ ★

A little before noon, Harry and Sarah walked the half mile of white sand road, stopping once to let a doe and her fawn cross the road.

"They're lovely," Sarah said, "but aren't they awfully small?"

"Florida whitetails are much smaller than northern deer."

"Why are they so much smaller?" Sarah looked around at the heavy green growth surrounding them. "There's plenty to eat."

"Good question. Bears, raccoons, deer, maybe panthers are smaller down here, too. It probably has something to do with the average temperature. Animals tend to be largest in the colder climates."

"How about giraffes and elephants, hippos and rhinoceros, never mind the ostrich?" Sarah asked.

"You've got me there," Harry said, delighted by her interest. "I think the woolly mammoth grew up to fourteen feet high at the shoulder, and the mastodon was shorter but more massively built than the modern Indian elephant. That's my best shot."

Sarah glanced up at the sun. "Let's go before I wilt. I can't hope to shrink."

Sanchez and Oh, Brother! were standing in the road waiting for them when they turned the last corner before reaching Tucker's place.

"Don't tell me they knew we were coming," Sarah said, stroking Oh, Brother!'s neck.

The mule stepped back and bent his head to look at her.

"What?" Sarah asked a little uneasily.

Just then Sanchez gave her a boost from behind with his nose. She yelped as she jumped.

"Okay," she said, stroking the mule's nose when she had caught her balance. "You did know." Then she turned to Harry, her face flaming, and said, "Don't you dare say, Honorary Dog."

"Okay," he replied, grinning recklessly.

Sanchez turned and led them up the driveway. Sarah walked beside the mule, resting a hand on his glossy shoulder.

"We saw a doe and her fawn," she said to him, then looked at her father as if she couldn't believe what she'd just done.

"It's the Tucker factor," Harry said with an easy laugh.

They found the old farmer in his pumpkin patch, watering the strong, green seedlings thrusting up from each hill. He was dressed in a carefully ironed, collarless, white shirt, faded bib overalls, and a straw hat with wisps of white hair curling from under the brim. He smiled a welcome, blue eyes dancing.

"I can't believe these plants have grown so big in such a short time," Harry remarked after the greetings were over.

"This is manure slurry," Tucker said, picking up a malodorous sprinkling can. "It smells to high heaven, but young pumpkin plants thrive on it. Just let me finish here and we'll go inside and see if the cat dragged anything home for lunch."

"Do you have a cat?" Sarah asked.

"No," Tucker said, "we've been talking about getting one, but Sanchez is holding back a little."

"You're teasing me," Sarah responded.

"Oh, no," Tucker said, glancing at the mule and the dog, watching from the edge of the patch and lowering his voice as he rinsed out the sprinkler with a garden hose, ran some of the water over his hands, and started towards the house. "You see, Sanchez has what might be called a genetic predisposition not to like cats, but Oh, Brother! has been working with him on the problem. I think he's making some progress."

"Do you want a cat?" Sarah asked.

Harry was relieved to see he wasn't the only person who didn't rebel at the suggestion that a mule was counseling a dog.

"I'm of two minds. Cats have decided views and a lot of personality, but they also kill birds and really can't seem to control themselves in that area."

He and Sarah, who was fond of cats, continued the conversation all the way into the kitchen. In fact, Tucker became so engrossed in the discussion that he forgot to introduce Sarah to the Plymouth Rock rooster General Longstreet and his hens or the hives of fancy Carniolan bees he walked among unscathed like Daniel in the lions' den.

Harry settled happily into one of Tucker's bentwood rockers and looked at a seed catalogue while Sarah and Tucker put lunch on the table, talking and working together as if they'd known one another a lifetime. Sanchez and Oh, Brother! stood with their heads under the stoop roof, looking in the screen door, apparently flabbergasted by the sight of a woman working in Tucker's kitchen.

While they ate, Tucker told them more about the bear.

"It's a young female, and I think she may be hanging around for the company." He paused to frown over what was coming next. "And she's thin as a snake. Sanchez and Oh, Brother! have had to discourage her a few times from getting into the hives. But one of these days, you know . . ." His voice trailed off.

"She's going to pull the wall off your hen house," Harry said, completing Tucker's sentence. "Or you're going to get up some morning and find her in your kitchen."

Sarah looked alarmed. "What are you going to do?" she asked.

"I'm thinking about putting a top on that old dog run and trapping her."

Harry dropped his fork with a clatter. "Tucker," he said a little louder than he intended, "you're not going to start messing with that bear. It was bad enough when you trapped Weissmuller."

"Weissmuller?" Sarah asked, forgetting her lunch. "As in Johnny Weissmuller?"

"He was a dog, but he was named after the man," Tucker

said. "His owner was shot, and Weissmuller escaped into the Hammock. Your father and I trapped him, and I built a strong run to house him in. Sanchez and Oh, Brother! gentled him, but it didn't stick. He ran away, and the game warden finally shot him for killing deer. We all miss him."

"I don't," Harry said, but the denial lacked conviction.

"He's only saying that because he doesn't want me to catch this bear," Tucker told Sarah. "He and Weissmuller became good friends. But let's change the subject. What's going on with the Alliance?"

"A man named Joshua Bates and his wife were killed last night," Sarah said crisply. "And what I want to know is if someone is shooting people in that Alliance, what's to keep them from shooting Harry?"

"Well," Tucker said, "I think they've already had a go at it."

"Harry!" Sarah broke out. "You never told me that. What happened?"

Harry gave her a very sanitized version of how he and Colleen McGraw had been shot at on the Okalatchee River.

"Mr. LaBeau," Sarah demanded when Harry was finished, "how much of what I just heard is the truth?"

"What he said was true, but what he left out tells you his intent was to deceive, and speaking of deception, call me Tucker. It will make me feel younger."

"I'll do it, not that you need to feel younger. You're fine just as you are."

"Thanks a lot," Harry protested when he finally managed to break into the conversation. "She already thinks my job stinks. Now she'll think I spend my days being shot at."

"*She* is sitting right here and able to speak for herself," Sarah said, "and *she* thinks, Tucker, her father is in considerable danger."

"Well, he gets himself in these spots from time to time," the old farmer said to Sarah with a reassuring smile, "but the good news is that Harry seems to have more lives than a cat."

"That doesn't make me feel a lot better," she replied.

"You've both exaggerated the risk," Harry said, putting a hand over hers.

"He's probably right," Tucker responded, passing Sarah the bowl of chicken salad.

Sarah sighed but put some on her nearly empty plate. So did the two men.

"I'm going to look like a sausage," she complained.

"It can't happen," Tucker said comfortably. "My cooking isn't fattening." Then he turned to Harry and asked, "What are you going to do about Bates?" Then he added, "I knew his wife's grandfather a little. Estes Hubble came here from the east coast and married one of the Finney girls."

"Where have I heard the name Hubble before?" Harry asked.

"Probably whenever people were talking about abuse of power," Tucker said with a sour laugh. "Estes Hubble founded the Blue Skies Realty something like fifty years ago. Everybody thought he was crazy, but the company's never stopped growing."

"Does the Hubble family still have an interest in the business?" Harry asked.

Tucker put down his fork and thought a minute. "I don't think there's many of that family left, but those still above ground own the company. I expect the Bates girl just came into a lot of money. That's not to say she wouldn't rather have her parents back," he added for Sarah's benefit.

"You must know a lot of people," she said.

"That happens to you if you live pretty much in one place and don't die," Tucker said with a straight face.

13

That night Harry went to a hastily called meeting of the Alliance Board. He asked Sarah to go with him, but she said she wanted some time alone, and Harry didn't press her. She had a husband to think about as well as an angry mother. Whether or not her brother figured into her concerns, he didn't know and didn't ask. He drove off the Hammock wondering how long they could go on pretending Clive didn't exist.

By the time he turned onto the Goodnight Road and began looking for Colleen's house, he had made up his mind that if Sarah didn't mention Clive in their next conversation, he would. No one answered his ring, and he opened the door and walked into a very loud argument, in which three of the four people standing around the coffee table in the living room were all talking at once. Colleen, who appeared to be staying out of the argument, came to greet him.

She was wearing dark slacks and a lavender blouse. Her hair had been styled in a new and attractive way, and she was taking more pains with her makeup. Harry approved and thought that Jim Snyder probably had something to do with the new presentation. He wanted to tell her how good she was looking but decided, given the circumstances, it would be a mistake.

"Isn't it terrible about Joshua and Crystal?" she said.

He agreed it was and asked what the fight was about.

"They started wrangling as soon as they got here," she told him in a resigned voice. "They're arguing about whether or not

Joshua's death has anything to do with Joyce Fields' murder. It's so damned inappropriate. . . ."

"It's a fairly common response to news that's this bad," he broke in. "Let's see if we can get them to stop."

Despite the intensity of the argument, at Harry's arrival, the three turned to him, and began appealing to him to support their individual claims. He made a T with his hands and said loudly, "Time out."

They all stopped speaking at once and looked at him with angry faces.

"How much do you know about what happened to Joshua and his wife?" he asked.

"They're dead. That's enough," Arlen Gott said belligerently, scowling at Harry.

"Oh, Arlen," Cora responded, forcing out a smile. "Don't be such a bear. All I know for certain, Harry, is that they were murdered."

Elaine agreed that was all she knew, and, grudgingly, Arlen admitted he had no details.

"Then I'll tell you what I know," Harry said, and he did. But he said nothing about the Hubble family connection, in part because he had not had time to think about it himself.

The Bates killing had been so clearly professional it raised serious questions as to whether or not it was connected to Joyce Fields' death. If it was, they were dealing with a level of danger he had not even suspected, much less prepared for.

"Should we think about dissolving the Alliance?" Cora asked in the silence following Harry's recitation.

Colleen started to protest, but Elaine cut her off. "It's a reasonable question," she said, avoiding looking at Cora, who appeared surprised by her support.

"I don't like the idea of cutting and running," Arlen grumbled, "but I'm not anxious to be shot either."

"Neither am I," Colleen said defiantly, "but I'm damned if I'll be scared off. Tomorrow, I'm joining a gun club and learning how to use a gun."

"Bravo," said Cora, clapping her hands. "I may join you."

"I'll need a shotgun," Elaine said, pulling off her glasses and waving them around, getting into the spirit of the thing.

"Brock!" Gott shouted. "Do something. They've lost their minds."

"I take it you're not quitting," Harry said when the women stopped laughing.

"That's right," they said in a ragged chorus. "We're sticking."

Gott seemed genuinely upset and was having trouble getting his words out.

Cora put a hand on his arm and said in a shockingly bad attempt at a motherly voice, "It's all right, Arlen, we'll protect you."

"Idiots!" Gott blurted, shaking off her hand and striding out of the room.

A moment later the front door slammed shut behind him.

"Oh, shit," Colleen said.

"It's all right," Cora said. "He'll come back."

"Yes," Elaine said, pulling herself to her full height and dropping a comforting hand on Colleen's shoulder. "They nearly always do, more's the pity."

When Harry arrived home, Sarah, looking concerned, met him at the door. She was barefoot and wearing a red terry cloth wraparound that to Harry's mind set off her dark hair to perfection.

"I hope you don't mind my not going with you," she said at once. "I wanted to, but I really did have to make some phone calls, and I wasn't sure that the meeting would end in time. . . ."

"It's all right," Harry said, breaking his own rule and putting an arm around her shoulders. "Nothing much happened, except they decided not to dissolve the Alliance—at least Colleen, Cora, and Elaine did. Arlen Gott was so mad with Colleen for threatening to learn how to shoot a handgun that he stormed out of the house. I don't know whether he'll quit the Alliance or not."

To his relief, Sarah had not pulled away from him, but when they reached the kitchen door, he was able to release her without it becoming an issue.

"I'm not prying, but did the calls go all right?" he asked, following her into the room.

"I don't know, but I want to wait a while before talking about it. There's coffee if you want it," she said.

"Good," he replied.

"Is Colleen really going to buy a gun and learn how to use it?" Sarah asked.

"She might. I don't know her well enough to say."

"I think I'd like her," Sarah responded, bringing their coffee to the table.

"You probably would, and I played Cupid there." The recollection cheered Harry.

"How so?"

"I introduced her to Jim Snyder, a captain in the Tequesta County Sheriff's Department and an old friend of mine. I had Jim figured for a lifelong bachelor, but he and Colleen seem to have some chemistry."

"What about you, Harry?" she asked a little too brightly. "Aside from the lifetime supply of bubble bath, I haven't seen any evidence of a woman's presence in this house."

"No, not since Katherine left, but I am seeing someone," Harry said, making a decision. "Her name is Cora Wingate. She owns a gallery in Avola and is on the Alliance Board of Directors."

Sarah rested her forearms on the table and asked with no trace of enthusiasm, "How long have you known her?"

"A few weeks."

"Is it serious?"

"I don't know."

"Can I meet her?"

"Of course."

"Okay." Sarah got up. "I'm tired. I'll see you in the morning."

"Sleep well."

Harry watched her walk out of the room. Just like her mother, Harry thought only half humorously. "Her back is more eloquent than her tongue."

Harry, Jim Snyder, and Frank Hodges came out onto the porch of Joshua Bates' house and waited while Hodges made sure the door had locked and replaced the crime scene tape.

"This has me seriously worried," Jim said, scowling at the quiet street and the neatly landscaped houses surrounding them.

"Well, it wasn't a pretty sight," Hodges said loudly. "That bedroom stinks of death, and the blood soaked into the sheet and the mattress doesn't help. Imagine the kid coming in and seeing that?"

"Where is she?" Harry asked.

"She's with her mother's sister up toward Tampa," Jim replied.

"When you talked with her on the morning her parents were killed, she didn't tell you anything helpful?" Harry asked.

"No. There was nothing she could tell us. One of the female deputies and I talked with her for about twenty minutes before Sue Ellen Burns came and took her away."

"You said she's in Tampa," Harry said.

"That's right," Hodges put in. "Sue Ellen's got three kids of her own. So her sister Alfreda Pendleton took Anna to stay with her."

"We know where she is if we need her," Jim said, "but I've got the feeling it will not be easy for us to talk with her again. For some reason the family is circling the wagons. But I'm not nearly as concerned about that as I am about the fact that whoever did the shooting got into the house, killed Bates and his wife, and, as far as our Crime Scene people can tell, left without leaving a trace. That's got me worried."

"The gun had to have had a silencer," Harry said.

"And whoever it was, it wasn't his first time out," Jim added.

"You've gotta think East Coast," Hodges said, pulling up his belt only to have it slide under his belly again.

"And I ask, why?" Jim said.

"Why it's from the East Coast?" Hodges asked.

"No. Why a professional shooter?"

"Unless Bates was involved in big time drug running, which I doubt, there's no obvious answer to your question," Harry said.

"Maybe Bates was screwing somebody's wife, and the guy found out," Hodges suggested. "It's usually sex—when it isn't money."

"Then it's somebody with money to burn," Jim said testily, "because a professional shooter doesn't come cheap."

"And there's still the question of whether or not the killing was connected to Bates' involvement with the Stoneman Douglas Alliance," Harry said, starting down the steps.

"As I said," Jim commented, following him with Hodges in tow, "I'm not feeling too good about this investigation."

"What investigation?" Hodges demanded with a barking laugh.

When they reached the driveway, Harry turned to the two policemen and said, "We're assuming here that Joshua was the intended victim and that his wife was shot for insurance, but what if it was the other way around?"

"That makes me feel even worse," Jim said. "What's behind it?"

"Bates' wife was a Hubble."

"So?" Hodges demanded.

"If it's not sex, it's money, Frank," Harry said.

14

"Have you got any plans for tomorrow?" Harry asked Sarah that evening as they were eating dinner.

"Nothing special," she replied. "I was thinking about the beach."

"I've got to go to Gainesville. Want to come along?"

"What's taking you to up there?"

Harry had noticed with a mixture of amusement and irritation that Sarah frequently responded to a direct question with another question. "An interview."

"Couldn't you do it by phone?"

God, just like her mother. "Yes, but she's an important link in Joyce Fields' murder, and I want to meet her."

"Who is she?"

"Marcia Graham. She's an ABD in biology at the University of Florida and was Joyce Fields' research assistant. I'm hoping she was also her confidant. We'll drive up, buy her dinner, talk, and come back the next day."

"Why aren't you taking Cora What's-her-name?"

"Sarah, do you want to go or not?"

"Sure."

"Good. It's an early start."

"You didn't say it was this early," Sarah grumbled when she thumped down the stairs the following morning carrying an overnight bag.

She was dressed in white pedal pushers, white sandals, and a blue, short sleeved blouse and had pulled her thick, dark hair into a ponytail.

"Breakfast is ready, except for the coffee, and you look great," Harry said.

"I'll make it. Thanks. No more conversation."

That suited Harry. He had things to think about. By the time they reached I-75, the sun was inching above the horizon. For the next two hours Sarah slept and Harry spent some of the time going over the things he wanted to ask Marcia Graham. He particularly wanted to know what the problem had been between Joyce Fields and her assistant Bob Walker. When he was done worrying that bone, he turned his mind to Joshua Bates and the Hubble family.

What he had been able to learn in addition to what Tucker had told him had come from Wetherell Clampett, who worked for Bevel's Sand and Gravel Company and was a walking PEOPLE magazine for Tequesta County. Clampett had once helped Harry with a case, and Harry thought he might help him again.

For Wetherell, gossip was a calling. Hubbard, Wetherell's father, was a friend of Tucker's, and what those two didn't know about Tequesta County families hadn't happened yet. Wetherell was assiduously inheriting his father's store of information.

Harry drove through Bevel security and found Wetherell in the stone crushing section of the operation where the sun was bleached to a dull silver by gray rock dust and the ground shook under the roar of the crushing machines and the rumble of the vast earthmovers.

"I remember my father talking about Estes Hubble," Wetherell told Harry, leaning back against his truck and settling in for a long talk. He was square jawed, grizzled, almost as broad as he was tall, and never in a hurry. He had hands like pie plates and wore enormous dungarees, a blue work shirt, and a frayed plastic straw hat that had once been white.

As soon as Harry had shouted what he wanted to know about the Hubbles, Wetherell shouted back, "Let's go into the super's shack. We can't have a decent talk out here."

Once inside, Wetherell settled them on upended dynamite boxes and began speaking with a seriousness usually reserved for sacred texts. "Old Estes died in 1970, leaving the business to his two sons, Millard and Philip, and a record of skullduggery to the rest of us that would have made a skunk smell good." Wetherell paused to chuckle and then went on. "Millard had two young boys at that time, and Philip had three daughters. Crystal Bates was one of them. Sue Ellen Hubble Burns and Alfreda Hubble Pendleton are the surviving sisters, both married."

"What about the boys?" Harry asked.

Wetherell took off his hat and ran his hand over his head as if he was seeking guidance and said, "Millard was a hell raiser. He went through women like a kid through popsicles, and his boys Rafe and Buford have took after him. At Estes' death, Millard, who was the older brother, became CEO of the company and Philip picked up the financial end of things."

"Any problems between them?"

"Plenty. Philip got so disgusted with his brother's shenanigans that he went to the law, and when the fight was over, their lawyers worked out a plan to put the business under hired management," Wetherell said with great satisfaction, "and that's how Adelaide Slocum comes to be CEO of Blue Skies Realty today. Millard and Philip still serve on the Board of Directors, but I don't think they've spoken directly to one another since the court fight."

Harry had wanted to ask how the young cousins got along,

but Fontaine Bevel, the quarry owner, came shouting into the shack, his once wild blond hair tamed and gray but his enthusiasm undiminished. He was so delighted to see Harry that he dragged him back to his office to show him pictures of his kids and the changes that had been made in the company since the days when Harry had saved him from going to jail.

"Isn't that Belle?" Harry asked, looking at the regal looking woman in a family picture and trying to keep from sounding too astonished.

"The one and only. I married Belle Chance in a Savannah church a month after the trial, and I don't know which one of us was more surprised," Fontaine said with a shout of laughter. "It scared us so bad we almost didn't sleep together that night, but then we said, 'What the hell,' and found neither one of us was dead."

Harry laughed and remembered how beautiful Belle Chance had looked that distant day on that stage at the Swamp Buggy Races when he and Helen Bradley . . . He stopped himself. It was a painful memory. He had been in love with Helen, but it hadn't worked out.

Sarah woke up and said, "Where are we?"

"About an hour north of Tampa," Harry said.

"I'm hungry."

"You've already eaten breakfast."

"It doesn't count."

"Why not?"

"It was too early."

"How old are you?" he asked.

"Eleven," she answered. "Did you ever eat at a Cracker Barrel restaurant?"

"Only to avoid dying from starvation."

"There's one at the next exit. What do you say?"

By this time she was smiling happily and looking around at the surrounding woods with interest.

"Sure," he said, laughing.

Perhaps, he thought, I'm going to find out after all what it was like bringing up a girl. This led him to remember that she was pregnant. He had stopped pretending that he did not want a grandchild, but he could not get past the fact that whether or not she terminated the pregnancy was a decision only she should make.

Over their second breakfast and with no prompting from Harry, Sarah finally began talking about Clive.

"I haven't said much about him, Harry, because there's no way of hiding the fact that he continues to believe that you wrecked our mother's life. And everything that has gone wrong in his life, he's piled on you."

"Has a lot gone wrong?"

"Enough. He had trouble through school with every male teacher he ever had. He was fired from his first two jobs, and he got his present job in Holbrook and Weeks' brokerage firm only because a guy who's married to one of Jennifer's friends called in some chips with the company's president and shoehorned Clive in."

"How long has he been in the brokerage house?"

"Two years. A record, but all he does is complain about how hard he has to work."

"Do you two get along okay?"

This conversation was not making Harry feel good, but he thought he wanted the information and may have made a mistake.

She gave a short, stiff laugh. "I love him, and he's Jennifer's darling boy, but I keep waiting for him to grow up."

Harry nodded, deciding that was enough family information

for one day and paid the check.

Marcia Graham was a short, curly haired woman with shrewd brown eyes and a solid, assertive body that was popping with confidence and competence. She shook their hands as if she was running for office.

"Thanks for coming up," she said to Harry, then to Sarah, "I've got a sister in Milwaukee. In fact, I've got somebody I'm related to in all the major cities in the country. My mother came from a family with ten kids and she had eight and felt guilty for having stopped short of a dozen. Until I reached junior high, I thought everybody slept three in a bed."

They were standing in the tiny living room of her walk-up apartment in Rosewood Gardens, a rackety apartment complex half a mile from the university.

"There were times in college when I thought so too," Sarah replied.

The two women laughed like co-conspirators. Harry, to his disgust, felt his face burn. His discomfort only increased their amusement.

"You said you're no longer working in the Fisheries lab. What happened?" he asked when he could get a word in.

"Robert Walker. He sent me packing after Joyce was killed."

"Why were he and Fields quarrelling?" Harry asked.

"I think, at bottom, it was because they were totally different people. He is a rules maven, and she was, for a scientist, much looser. But what they fought over was politics. He never wanted the department to be seen as favoring anything that threatened the power structure."

"What is that?" Sarah asked, possibly naively.

"Oh, well, the people in that Southern Florida Development Association and the legislators they've put in office. Joyce saw everything in terms of finding out what the problem was, who and what was causing it, and slamming them hard. It was a war with her."

"Sounds right," Harry said. "What about the research?"

Marcia smiled broadly, her brown eyes dancing. "I took it with me, and by the time asshole Walker finds it's gone, I will have processed the last of Joyce's raw data and converted it into text, formulas, and graphics. I also photocopied her notebooks. If he demands the raw data back, he can have it. My dissertation is safe."

They talked for a few minutes and then Harry made arrangements to pick up Marcia for dinner, and he and Sarah went in search of a motel. Over dinner, Marcia gave them more details about where Fields' research had been taking her.

"She had pretty well wrapped it up by the time she was killed," Marcia said, her eyes filling.

"I'm sorry," Harry said. "How long did you work with her?"

"Three years," Marcia replied, using her napkin to dry her eyes.

"That's a long time," Sarah said. "Were you close?"

"She wasn't easy, but she was the most generous person and the hardest working that I have ever known. She was only my advisor, but she looked after me as if I were her kid. And she would have hated my crying over her," she said, forcing herself to smile.

"Have you any idea what her conclusions would have been had she lived to write them down?" Harry asked.

"It's all there," Marcia said defensively. "Before she died, she had done the work. We knew a month ago what was wrong with the river and what needed to be done to remedy the situation."

"Why didn't she tell Colleen McGraw?" Harry asked in surprise.

"But it was all in the report," Marcia said. "Didn't Colleen show it to you?"

15

"But there's no mystery to it, Harry," Colleen protested, digging in her desk until she found what she was looking for and carrying the folder back to where Harry was sitting.

She sat down and passed it to him. "This is what Joyce gave me. I suppose it's valid."

"How long have you had this?" Harry asked, turning over the loose pages, filled with charts, tables, and explanations of what the numbers meant.

He closed the folder, feeling a hollow place where his stomach belonged.

"Joyce gave it to me two weeks before she died," she replied.

He looked up. "Who besides you and Marcia have seen it?"

She seemed surprised by the sharpness in his voice. "I gave Josh and Arlen copies and made them promise not to tell anyone about it."

"Have Cora and Elaine seen it?" Colleen shook her head. "Why not?"

"I . . . I haven't made up my mind what to do with it. No. After I showed it to Josh and Arlen, I got cold feet. I was sorry I'd shown it to them."

"Is that why you didn't tell me about it?" he demanded.

She flopped awkwardly into the chair facing him and made a face.

"I was frightened by it," she said in a barely audible voice, unfolding herself into a more or less upright position. "And when Joyce was killed, I was even more scared."

Harry waited for her to go on. When she didn't, he said, "I can understand why Fields' death might have upset you, but why did the report disturb you?"

"Because it confirms all our worst fears and adds things we hadn't thought of. The river's dying, Harry. It's being poisoned, and everybody's to blame!"

She was almost shouting by the time she stopped speaking.

"Have you told Jim about any of this?" Harry asked.

"No."

"You should have told both of us," he said, keeping his anger out of his voice.

"I don't see why," she said defiantly. "The report is Alliance property."

Harry let that go. "Did you show the report to Gott and Bates before or after Fields was killed?"

She paused a moment, frowning at him. "Before. What difference does it make?"

"Her death may be directly connected to what's in the report."

"I don't see how," Colleen protested. "Only Josh, Arlen, Marcia and I have seen it, and it's not possible any one of us could have killed Joyce."

"Let me ask you again why you didn't show the report to Cora and Elaine," Harry said gently.

"For two reasons, I couldn't decide what the Alliance should do with the report, and I was afraid the report might somehow get out, even be published."

"And you were afraid that you and the Alliance might come in for even more trouble than you have had already."

"Yes. That's right. I wanted time to think. Then when Joyce was killed . . ." Suddenly, the color drained from her face. "Oh, my God," she said. "You think either Arlen or Josh showed it to someone, and that may have led to Joyce and Josh's deaths."

"Possibly, but we're a long way from knowing that."

Jim found Harry on his lanai poring over the Alliance file.

"I thought I'd better stop here on my way to the University," he said.

Harry noted that Jim had carefully avoided saying he was on his way to talk to Colleen, a conversation that was not going to be easy for either of them.

"Sit down," Harry said, closing the file and waving it at one of the lounge chairs.

Jim folded himself into his seat, dropping his hat on a bony knee. "Things have just gotten a lot more complicated," he said.

"Yes," Harry said. "Have you read Fields' report?"

"No, but from what you say it's pretty incendiary stuff."

Harry agreed and then asked, "Did your people find Bates' copy?"

"I don't know. The Crime Scene team has all the papers."

"It would be good to know," Harry observed as neutrally as possible.

Before he finished speaking, Jim was making the call. "They'll get someone on it," he said with a resigned sigh when he hung up.

"You know that Colleen gave another copy to Arlen Gott."

Jim nodded. "I'm calling him in. Have you talked with him yet?"

"No," Harry answered. "I got sidetracked by the newspaper thief. And before I'm finished with it, Fisher is going to owe me, big time."

Jim laughed, losing his worried frown for the first time since sitting down. "Are you making any progress?"

"No. I told the building manager to put up a surveillance camera and run through the tape every morning until they catch whoever it is."

"But . . . ?"

"The Board has to approve the expenditure. While they were discussing it, a fight broke out over whether or not a surveillance camera was an excessive intrusion on privacy, unjustified by the theft of a few newspapers. One of the members suggested that the Association just buy an extra copy of the paper, which would be cheaper than the camera."

"Not bad," Jim said with a smile.

"Maybe, but that led to another, more acrimonious, disagreement over whether or not Association funds could be used for such a purpose and whether or not it was an unprincipled act, aiding and abetting theft."

"Lord, Lord," Jim said, his eyes wide.

"That's what I said," Harry replied, "only I invoked the Son."

Jim got to his feet. "I don't really want to go out there," he said, the frown returning.

"You want some company?"

"No, but it's good of you to offer. I left Frank at the office. Technically, she and Gott have committed an actionable offense."

"Withholding evidence," Harry said.

"That's it."

"I doubt it ever crossed their minds."

Jim shook his head and sighed. "Two pretty highly educated and intelligent people closely connected with both murders . . ."

His voice drifted off, and he stood staring out the screen door, turning his hat in his hands.

Reluctantly, Harry refrained from saying what he thought should happen. Instead, he put a hand on his friend's shoulder and said, "When you get there, you'll know what to do."

"And what will that be?"

There was no happiness in Jim's voice.

"Keats said it best," Harry replied, partially breaking his promise to keep his mouth shut, " 'I am certain of nothing but the holiness of the heart's affections. . . .' "

"Oh, that makes me feel a lot better, Harry. You know, your daughter's right. You are weird."

As Jim strode across the lawn toward his cruiser, Harry called after him, "Think about it." But Jim just walked faster.

Harry went back into the house, miffed with Sarah for having told Jim that her father was weird. The phone rang. He picked it up, still thinking about Jim's comment.

"Hello, Harry."

Her voice had not changed. There was a moment when Harry thought the years had unraveled, felt panic building, and fought it down. He took a deep breath to steady himself and answered.

"Hello, Jennifer. Are you calling Sarah?"

"No, Harry. I'm calling you."

Several responses, bright with arterial blood, occurred to Harry. He rejected them and asked, "Why?"

The question was more summation than inquiry.

"You've lied your way into my daughter's life."

"I haven't lied to anyone, Jennifer." Harry's voice climbed a little despite his best efforts to stay calm.

"Why should I believe a murderer?" she shouted. "You're already coming between Sarah and David."

"I'd have no reason to do that," he answered.

"You don't need a reason to be destructive." She was breathing heavily. He could feel her anger like a presence in the room. "And there's another thing," she said, her voice dropping and becoming more intense. "Stay away from my son."

Slowly and very gently, Harry hung up the phone.

16

Harry's initial impulse was not to tell Sarah about the call. Reflection changed his mind. They were taking an after dinner walk along the Puc Puggy, something that Sarah, to his surprise, had come to enjoy, when he broke the news.

"What did she want?" Sarah demanded, forgetting the female mottled duck that had brought her four young ones out of the nest to feed on the soft green algae at the edge of the Creek.

"She said I was coming between you and David."

"Why?"

"She's very angry," he replied, hedging.

Sarah grabbed his arm. "Harry, what did she say?"

"She was angry and, I think, frightened. I don't think . . ."

"Harry!"

"I've told you the gist of it. There's nothing to be gained by . . ."

"Stop right there," she said, her dark eyes boring into him. "Tell me exactly what she said. If you don't, I'll brood on it and worry myself sick. Now, what did she say?"

He heard the vulnerable child in the strong, competent woman's voice and felt a rush of love for both of them. "She said I had lied my way into your life, that I was a destroyer, and I would ruin your life the way I had wrecked hers. She also told me to stay away from Clive."

Sarah's eyes filled with tears, and she said in a breaking voice, "Oh, Harry, I'm so sorry. What did you say?"

"I hung up."

Half laughing, half crying, she said, "I wish I could."

"I don't think we'll be arrested. My feeling is that the assistant District Attorney is not going to press charges. But I've talked with a lawyer, just in case," Gott said.

Then he finished his summary of his and Colleen's meeting with Jim and leaned back in his chair, more subdued than Harry had ever seen him. The Alliance Board had met again, and those present were very aware of the gap left by Joshua Bates' absence.

"When Jim, er, Captain Snyder talked to me," Colleen said, blushing slightly, "I felt he was doing his best to be supportive, but Arlen's assessment may be a little optimistic. We're talking about three murders here, and if the state ever gets to the point of indicting someone, Arlen and I may be swept in on a charge of obstructing justice. What do you think, Harry?"

"It's very hard to say. Harley Dillard, the DA, is a thorough man, but I've always found him fair. I don't think there's much chance that either of you is looking at a conviction although the indictments may come down. I think to some extent it depends on whether or not Bates' copy of Fields' report is ever traced."

"Was it taken at the time of the murder?" Cora asked.

"The police can't say. It wasn't in his files at his office. There was an empty folder in one of Bates' files in his home, labeled FIELDS' REPORT, which suggests he either gave it to someone or it was stolen. If it was stolen, it was probably taken the night of the murder. If it wasn't, then Joshua and his wife may have been killed for nothing."

"That's assuming he was killed because of his connection with the Alliance," Elaine Porter said.

For a few minutes there was a spirited argument over Porter's comment, interrupted at last by Colleen, who said, "Harry's right. We don't have enough information to come to a satisfactory conclusion. Let's do what we came here to do, talk about Joyce's report. I should have given it to all of you, and I certainly should have given it to the police after Joyce was killed."

She passed stapled copies of the report to Cora and Elaine, who took them with fairly good grace, considering that they had only a half hour earlier learned they had been deliberately passed over when Colleen gave copies to Bates and Gott. They were not, surprisingly, dissatisfied with Colleen's explanation of why she had done it.

"If it's all right with the rest of you, I'll take us through the main points and then open the meeting to a discussion of our next step," she said, "but first I want to offer you my resignation. . . ."

Her voice failed her momentarily. "I've acted very unprofessionally," she said, but Cora interrupted her, seconded by Arlen and Elaine.

"You're staying," Cora said flatly.

"Get on with it," Elaine added with spirit.

"All nonsense," Arlen put in, making everyone laugh.

Harry listened to Colleen's summary with admiration. She was in command of the subject matter, and her presentation of it was a tribute to her organizational skills. The library, he thought, must run like a very good clock.

"To reduce Joyce's finding to their essentials," Colleen said, preparing to wind up her presentation, "I would say that she established that the Okalatchee is in serious trouble. The most dramatic evidence of its condition is the outbreaks of *Pfiesteria piscicida,* which has resulted in repeated and extensive fish kills."

Cora said, "I listened, but I'm still not sure what this *Pfiesteria* thing is and what it does."

"Cora, maybe you should stick to your paintings—" Arlen began only to be cut off by Elaine.

"Don't be so damned condescending, Arlen" she said. "Colleen, answer the question."

Well, Harry thought, secretly delighted by Elaine's response, Cora has gained a friend. And Cora stared blankly at Elaine for a moment and then broke into one of her brilliant smiles.

"Thank you, Elaine," she said.

"Sisterhood," Elaine replied, smiling despite herself.

Even Arlen grinned.

"Well, here's my best effort," Colleen said quickly. "When it's active, it's a very aggressive, single celled predator, occurring naturally in the water and mud of Florida rivers and estuaries. Under ordinary conditions it poses little or no threat to fish and goes about its business of eating bacteria, algae, and other very small animals like itself. But under certain conditions it becomes toxic and attacks fish, opening sores and lesions on the fish and feeding on the discharges from those injuries."

"What turns it toxic?" Arlen demanded, coming out of his brown study.

"Harry, help me here," Colleen said.

"Sure, in a healthy river or estuary, it only happens when schooling fish congregate in numbers in one location to feed. As they defecate, their droppings release chemicals into the water that prompts a change in the *Pfiesteria* cells. As the stimulated cells swim toward the fish, they emit powerful toxins that make the fish lethargic."

"Disgusting," Elaine said.

"Pretty remarkable as well," Harry insisted. "The toxins also damage the fish's skin, creating sores and even hemorrhaging. The *Pfiesteria* then feed on the blood, tissue, and sloughed bits of skin. When the fish die, the cells transform themselves again into a flagellated form and feed on the dead fish. Pretty remarkable creatures."

"Frightening!" Cora exclaimed. "What else can the wretched things do?"

"When conditions become threatening, say from a storm or falling water levels, they can grow a thicker skin and sink into the mud as dormant cysts."

"And that's not the end of it," Colleen broke in. "Humans exposed for any extended time to water infested with *Pfiesteria* in their toxic stage can develop sores as well, and if they breathe air with the toxins released into it by wave action, they can sicken and die."

"But the Okalatchee is moving water," Cora protested. "How can what you've just described be happening in it?"

"The Okalatchee is now carrying such a burden of pollution," Colleen replied, "that the *Pfiesteria* are being stimulated to change into their toxic form without being surrounded by dense schools of fish. The river is so out of whack that it is engineering the destruction of its own inhabitants."

"Does Joyce say what the pollutants are?" Arlen asked.

"The principal culprits are nitrogen, phosphorous, and human and animal fecal matter," Harry answered. "There's also a chemical factory of trace pollutants such as pesticides and herbicides, heavy metals, and things we don't even know about yet."

"Coming from?" Elaine inquired, her ordinarily calm expression creased with concern.

"Farms, ranches, mines, landfills, lawns, roads, yards, faulty septic systems, whatever rain falls on and washes into the system," Harry replied.

"That suggests that unless we gain control over the entire river, its tributaries, and its watershed, we're not going to be able to bring it back to health," Cora said with a note of hopelessness in her voice.

"That's right," Colleen said. "So what are we going to do

with this report?"

There was a long silence before Elaine spoke. "We're almost certain Joyce Fields died for this." She held up the report and went on holding it as she finished speaking. "There's a real possibility Josh and his wife died because of it, too. I don't want them to have wasted their lives. I say we publish it."

"And I'm angry," Cora put in loudly. "I agree with Elaine. Let's publish it. To think that we could have been so careless, so *stupid* that we let this happen. I want the whole damned world to know."

"Okay," Arlen responded, "I'm with you, but let's open this discussion to the membership. We gain two ways. We fully alert the membership, and we publicize the report even before issuing it."

"Then I'll call a meeting and open it to the public and invite the media," Colleen said, jumping to her feet. "If we're going to do this, let's make all the noise we can, and in the process of getting to a vote, we make sure the Association won't be able to bury Joyce's report no matter how hard they try."

Harry stood up to shake hands with everyone, and Cora was so carried away with enthusiasm that she threw her arms around Harry's neck and kissed him. When she let him go, she found Arlen, Colleen, and Elaine staring at her with shocked expressions. Harry's face was very red.

"Oh, shit," she said, which set the rest of them free to laugh as hard as they wanted to. Even Arlen joined in.

The next day, Harry had an appointment in Judge Willard Clancy's courtroom where the case of Viking Insurance Company vs. Strether Humphrey was being tried. Viking was seeking to prove that Humphrey was not entitled to the disability payments he had been awarded by a previous court decision, involving damages due after a ninety-year-old man in a Cadillac sedan flattened Humphrey as he was crossing a downtown intersection on the WALK light.

Viking was the driver's insurer and argued that the light was green and Humphrey was jaywalking. Five witnesses said otherwise. Two months later Viking hired Harry to conduct a surveillance of Humphrey in the hope of catching him doing somersaults on his front lawn. Instead, Harry found him in a neck brace, limping painfully around his patio, dragging a folding chair behind him and having to sit down every five minutes. When he reported his findings to Viking, the company fired him and was stiffing him for his fee.

Having thought over the situation, Harry called Humphrey's attorney and offered him at no cost the dated photographs he had taken of Humphrey inching across his patio in a travesty of exercise. As proof that no good deed goes unpunished, Harry was subpoenaed to testify. He had to wait an hour on a hard bench before being called but then had the wonderfully satisfying experience of telling the court about what Viking had hired him to do and how they had not paid him for his services.

The jury was out less than thirty minutes and found unanimously for Humphrey. Judge Clancy gave the Viking attorneys an earful and banged his gavel with unusual vigor in delivering the finding. Harry left the Court Building feeling that things might not be as bad as he was inclined to believe. His better than average mood lasted only until he reached the Rover and found that someone had keyed the driver's door while he had been making the world a better place.

When he got home he found two messages, a written note from Sarah and a telephone message from Colleen. Sarah had gone to Shark Valley, a National Park on the East Trail, set in the center of the Everglades. It was a full day's excursion, and Harry was glad she had taken his suggestion to visit the park. The alligators alone made the trip worth the effort. And if she rented a bicycle and pedaled the dirt road that circled out into the vast ocean of grass and water, she would share something of what the Seminoles experienced, poling their pirogues through that sun drenched world.

The second message was from Colleen. She was scheduling an open meeting of the Stoneman Douglas Alliance for Wednesday of the following week and would have posters distributed and announcements of it carried on the public service slots of all the local radio and television stations.

"I've sent copies of Joyce's report to Adelaide Slocum," she said. "That should put the cat amongst the pigeons."

Harry was still listening to his messages when Arlen Gott called.

"Brock, I've been acting like an asshole. I apologize. Now I've got something constructive to suggest."

"I'm listening," Harry answered, having decided not to comment on the anatomical comparison.

"I've got some skills as a researcher, and Elaine Porter is an accountant with a major firm. She has access to a lot of business information in Tequesta County. I've mentioned our collaborating on something like this. She's willing. What do you say to our looking into Joshua Bates' and his wife's relationship to Blue Skies Realty?"

"If you do it, you're going to have to keep your head down, Arlen. Josh and Crystal may have been killed over that relationship."

"Or the Stoneman Douglas Alliance connection. If it's the latter, we may be targets anyway. May as well make ourselves part of the solution while we wait."

"I'm serious, Arlen. Don't broadcast what you're doing."

"All right. One of us will talk to you when we have something to report."

Harry hung up thinking Arlen and Elaine were probably wasting their time.

17

The meeting was held in the Wildewood Community Center. Half an hour before the meeting began, all the three hundred seats that had been set up in the Assembly Room were filled, and by the time Colleen called for order, the standing room was jammed. The speaker's podium bristled with television and radio mikes, and the three major local television stations had their cameras ready for action.

"Are these people all Alliance members?" Sarah asked Harry, just before Colleen grasped the Assembly Room's brass school bell and rang it, to quiet the din.

She and her father were seated in the front row, and Sarah was half out of her chair, looking around at the crowd.

"Not half," he answered.

"Then why are they here?"

"Mostly to make trouble," Harry answered.

Before he could say more, Colleen convened the meeting. When the formal business was concluded, Colleen said, "We are here to decide what should be done with the report submitted to the Alliance by the late Dr. Joyce Fields on the condition of the Okalatchee River. Some of you have already seen the report. For those of you who have not, I have asked Marcia Graham, who was Dr. Fields' assistant during the months they worked on the river, to explain the chief findings of the report to you. Marcia is an ABD at the University of Florida, Department of Biology. Her area of specialization is ichthyology. She is currently completing her dissertation, much of which is based on the research she did while working for Joyce Fields. Marcia, please begin."

While Colleen was speaking, the audience had been growing increasingly restless. As soon as Colleen sat down, a tall, thin man in dungarees and a white T-shirt shouted, "Why should anyone here care what this Dr. Whoever has to say about our river?"

Cheers and jeers immediately erupted across the hall, and arguments broke out even before the clapping and booing had died down. Marcia, who had just reached the speaker's rostrum, froze. Colleen started for the rostrum.

"Settle down!" a stentorian voice, trained for decades in quieting lecture halls stuffed with rebellious undergraduates, rose over and quelled the growing uproar.

Arlen Gott was on his feet, scowling at the crowd.

"That's better," he rumbled into the restless silence, leaning forward over the table. "The question was a good one, and if the gentleman who asked it and the rest of you listen to what Ms. Graham has to say, you'll soon have your answer."

Colleen smiled encouragement at Marcia, who was now looking at the crowd as the Christians once looked at the lions. Sarah, who was sitting not more than ten feet from where Marcia was standing, said. "Go for it, Marcia."

Marcia grinned and pulled the mike down so that she could speak into it. Harry began clapping, and the applause spread quickly through the room.

"I'm going to tell you what Dr. Fields and I looked at and what we found," Marcia began a little hesitantly, "but I won't talk now about the supporting science that led to the report's conclusions. I'll only say it's sound. If it wasn't, Joyce Fields, who was one of the most capable biologists I've ever met, would never have put her name on it."

Then with growing confidence she launched into her presentation and was soon addressing a rapt audience. The presentation took fifteen minutes. When it was over, most of the audience applauded enthusiastically.

"Thank you," she said. "If you have any questions, I'll try to answer them."

A forest of hands shot up.

The questions mostly dealt with the causes and effects of the various problems identified by the report. Some veered off the subject into boat speeds on the river, manatee protection or lack thereof, and land use issues, but Colleen deflected them and kept the focus on the report.

Getting a motion proved less difficult than Harry thought it would be, and Colleen, with the help of the rest of the Board, especially Cora and Elaine, who proved to be a formidable team when working together, soon had one that Arlen quickly seconded.

Colleen read the motion: "It is moved and seconded that Dr. Joyce Fields' report on the current health of the Okalatchee River, commissioned by the Board of Directors, be as widely published in the visual and print media and by all other means as our funds permit."

For a moment the room hung in silence. Then Adelaide Slocum was on her feet.

"Madam President," she began in a voice that needed no amplification to be heard but which carried no hint of hostility, "I am Adelaide Slocum, Chief Executive Officer of Blue Skies Realty and President of the Southwest Florida Development Association. What was the Alliance's purpose in having this study made, and why are you now seeking to distribute it to the general public? I request the privilege of responding to your answer."

Colleen replied that visual and anecdotal evidence collected by the Alliance indicated the river had problems severe enough to demand a scientific assessment of the river. The report revealed problems far deeper and more widespread than anyone on the Alliance Board had suspected. The purpose in distributing the report is to alert the communities bordering the river to the seriousness of its condition. She then gave the floor back to Slocum.

Slocum thanked her, and in the same powerful but unemotional voice said, "Isn't it also part of the Alliance's intent to lay the groundwork for a campaign to persuade the Florida Legislature as well as the EPA, and other federal and state agencies to severely limit land use the entire length of the river? And isn't it also true that the Alliance intends to do everything it can to control the kinds and quantity of effluents that may be allowed to enter the entire river drainage? And, finally, isn't it true that you are attempting to recruit the St. John's River Coalition to help you in your efforts, in short, bringing in outsiders?"

Without hesitation, Colleen said, "Yes it is. The river is already very sick, and if drastic steps are not taken to reverse the trend, it will die. If that happens, the commercial fisheries in Avola Bay will perish, a host of environmental calamities will accompany the destruction, and the health of every person living in the Okalatchee basin will be placed at risk. And I do not apologize for seeking help from the Coalition. Their record in defense of the environment of this state is superb."

When the uproar that followed Colleen's answer subsided, Slocum was on her feet again, and without waiting to be recognized, she said, "Then you should know that the Association will do everything in its power to oppose you."

For the next hour Slocum's supporters and the Alliance supporters engaged in a heated, rancorous argument, most of which did nothing to advance understanding of the problems facing the river and those who lived and made their living on or near it. But by the time Colleen banged her gavel, ending the discussion, the two sides had laid out the lines of battle and demonstrated how difficult compromise would be.

Colleen put the motion to a vote, and the Board voted unanimously in favor of it. That produced more cheering and booing, but the vote was cast, and the battle was joined.

"I think your job just got a lot more difficult, Harry," Sarah said as they were driving home. "That Slocum woman is a real tiger." Then, without waiting for Harry's comment on what she had said, she asked, "When are you going to introduce me to Cora Wingate?"

"Can you wait until tomorrow?" Harry asked.

18

"Am I that much of a threat?" Sarah asked when Harry told her Cora had invited them for lunch.

"What do you mean?" Harry demanded, feeling a little threatened himself.

Sarah cocked her head and shot her father a quizzical look. "I think it's obvious. She's retreated to her castle."

"Possibly, but don't judge her too harshly for it."

"I'm not judging her at all."

Harry thought that was unlikely. But the lunch went well. Cora was gracious and Sarah generous in her praise of the apartment and Cora's paintings. To Harry's surprise Sarah knew enough about contemporary art to ask questions that soon had Cora talking freely and enthusiastically about her collection. It was Harry who finally said it was time to leave.

Sarah was silent as they rode down the elevator, and by the time they reached the Rover, Harry was out of patience. "Well, what do you think?"

"She's an interesting woman."

"Now who's being defensive?"

Sarah pushed back in her seat and sighed. "Harry, I don't know what to say."

"What don't you like about her?"

"Oh, I like her well enough. She's intelligent, she's amusing, and God knows she's rich."

Although Harry was listening closely there was dissatisfaction in Sarah's voice that wasn't showing up in her words. "But?" he asked.

"The night I arrived, I asked you a question that you said I wasn't entitled to ask because I didn't know you well enough. As I recall, it had to do with what you called our history and I called our lack of it. Are we at the point yet where we can ask one another possibly disturbing personal questions?"

"I trust you, but do you trust me?" Harry responded, interested in where she was going.

"Yes."

"Good. Ask the question."

"What do you want from Cora Wingate?"

"Companionship."

"That's it?"

"I'm not sure, and I don't know why you're asking the question."

"I think she's in love with you," Sarah responded firmly.

"You learned that in the hour and a half we were together, talking about publishing, art, and my hermit tendencies?" he asked.

"It's not a joke, Harry," she said, sounding huffy.

"Cora and I are okay."

"But where is your relationship going?" she demanded.

"Sarah, at our age, we don't have to ask that question. I think Cora would agree with me."

Sarah eyed him skeptically and said, "Ask her and tell me what she says."

Harry spent the rest of the afternoon with the Piney Woods Condominium Association, trying to persuade the Board of Directors this wasn't a situation that was likely to involve the Supreme Court and that their decision to catch the newspaper bandit by stealth and surveillance would not put the Bill of

Rights in jeopardy.

"But we're a tightly knit community here, Mr. Brock," Bill Falwell told Harry with a worried frown.

Falwell was a large, bald, very fat man with a face like a bulldog and for whom the shortcomings of his fellow men was a constant, unpleasant surprise.

The other four members of the Board nodded in assent and then fell to arguing in terms that made it clear that if the Board was representative of the association membership, they were a community knit together by mutual loathing.

Harry came away from the meeting reeling. Driving home, he determined that he would have to solve this on his own before it destroyed his mind, if he had any left.

He had a message to call Hodges.

"The deputies on Marine Patrol have talked with Howard Westheimer," Hodges said. "Westheimer's the guy who found the boat you shot up."

"What have you got?" Harry asked.

"The boat was stolen a month ago from a small crabbing outfit in Punta Rassa. The owner doesn't have any idea who took it. Their security is a sieve. Nobody we talked to in the marina saw anything or even knew a boat was missing. It would take a miracle to find out who lifted the boat."

"Anything in it of any help?"

"Nope. The rifle had no serial number. What hadn't floated off had been dumped or carried away."

"Westheimer is clean?"

"The Captain talked to him and said something about a hound's tooth."

"A dead end."

"So it seems."

That evening Harry took Sarah out for dinner. After they had eaten, they walked out on the Avola pier. A waning moon silvered the water, and a quiet group of strollers were scattered along its length.

"A penny," Sarah said, taking Harry's arm.

"I'm sorry," he replied. "I was thinking that I don't have any idea who killed Joyce Fields and Joshua Bates or who took a shot at Colleen and me."

"Who was that you were talking with just before we left for town? Was he any help?"

"It was Bob Walker, the man who was Joyce Fields' assistant and now has her job. I wanted to find out whether or not I could discount him as a suspect in Fields' death."

"And?"

"By the time I finished talking with him, he had become so obnoxious, I wanted to make him a suspect just so I could go up there and persecute him."

Sarah laughed. "But you can't."

"No. He's one of those fools who has ideology where his brains should be, but he's no killer."

"What ideology?" Sara asked.

"He's still furious with Fields for having allowed her research to be used by the Stoneman Douglas Alliance. I asked him what she should have done with it, and he said it shouldn't have been done at all. In his view the commission exists to serve the needs of Florida's commercial interests. I hung up."

They had reached the end of the pier and leaned their arms on the railings to watch the sunset and the half dozen dolphins playing and feeding just beyond the fishermen's lines.

"What do you do now?" Sarah inquired after Harry had explained that the dolphins were territorial and that their pod lived on this stretch of coast more or less permanently.

"As pretty much a last resort, I'm going to talk with the Hubble family. Joshua Bates' wife Crystal was one of three

Hubble sisters, along with two brothers, who inherited the Hubble estate when their parents died. I believe that even split five ways it comes to a lot of money."

"It sounds fairly sordid," Sarah replied, turning back to the sunset.

The dolphins were moving north, their dark backs flashing fire when they rolled into the crimson light.

"I suppose it is," Harry said, "but so are most human activities when looked at closely."

"Harry!" Sarah said in a shocked voice as she spun around to stare at him.

"It's not cynicism," he said quickly. "It's experience. Shall we change the subject?"

"Yes."

"Jennifer's call has been worrying me. Am I contributing to the troubles between you and David?"

She dropped a hand on his arm and said, "Of course not. You have no idea how wonderful it is to be with someone who's not trying to manipulate me. But since you've asked, what do you think I should do about David? You've been very cagey about giving me your thoughts on the subject."

"Probably because I don't know what to say," he said.

They were leaning on the railing, shoulders touching, watching the sun go down. And unwilling to leave her hanging, he added, "My best shot is to say, do what you think is best for you."

"I'm going to try," she said. "Now, what about the pregnancy?"

Harry groaned. "I'm never going to be pregnant and that fact severely compromises whatever I say. But here goes—and this may be where my objectivity fails the test—there's no rush, so think hard."

"But what do you think I should do?"

"Have the baby."

"It's not a baby, Harry, and saying so isn't worthy of you."

"What do you mean?"

"It's a fetus and will be as long as it's a part of me. When and if it's born, it will be a baby."

"Okay. Carry it to term. It's yours—and David's. You must have wanted it."

"We did. At least I did, but that was when I still thought David and I could make a go of things."

"And you thought having a baby would help you to accomplish that?"

"Yes. How upset would you be if I decided to have an abortion?"

Her voice was steady, but Harry wasn't fooled.

"I would be very disappointed, but if you were sure it was what you wanted, I would not be upset with you at all. I love you, Sarah, and I'm going to go on loving you."

"What about David and Jennifer?" she asked, leaning harder on him.

"Is she having the baby?"

"No."

"Then that takes care of Jennifer." He caught one of her hands in his. "If your marriage to David were solid, I would urge you to discuss it with him. But in the end my advice would still be this: Take your time. Think carefully, consult your head and your heart, and then do what you think will be best for you."

"Then you're saying that in the end it's up to me."

"Exactly."

19

The next morning while Sarah, gradually adapting to life on the Hammock, was sitting on the lanai with a cup of coffee, watching the sun come up, Sanchez arrived with a note from Tucker.

"Tucker says he needs two more pairs of hands," she told Harry, who had pushed back the breakfast dishes to give himself writing room, was working on a crude genealogy of the Hubble family.

"I'll go," Harry said, "and when the chores are finished, I'll get him to help me with this list of names."

"I'm going too," Sarah replied, starting to clear the table.

"Okay, but I don't want you doing any heavy lifting."

"Fussbudget," she scoffed, smiling as she said it, obviously pleased by his concern.

Once they had cleared away the breakfast things and given Sanchez two Milk-Bones, they set off on foot into the lovely morning.

"What I need is some help lifting these sections of hurricane fence to roof this in," Tucker told them when they were gathered inside the enclosure.

Tucker had built a pair of benches, one for each side of the run, and put them on the cement floor inside the wire walls, to stand on.

"You put on the clamps and bolt them in place," Tucker said to Sarah, pointing at a wooden box between them filled with U clamps, bolts, and nuts, "and Harry and I will lift the sections into position."

"Right, Chief," Sarah said, picking up a wrench and looking at it as if it was the first time she'd ever seen one.

"Don't worry," Tucker told her, "Your father and I will tell you how to do it."

"All my worries are over," she replied.

For the next twenty minutes the two men worked holding the wire rectangles in place while Sarah placed the clamps where Tucker told her, put the bolts through the holes in the clamps, and locked them in place with heavy nuts, twisting them tight with her wrench. When the work was done, Tucker wiped his face with a huge white handkerchief and said, "I'm ready to say right now that this place would hold an elephant."

"You know it's against the law to trap and cage a bear," Harry responded, making one last try at changing Tucker's mind.

"I'm just trying to keep that poor animal alive until I can get a vet to look at her. After I've fed her up a little, I'll turn her loose."

"And have a friend for life," Harry said.

"What do you mean?" Sarah demanded, sounding a little angry.

"He means she might grow partial to being fed on a regular basis and having a dry, snug place to sleep when it rains," Tucker replied. "But don't worry, when she's ready to make do on her own, Guy Bridges, our game warden, will truck her out to the Big Cyprus where she'll forget all about us."

"Dream on," Harry grumbled, but gave up the argument.

"What are you going to feed her?" Sarah asked as they walked toward the house.

"Just about what you and I and a pig eats," Tucker said with a broad grin. "There's not a straw's difference among us."

"Should I be offended?" Sarah asked.

"No. To be compared favorably with a pig is a compliment," he told her with a smile.

Over tea, Harry pulled his list out of his pocket and, spreading it on the table in Tucker's kitchen, began talking about the Hubbles.

"From conversations with you and Wetherell Clampett and working in the archives of *The Avola Banner,*" Harry said, "I've learned there are three generations of Hubbles living who have already inherited a share of old Estes Hubble's fortune or are in line to do so."

Tucker nodded while Harry was speaking and then stared up at the ceiling as if searching for something before saying, "That would be Millard, Estes' only surviving son, his other son Philip having died, and Philip's two living daughters Sue Ellen Burns and Alfreda Pendleton." He interrupted his study of the ceiling to pour them all more tea then said to Sarah, "Philip had another girl, Crystal, but she and her husband were murdered a short time back—a terrible thing. They had a daughter. What's her name, Harry?"

"Anna," he said to Sarah. "We've talked about her. Unless there's some quirk in the will, she will in time inherit her mother's share of the Hubble estate."

"Yes," Tucker said, "and I believe she's now staying with her aunt Alfreda Pendleton, who lives in Tampa."

Harry nodded. "That's what Jim told me. It seems a little odd to me that Sue Ellen, who lives in Avola, didn't take her in. Of course, she's got three of her own, but so does Alfreda, all still school age."

"Maybe they thought the child would recover more quickly in new surroundings," Sarah suggested.

"I'd like that to be true," Tucker said.

"Why wouldn't it be?" Sarah asked, showing surprise.

"Because although I'm a great admirer of Occam and his

razor, a simple solution is usually an oxymoron."

"I don't see why that would be true in this case!" Sarah protested.

"I think Tucker means that where there is a lot of money involved, motives tend to become complex."

"I didn't want to mention it," Tucker added with a frown, "but there may be reason to fear that the child's in harm's way."

"Is that possible?" Sarah asked, turning to her father.

"I'm afraid so. As I said, there's a lot of money involved."

Sarah looked troubled, but she didn't pursue the point.

"You've mentioned everyone on my list. Are there others I need to think about?" Harry asked Tucker.

"Probably, but they're not family. Who are you going to speak with first?"

"Millard, I think."

Tucker nodded. "When you've got to deal with a snake, it's a good idea to start with the head."

"Why was Tucker so harsh in seconding your decision to interview Millard Hubble?" Sarah asked as she and Harry were walking home.

"The Hubbles have been major stakeholders in Tequesta County for fifty years. I don't know the details, but from the beginning their names have been associated with shady dealings."

"The tone of Tucker's voice surprised me," Sarah said. "He seems to be so tolerant."

"Not where the suborning of public officials is concerned, and as I understand it, Estes Hubble made more money from bilking the public than he did selling real estate."

The next morning, Harry called Millard Hubble's office and was surprised when the man answered the phone. Wetherell had warned Harry that Millard had more sharp edges than a bench saw, but when Harry introduced himself and asked if Millard had time to talk with him, the man said in strong but friendly voice, "These days I've got nothing but time. Come in now if that suits you."

Millard Hubble was a big man and had been bigger. Harry judged him to be in his early sixties. His dark suit, a good one, hung a little loose on him, and he didn't quite fill his shirt collar, but his dark eyes were clear and sharp, and his hair, which was thick and worn long, still had a lot of black in it, as did his mustache. Harry's first impression was that there was Indian blood not far back in his family's past.

After shaking hands and waving Harry into a leather chair, he said, "What do you think of the desk?"

"Oak, isn't it?" Harry responded. "And clearly an antique."

"That's right," Hubble said, walking around the desk to his chair. "It belonged to my father and his father before him. Have you noticed the other things?"

His gesture took in the large room. Three walls were mounted with Indian spears and shields, scalp locks, knives, coup sticks, pipes, medicine pouches, and war clubs. Behind Hubble were two Caitlin paintings. Scattered around the room were several large bronzes of horses and Indians.

"Are those Remingtons?" Harry asked

"Yes," Hubble answered. "They're museum grade, as are most of the items in the inventory. The pipes and the weapons in this room came to me from my great grandfather."

"Was he a collector?" Harry asked.

"You could say that," Hubble answered with a chuckle. "He was an Indian agent in the Wind River country and married an Arapaho woman, a fact that I'm proud of. Most of the things you see came from her people and the Shoshone, but I've extended the collection significantly. What you see here is only a sampling of what I have. Much of it is out on loan more than it is with me."

"That must be gratifying," Harry observed, beginning not to like Millard Hubble.

"I devote most of my time to keeping track of it and adding where I can," Hubble continued, speaking as if the room was full of people then focusing again on Harry. "I accumulate, Brock. I never sell."

Harry sat and waited for Hubble to go on. When he didn't, Harry said, "You must be very busy. Let me ask you if you're still willing to talk about Joshua Bates and your niece Crystal's murders?"

Hubble turned to look out the window to Harry's left. In profile his Indian inheritance was even more evident. Harry suspected Hubble was aware of the effect. What he was trying to achieve was less obvious.

"I might be," Hubble replied, turning back and regarding Harry with a flat stare, "but first, what business is it of yours?"

The heavy voice had grown cold.

"I'm working for Colleen McGraw, President of the Stoneman Douglas Alliance," Harry answered. "On the day I went to work for her we were shot at. Shortly after that, Joyce Fields' body was found in the Okalatchee. Then Josh Bates, who, as you know, was a member of the Alliance's Board of Directors, and your niece Crystal were murdered. I'm trying to find out whether or not the shooting and the killings are connected because until I know that, I can't solve the problem of how best to protect Ms. McGraw."

"Do you have any evidence that any of these events are connected?" Hubble asked.

"No."

"I didn't think so," Hubble said, getting slowly to his feet. "Let me tell you something, Brock, I didn't approve of Bates getting mixed up with that Alliance bunch. I told him so, but he didn't listen. They're left wing troublemakers. Know-nothings! Most of them haven't done a decent day's work in their lives or met a payroll. And they're interfering with good people who are trying to make an honest living."

His dark face had paled, and he paused, leaning his weight on the desk, catching his breath. For the first time Harry saw the man's frailty. But Hubble gathered himself and continued. "When you poke into people's lives like that, Brock, it shouldn't be a surprise if you get hurt."

"Do you think that's why Joshua and Crystal were murdered?" Harry asked quietly.

"How would I know why they were killed?" Hubble demanded, his voice rising.

"I don't know," Harry said.

Hubble scowled at the answer. "Don't become a nuisance, Brock."

"The last time I ate here," Cora said to Harry, looking up into the cool, leafy shadows above their heads, "one of those birds pooped on the table."

The birds were several pairs of collared doves, whose lugubrious and bubbling calls, *pace* their bathroom habits, added pleasantly to the woodsy atmosphere at Oppenheimer's, a small, quiet, shaded restaurant with outside seating arranged under two huge fichus trees.

"No extra charge," Harry said with a straight face as they sat down.

"But it detracted from the panna cotta, which I shouldn't have been eating anyway," Cora responded, this time with a smile.

She was wearing a pale pink, sleeveless shift and a white coral necklace, a combination that Harry particularly liked.

"By the way," he said, passing her a menu, "you look very

lovely, and your hair looks great. What have you done to it?"

"I've had it streaked," she said, blushing slightly, "and thank you, Harry, I almost believe you."

"Believe me," he said.

They chose a wine, and when that came, they ordered.

"Bring me up to date on Sarah," Cora said.

"She's pregnant."

"You don't sound very happy."

"That's because she may not be going to keep it."

"Is it a health issue?"

"No. She may be going to leave her husband. And I don't know why I'm telling you this. I'm sorry."

Cora tilted her head a bit and stared at Harry in a way that made him uneasy.

"What's the matter?" he asked.

"First I wondered why it had taken you so long to tell me, and now that you have, why you regret it."

"The thing is, I need to talk about this," he replied. "I've wanted to tell you for a while now, but at first I thought that might not be fair to Sarah. Now I feel as if I'm taking advantage of you."

"You haven't been taking advantage of me nearly enough lately," she said, widening her eyes in false innocence, "so keep talking, take advantage, and if by the end of lunch you're feeling more comfortable with the concept . . ."

"Now look what you've done," Harry said, feeling his face burn.

"I love it," she said, finally breaking into a grin.

Lunch came, and as they ate, Harry began telling her about Sarah's problems with David. He had just said that the situation had created a dilemma for her over the pregnancy when Cora interrupted him.

"I get it, Harry," she said with marked impatience, breaking apart a roll as if she was pulling the head off a chicken. "Sarah has a problem, but I don't see what it has to do with you or me."

"I agree it's not your problem," Harry shot back, "but she's my daughter, and I'm involved."

"You're beginning to sound as if you've found a vocation."

"What does that mean?" The comment stung because Harry suspected there was some truth in it, and having it pointed out made him angry.

"Face it, Harry," Cora replied, doing more damage to the roll. "She's a thirty-year-old woman, and from my limited observation of her, a very competent one. Also, your not wanting her to terminate the pregnancy can only make things more difficult for her."

"So?"

Harry immediately regretted that response, but Cora smothered his effort to say something less cretinous.

"*So,* when the time comes, she'll make her own decision, and you'd better be very careful how you put your oar in. If you're not going to eat those olives, can I have them?"

Harry pushed his plate toward her and tried to feel offended by her summation. Cora speared the olives and ate them with relish.

"There's something missing," Harry said.

"The marinade needs more salt," she replied, dabbing her mouth with the napkin. "Why aren't you eating?"

"I'm not hungry. If you're right, why do I feel so lousy?" Harry demanded.

"It's not the marinade is it?" she said. "I've hurt your feelings and trampled on your new-found fatherhood."

"That's a little nasty."

"I suppose it is," she agreed in a subdued voice. "I'm sorry, Harry, but there's no use pretending. Where Sarah's concerned,

I'm not going to be on her side, and building on that, I'm probably not going to be much help to you."

"Okay, Cora," Harry replied, "but I've got five kids and two ex-wives. I don't see much of them, but they're there. If you want me, you get them too."

If he had taken the time to ask Cora why she felt the way she did about Sarah or even to be a little less cryptic in her response, things might have gone better. But he didn't because he thought she was telling him she wasn't interested in becoming involved in his family.

"I don't know why you said that to me, Harry," she snapped, "but I don't like being threatened. Please take me home."

Harry spent a lot of the next day, rerunning the tape of how he and Cora ended their meal. It did not become any more pleasant with repetition. But because he was still in his self-righteous mode, he devoted most of his internal commentary to justifying to himself what he'd said to her in the restaurant and his having let her get out of the Rover without having made any effort to break the icy silence in which he had driven her home. Despite the arguments he mustered in his own support, he could recall times when he had felt better.

That evening Harry got a call from Arlen Gott.

"The relationship appears to be straightforward," Gott said without preamble. "Crystal Hubble Bates inherited a third of her parents' interest, including voting rights, in the Blue Skies Realty Company. Because Joshua and Crystal Bates' will has not yet been probated, Elaine and I weren't able to find out who Anna's guardian will be, but Elaine thinks she will probably inherit her parents' holdings in Blue Skies."

"Good work," Harry said. "What are the chances of your finding out what voting weight Anna would have in Blue Skies if she did inherit those rights?"

"In answer to your first question, moderately good. Also, I think how the company votes its shares is probably a matter of record. How's the investigation going?"

"For the first time, I see some movement. It's not the time to say much more, but I'm hopeful."

Harry was surprised to find that saying it made him aware he really was hopeful.

He and Sarah had developed the pleasant habit of eating breakfast on the lanai. Sarah poured the coffee and said as she sat down, "I had a talk with Colleen yesterday. I was bored with the beach and drove out to the campus. She's not feeling very good."

"More bad mail?" Harry asked, buttering his toast.

"No, it's not that. She's concerned about Jim."

"Oh?" He thought about his talk with Jim and became more interested.

"They're not quarrelling," she said. "If I've understood her, it's just because they're getting along so well that she's worried—if that makes any sense."

"Jim said something pretty much like that to me," Harry responded in surprise. "He's concerned about not being as well educated as Colleen."

"Exactly!" Sarah said, flourishing her spoon. "Only she's concerned they won't have enough common interests to carry them beyond this stage of the relationship."

"Why are they so concerned?" Harry asked, pouring half and half on his oatmeal.

"That's doing your arteries serious damage," Sarah said sternly.

"I know. Answer my question."

Sarah put down her spoon, folded her hands under her chin, and said thoughtfully, "I think they really like each other and are scared they're not going to make it work."

"Are they sleeping together?"

She recovered her spoon and scraped out the inside of her egg, eyeing him suspiciously. "Are you trying to be funny?"

"You mean they're not?"

"No, Father, I don't."

"I didn't really think they weren't."

"I'm relieved to hear it."

20

Over the next few days Harry kept rethinking Cora's comment. At first he assumed she had meant that she had no experience raising a daughter, but after more thought he decided she had either been establishing a boundary or warning him not to bring his family concerns into their relationship.

But her anger seemed excessive. In fact, he was still telling himself that he was the innocent and injured party and that he was not going to fold on this one because if he did, who knew what she would get up to next? Instead of worrying about it, he decided to try to find out who was stealing newspapers at the Piney Woods Condo Association.

Bill Falwell was becoming a real pain with his agonizing over privacy versus the Association's need to apprehend the thief. Grumbling about Falwell helped him to avoid determining his exact role in his quarrel with Cora.

"I'm giving you a choice, Mr. Falwell," Harry said as sternly as he could when he and Falwell were seated in the Board Room. "Either let me catch the thief or let me go."

Falwell squirmed on his chair and grimaced in pain, his round face bright with sweat. "I'm not sure that I can. . . ." he began.

"You can," Harry said flatly, "and you're going to. Do you want this person caught or not?"

Falwell nodded and groaned miserably, as if caught out in an indecency.

"I'll need a key to the building," Harry said quickly, pressing his advantage.

Falwell pulled a huge bunch of keys from his pocket, freed one from the ring, and passed it to Harry. "What . . . ?"

"It's better you don't know," Harry assured him, pushing to his feet.

As soon as he was in the Rover, Harry called Ernesto Piedra, a handsome young man with a head of beautiful black curls, acquired only his mother knew where. Piedra's continuously increasing *cometidos* had led him to abandon the tomato fields for more solitary but also more profitable night work. The new work occasionally brought him in contact with the police and occasional periods of enforced unemployment.

A sleepy and heavily accented voice said, "Hello."

A young woman's voice that sounded to Harry as if she was speaking through bedclothes complained in muffled Spanish and fell silent again.

"Hello, Piedra," Harry said, breaking into a smile in spite of himself. "Are you making more responsibilities?"

"Last night perhaps," Piedra answered sheepishly, "but now, Harry, I am trying to sleep."

"I've got a night job for you with no risk of arrest."

"How much?"

"A hundred. You will have to be in a place by three a. m. and stay awake until you see someone picking up a newspaper. You will take as many pictures as you can of him holding the paper. Then you will run like hell."

"I'll do it, *pero, por favor,* I sleep now."

"All right. I'll meet you at the usual place about four this afternoon."

"Si. Hasta luego."

The woman Harry had heard before, apparently free now from the bedding, said in a soft, lilting voice, "Er-nes-to," suggesting to Harry that Piedra would not be sleeping soon.

"This is the place," Harry said, driving under the *porte cochere* of the Piney Woods Condo Association and pointing through the glass doors of the lobby. "The papers are dropped here about four a.m. Whoever's been stealing them, opens the door, carries the papers inside, takes the one he wants, and leaves."

"Why does he take them inside?" Piedra asked, wearing a puzzled expression.

"I don't know," Harry said. "For that matter, why would anyone with the money to live here steal a newspaper?"

"A tontas y a locas," Piedra said, shaking his head.

Driving back into town, Harry went over again with Piedra what he was to do, and as Piedra was getting out of the Rover, Harry gave him a key and a camera.

"Don't screw this up, Ernesto," Harry said, "remember your *cometidos.*"

"No problem, Harry," Piedra answered with a grin. *"Muy facile."*

And apparently it was because the next morning Piedra returned the key and the camera to Harry and said he had taken three pictures before *el hombre viejo* had put the paper in front of his face and run.

Harry thanked Piedra, gave him the hundred, and hurried off to have the film developed.

"This is your man," Harry said, passing the prints to Bill Falwell.

"Barry Kolinsky!" Falwell exploded, his face flaming. "I should have guessed. The old bastard is nothing but trouble."

"Well, you've got him nailed," Harry said with a relieved laugh, shaking Falwell's hand and almost running for the door.

Harry drove back to the Hammock through a blazing noonday

sun, and found a nervous Sarah waiting for him on the lanai.

"I'm glad you're back, Harry," she said in a rush. "Colleen's been calling, and she sounded to me scared half to death."

"What's happened?"

"This morning, the mailman found a rattlesnake in her mailbox. He threw her mail on the ground and began shouting about a lawsuit. The snake's still in the mailbox."

"I'd better see her," Harry said. "Where is she now?"

"At home, but that's not all. Her e-mail is suddenly full of really nasty stuff."

Harry turned and pushed open the screen door. "Okay, I'll talk to her."

"Wait for me," Sarah said. "She could probably use some female support."

"I've been neglecting you," Harry said once they were in the Rover. "What's new?"

She sighed and frowned out the window. "I've had another talk with Jennifer, and it was worse than the first one."

"Does she want you to come back to Milwaukee?"

"She wants me back with David and away from you. You'd think I was breaking all the Commandments by staying here. Thank God I only have to deal with her on the phone."

Harry started to say, Add my name to those giving thanks, then thought better of it.

"I don't know how much more of this I can take," Colleen said in an unsteady voice as Sarah, who had just jumped out of the Rover, gave her a hug.

"You're going to get some help," Harry said.

"And Harry's going to get rid of that rattler," Sarah added, stepping back to grasp Colleen's hands.

"Right," Harry echoed, having conveniently forgotten the snake in the mailbox. "I guess it's still in there."

Colleen nodded, her green eyes brimming. "The poor thing.

How can people be so dreadful?"

"With very little effort," Harry answered. "Have you got a pair of leather gardening gloves?"

"In the garage," she responded.

Harry found the gloves on a potting bench and put both of them on one hand. Looking around he found a burlap sack that had contained tulip bulbs. He wrapped his wrist and forearm with the bag, and as ready as he was going to be, strode to the mailbox, doing his best to keep pictures of striking rattlesnakes, fangs thrust forward, out of his mind. Sarah was standing in front of the box with Colleen, waiting eagerly. Harry noted cynically that Colleen was probably more concerned about the snake than she was about him.

"Don't stand behind me," he warned Sarah. "I may need running room."

Sarah thought he was joking and laughed appreciatively.

"Be careful," Colleen said in a worried voice.

Harry couldn't see how it was possible to be careful and at the same time to reach blindly into a mailbox full of a seriously irritated rattlesnake.

"Here goes," he said, and with his left hand wrapped in the burlap bag, he pulled open the gate on the box and reached inside with his gloved hand opened as wide as he could extend his fingers.

There was a warning buzz from inside the box, and an instant later something hit his palm, and he grabbed and pulled. Three feet of violently twisting snake poured out of the box, its head in Harry's grip. It hung for a moment from Harry's hand, but with a sudden, convulsive movement, it freed itself, fell to the ground, and tried to escape into the street.

"Grab him, Harry!" Sarah shouted.

"Don't hurt him," Colleen cried.

Harry tossed Sarah the sack.

"Hold it open," he told her and in three long strides overtook the snake and grasped it firmly behind the head with his gloved hand.

Sarah ran up and holding the bag out as far in front of her as she could, watched wide-eyed as Harry dropped the snake into the sack and squeezed shut the top.

"We need some string," he told Colleen.

A few minutes later the snake was lying quietly in its sack on the Rover's back seat.

"My hero!" Sarah said with a bright laugh and kissed Harry on the cheek.

Even Colleen was smiling. "Thank you, Harry," she told him, wiping away the last of her tears. "God, I'm a mess. Come inside, I'll make us some coffee and tell you what's been going on."

Colleen showed them a window at the back of the house that had been smashed by a rock, a handful of e-mails, calling her nasty names, and a letter threatening to torch her house. If that didn't persuade her to back away from the Alliance's efforts to stop interfering in river issues that didn't concern the Alliance, the letter continued, she could expect worse.

"Has Jim seen these?" Harry asked when he had read them.

Sarah had been reading over her father's shoulder, and snatching them angrily out of his hands and shaking them at him she said, her eyes snapping, "I think whoever wrote this filth should be hung on a tree."

"The same thought's occurred to me," Colleen replied with a short, harsh laugh. Then she answered Harry. "He's seen some of them, but there's not much he can do. The telephone calls have been from public phones, in filling stations mostly."

"Did he say where they were located?"

"Upriver mostly, back of nowhere places."

"Do you want to come and stay with us for a while?" Sarah

asked. "That wouldn't be a problem, would it Harry?"

"We'd be glad to have you come," Harry said quickly, pleased with Sarah for having suggested it.

But Colleen thanked them and refused. "I'm at the University most of the day, and at night I've got Alliance work to look after, not to mention what I bring home from the library and the night functions the library sponsors."

"If you change your mind," Sarah insisted, "you know where we are."

Harry and Sarah left Colleen apparently feeling much less distressed than when they arrived. As they drove away, Sarah asked, "How much danger is she really in, Harry? I feel bad about leaving her there alone."

"It's hard to say. Trying to protect someone from the kind of harassment Colleen's been getting is very difficult. So far, except for the snake, she hasn't been in any real physical danger. Cranks abound and are seldom dangerous."

"Except when they're not," Sarah replied. "Of course, she's not exactly alone."

"What do you mean?"

"She didn't want to spend her nights with us," Sarah said, grinning.

"Jim!" Harry shouted.

Once they had crossed the bridge onto the Hammock, Harry stopped the Rover and with Sarah determined to help, shook the rattler out of the sack and into the long grass beside the Creek.

"He looks more at home here," she said, standing with hands on her hips, watching the snake move slowly away.

As she was speaking, Jim Snyder came over the bridge in a cruiser and stopped beside the Rover.

"Harry, Sarah," he said in an unusually formal voice. Then,

not waiting for a response, he asked, "Harry, can you give me a few minutes?"

Harry said he could, and Jim nodded.

"I'll go ahead and wait for you at the house."

Once back in the Rover, Sarah asked in a subdued voice as if Jim might hear her, "What's that all about? He looks gloomy as a rainy Christmas."

"I don't know. He's generally solemn, but something's certainly troubling him."

"Then I'll leave you two to yourselves," Sarah responded. "I've got some calls to make. In case you haven't noticed, I've been neglecting my job. I think it's time I let them know I'm still alive."

"You're still planning to go back to it?" Harry asked, doing his best to make the question sound as casual as possible.

"Are you getting tired of having me around?" she responded.

"The opposite," Harry said truthfully, "I'm afraid you're getting ready to leave."

"You should be so lucky."

Once they were all in the house and the civilities were over, Sarah went upstairs and Harry took Jim back onto the lanai. The first thing he did when they were settled was to tell Jim everything that had happened with Colleen. Jim listened, asked a few questions, and didn't smile even when Harry described the episode with the rattler.

"So that's about it," Harry concluded. "We can talk about the telephone calls later if you want to, but I have the feeling there's something more important you want to get to."

"I suppose there is, but before I start—if I start—I want to be sure I have your permission to discuss it with you." Jim paused.

Harry decided he had better just wait for Jim to finish whatever it was he was struggling with. One thing he knew for certain, he had never seen Jim this upset.

"Well, the thing is, it's about Colleen. That is, it's about Colleen and me, and I've got to be sure you don't think I'm taking advantage of our friendship by bringing it up."

Harry choked back an impulse to laugh. He had known Jim Snyder for a long time, and he had burdened Jim with his personal problems dozens and dozens of times. It had never occurred to him to ask Jim if he was imposing on him. Another of his Yankee failings.

"Not at all," Harry said as seriously as he could. "You've had to listen to my complaints times enough. I only hope I can be as helpful as you've been to me over the years."

"Thank you, Harry," Jim said, his face red and his ears threatening to burst into flames. "Then I'll do it. At least I'll try to do it."

Effort was apparently required because before starting, he took a deep breath.

"You see," he began, avoiding Harry's eyes, "Colleen and I . . . that is, I have feelings for Colleen." That obstacle behind him, he seemed to gather courage because he looked at Harry, who was nodding encouragingly, and said, "The thing is, I've fallen pretty hard, and without taking liberties or making false assumptions. . . ."

He frowned and seemed to stick.

"She's told you she loves you."

"Yes," Jim said with a look of relief. "And I think she really does—that is, as far as it's possible to really know how another person feels."

"Of course," Harry said, interrupting what might have developed into a long digression and anxious to have Jim say what he really wanted to say. "I think there's a *but* making its way to the surface."

"That's it," Jim replied with a loud sigh.

"Let's have it," Harry insisted.

"Well, the thing is we come from very different places."

Unable to resist, Harry said, "You mean there aren't many stills in eastern New Jersey."

"Don't you start up!" Jim protested. "I'm serious here."

"I'm sorry," Harry said as quickly as he could. "Just don't start telling me that your mother would rise from her grave and come hunting you if she knew you were thinking of marrying a northerner."

In the years he'd lived in Florida, Harry's skin had been sandpapered pretty thin on the subject of damned Yankees. Jim managed a laugh, which was what Harry was hoping for.

"I never thought of that. It's got more to do with the fact Colleen's got a Ph.D., and I've got a high school diploma, at least I had one once. The Lord alone knows where it is now."

"Well, yes, she's got a bunch of degrees. What does she say about it?"

"I haven't mentioned it."

"I take it she hasn't either."

"No, but . . ."

"Wait," Harry said. "As Findlay Jay used to say, 'One thing at a time.' Do you think she's troubled by the differences in your formal education?"

Jim looked puzzled. "I don't know."

"Okay. Are you and she quarrelling about anything?"

"Lord, no. What made you think that?"

"I didn't think it. I was just trying to get an idea of how you two got along."

"We get along fine."

"Then why are you worrying?"

"I've got a feeling I ought to. Down the road . . ."

"How far down that road can you see?"

Jim laughed. "Well, maybe you're right." He got to his feet.

"Thanks for listening, Harry. It's been a help. Now, before I go, let's hear about those phone calls Colleen's been getting."

21

After Jim left, Harry told Sarah to eat lunch without him and drove to the Hook. He and Jim had agreed that because they had no new leads, their only choices were to go back over old ground to see if they'd missed anything. Harry would work the Hook and Jim would send Hodges back to the Fielding Crab and Bait Company, to look harder at their rental records.

Harry decided to begin with John Dee Rudd. He found Rudd supervising three men who had dismasted a twenty-foot day sailor, hauled her up the slip and had her rolled over onto her gunwales, preparing to scrape and paint her. Rudd saw Harry coming along the dock and came up a short set of stairs to meet him.

"Hello, Brock," the big man said. "What brings you out here?"

"Same old trouble only more of it."

"Get shot at again?"

Harry caught the same sneer in Rudd's voice that had been there when they first met, but he was no closer to knowing whether it was deliberate or not. The broad, bland face with the small, sliding black eyes told him nothing.

"Colleen McGraw's had a rattlesnake put in her mailbox, a rock thrown through one of her windows, and a bunch of nastiness in letters and e-mails sent her way. Can you shed any light on her difficulties?"

Judd pulled his hands out of his pockets and growled, "Are you saying I had something to do with what's been happening to McGraw?"

"No, I'm asking for help. I'd like to get this stopped before something really serious happens, and that doesn't say I don't think putting a poisonous snake in a mailbox is serious."

Harry said as much as he did, in part, to let Rudd cool off. He did not want the big lummox trying to break his back, and he didn't want to shoot him to keep it from happening.

"Why would I want to help you do that?" Rudd demanded, unclenching his fists and losing some of his growl.

"Joyce Fields is dead. So are Joshua and Crystal Bates although I'm not sure their deaths are linked to what's going on here on the river. I also think you're a sensible man."

"What's that got to do with the price of fish?" Rudd actually grinned.

"No one in command of his faculties wants people being killed in their neighborhood. And who's better placed than you to know what's going on in the Hook or anywhere else on the river, come to that."

Judd shrugged his heavy shoulders and shook his head. "Even if I wanted to help you, Brock—name names and that kind of thing—I couldn't do it without risking getting shot or burned out."

"All right," Harry said, disappointed but not surprised. "If you change your mind, you know where to reach me."

Rudd nodded, and Harry left. He was getting into the Rover when someone said, "Mr. Brock, can I talk with you a minute?"

Harry turned his head and saw Bobby Scrubbs standing in the shadows between two fishing shacks about ten feet from where Harry was parked.

"If you don't want Rudd and some other men to see you talking to me, you better name a place where I can find you."

"Okay, when you drive out, turn right the first chance you get. Then turn right again. I'll be down at the end of the alley."

"You skipping school again?" Harry asked the gangling, blond youngster when he joined him beside an abandoned slip, hidden from Rudd's boatyard by a thick stand of Australian pines. Mangroves and buttonwood trees shielded them from the buildings further east on the river.

Bobby grinned sheepishly. "No, the teachers are having a workshop day."

A flock of laughing gulls swept low over the pines, calling raucously.

"Before this goes any farther," Harry said sternly, "I want to be sure you understand that talking with me won't win you any friends around here."

"I know," Bobby answered, pulling himself up a little straighter, "but I'm worried about Fannon."

"That would be Fannon Jones, right?"

"Yes. He's been bragging on his father and what him and some of the others are going to do to stop the Alliance and Tallahassee from changing how things are run on the Okalatchee."

"What kinds of things?"

Bobby shifted his feet and seemed to lose some of his confidence. "Well, Fannon's been saying that what happened to that woman we found ain't the end of it, that this group is going to start bearing down hard."

"Why should that make you concerned about your friend?"

"Because if it goes the way he says, Fannon's father is going to find himself in a bunch of trouble." Bobby hesitated. "At least that's what my father says. He's real worked up about it."

"Is your father part of the group?"

"No, he won't have nothing to do with it although they been pestering him to join. My mother don't like it one bit."

Harry thought a minute what he could ask the boy without taking advantage of the situation. "Are the people in the group all from the Hook?"

"Oh, no. They come from all up the river."

"They don't have a name?"

"I've heard the River Watch, but I ain't sure."

Harry nodded, thinking that Rudd probably knew exactly what the name was. "What do you want me to do?"

"Whatever you can to stop this thing from getting to where Mr. Jones has to go to jail. They ain't got much as it is, Mr. Brock. If he goes to jail, I don't know how Fannon and his mother will get by. I thought maybe you could tell those Alliance people to back off. You know the McGraw woman, don't you? Wasn't the two of you shot at?"

"Yes, we were," Harry answered, trying to think of something to say that might make the boy feel better without lying to him. "All right, Bobby," he said finally. "I'll do everything I can to keep this business from getting any more dangerous than it already is. But I can't promise it won't. Do you understand?"

"Sure. I see that."

"All right, now listen carefully. This is important. I want you to tell your father you talked to me and what both of us said. Can you do that?"

"I can, but I don't think he'll like it."

"Probably not, but he'll be glad you told him the truth. Don't you breathe a word of this talk we've had to another person. Do you understand?"

"I ain't likely to. I don't want Fannon's father coming after me."

"No, you don't. You did the right thing to talk to me. Thank you. It was a brave thing to do for your friend. Is there anything else you want to say to me?"

"No. I can't think of anything."

"Then I'm going to drive out of here, but you wait at least fifteen minutes before you follow me. Leave by the same way you came in here, and if you can, don't let anybody see you. Okay?"

The boy nodded.

"Good. If you ever need me, you call me. I'm in the book. Remember what I said, tell your father and nobody else."

"Sure, Mr. Brock. Thanks."

Harry shook the boy's hand and drove away, already worrying about how much harm he'd done Bobby Scrubbs by talking to him. Somebody was sure to have seen the Rover drive down that alley, and somebody would probably see Bobby leaving it.

On his way home Harry called Jim Snyder and told him about his conversations with Rudd and with Scrubbs.

"It's a major break for us," Jim said with as much excitement as he ever showed. "Now we know there's some kind of organized resistance outside of the Development Association, it's going to be easier to find it."

"I'll talk to Rudd again and lean a little harder. He doesn't want to make his neighbors mad with him, but I don't think he's part of the group."

"Good, and I'll pass along what you've told me to Hodges and tell him to wring out those people at Fielding's Crab & Bait. With luck we'll get more information on that shooter. Stay in touch."

The next day Harry did talk with Rudd. This time he found the man in his shop with a clipboard in his hand, working on an inventory. The shop smelled of rope, paint, and sailcloth, with an overlay of old hardware store.

"I'm going to charge you rent pretty damned soon," Rudd complained, tossing the clipboard onto a counter and scowling at Harry.

"Fair enough," Harry said. "I've got some questions for you, Rudd. You can either answer them here quietly, or a couple of

Sheriff's deputies can come and get you with a siren blasting, to be sure everybody knows you'll be talking to the police."

"Shit!" Rudd said and slammed a thick hand down on the counter and bounced the clipboard.

"Your choice," Harry said calmly.

Rudd flung himself around a bit more then settled down and pointed Harry toward a small office off the shop. Rudd dropped into an aged wooden swivel chair behind his desk, and Harry sat on a battered folding chair.

"Let's hear it," Rudd said, scowling blacker than ever.

"Do you belong to the River Watch group here in the Hook that's planning to terrorize and possibly kill people associated with the Stoneman Douglas Alliance and anyone else trying to get the state more involved in managing the Okalatchee and its drainage basins?"

"I'm not planning to kill nobody," Judd shouted, then shot a look into the shop and dropped his voice. "No, I don't belong to those property rights activists, as they call themselves, and I sure as hell ain't going to terrorize anybody. What I'm trying to do here is run a business and make a living. What I don't want is trouble."

Harry shook his head, unmoved by Rudd's complaint. "That's not how it looks to me or how Captain Snyder will see it. You've been telling me you didn't know anything about a group. It's possible someone in that bunch shot Joyce Fields. If it was, you'll be an accessory to murder."

Rudd leaned over the desk toward Harry, his face pale. "You've got to believe me on this, Brock. I've got no idea who killed that Fields woman, and I don't belong to any group."

"What would Derwood have to say about what you've just told me?"

Rudd pulled back in alarm. "Jesus Christ, don't bring that crazy bastard into this."

"He's a member of the group. He knows if you are. Is he the head of it?"

Harry was surprised to see how shaken Rudd was. The sneering had vanished.

"I don't know who's the head of it, but it's no damned secret what they've been up to. God damn it, Brock, there's men all up and down the river in on it. At the start it was an effort by people to keep the river the way it's always been. They're mostly little people who banded together to keep from being trod on."

Harry ignored the editorial. "You said, 'At the start.' What's changed?"

Rudd had begun to sweat. "It looks like Derwood and others like him might be taking it over, and there's money coming from somewhere. People are getting fax machines who didn't used to have a telephone."

"Where's the money coming from?"

Rudd's face closed into a stubborn scowl. "I don't know."

Harry got up, certain Rudd was lying, but deciding he had heard enough. He would come back to the money issue later.

"No one in the Hook is going to learn from me that we've had this talk, and as long as I don't find out you've been lying, they won't."

Rudd shrugged his shoulders.

"This is a promise," Harry said, pausing at the office door. "Some people are going jail before this is over. Make sure you're not one of them."

On his way home, Harry got a call from Elaine Porter.

"The research paid off," she said with obvious satisfaction. "Old Beetle's Boat Yard and the Fielding's Crab and Bait Company are owned by the Freeland Property Development Company."

"Which belongs to Rafe Hubble," Harry said.

"Right. I've also discovered that Freeland and Blue Skies

Realty own thousands of acres of property along the Okalatchee, and a lot of the holdings are in the names of subsidiary companies that don't seem to have any function except to hold the properties. I don't see why Blue Skies and Freeland have gone to all the trouble. Arlen insists it's done all the time, usually legitimately. In this case, I'm not so sure."

"Neither am I, Elaine. Thanks for the good work, but be sure you and Arlen keep what you've learned to yourselves. If you find anything more, call me."

It occurred to Harry that having those shell companies might give someone a chance to spend money that couldn't easily be traced to Blue Skies or Freeland. Not a bad morning's work, Harry thought as he bumped over the bridge onto the Hammock.

The next morning Sarah and Harry were having breakfast on the lanai, which had become a habit once Sarah's days filled up to the point she began getting up with her father in order to do everything she wanted to do, when Sanchez trotted into the yard with his head high and woofed officiously at them.

"You get the note. I'll get the biscuits," Harry said.

"Whooee! Tucker's caught the bear," Sarah said, laughing and waving the note at Harry when he reappeared with Sanchez's treats and a bowl of water.

Harry groaned while Sanchez woofed again and grinned before starting his second breakfast.

"And he wants us to come over," Sarah added with a mischievous grin.

"Of course," Harry responded.

Taking the note, he went into the house and scribbled an answer on the note, went back to the yard, and tied it into the dog's red bandana. Sanchez finished off his snack with a loud drink of water and before heading for home, walked over to give

Sarah a friendly boost, but she caught his nose and he backed up and grinned at Harry, who stroked his head and sent him on his way.

"I swear that dog talks," she said as she and her father watched the big hound trot out of the yard. "What did you put in the note?"

"I told him we'd be over when we finished breakfast."

"Is this going to be an all morning thing?" Sarah asked.

"I don't think so. Why?"

"I had something planned with Colleen that was going to include lunch."

"You should make that all right," Harry said as they went back to their breakfasts. "Speaking of Colleen, how is she feeling?"

"Not bad, considering, but, actually, I was going to see her because I think she's been pretty worried."

"Has she had more threats and nasty notes?"

"No. I think she's still worried about her and Jim."

Harry stopped buttering his toast to say, "Jim's worried about the same thing. Does she want to break up with him?"

"No. Just the opposite. I think she is becoming very serious about him."

"Is she worried he isn't as interested in her?"

"I don't think it's that either. If I've got it right, she's worried that the differences in their education are going to prevent their relationship from developing."

"He's worried about the same thing. Only he thinks she's not going to be able to stay interested in him. I thought at first it was a regional, cultural thing, but Jim swears that's not the case."

"Another failure of communication," Sarah said a little bitterly.

"Do you want to try some matchmaking?" Harry asked, half joking.

"Maybe," Sarah said, grinning at her father, "although it may be a case of the halt leading the blind."

"Let's do it, but first we've got a bear problem to solve."

"I hated to do it to her," Tucker said, "but if she gets any thinner, she'll die."

The three people and Oh, Brother! and Sanchez were gathered around the box trap Tucker had used to catch Weissmuller. Only instead of a dead cat, Tucker had used a loaf of oatmeal bread soaked with honey for bait. The present occupant of the trap was no happier than Weissmuller had been with its predicament, but instead of turning the bait into confetti as Weissmuller had done with the cat, the bear had eaten the bread and then tried to wreck the cage with no more luck, so far, than the former occupant. In fact, she was still crashing into the wire, bawling furiously, and occasionally clouting the framing with her paw so hard the cage rocked on its skids.

"The poor thing is skin and bones," Sarah said in a tone of voice that suggested someone was responsible.

"Blame her mother," Harry said unsympathetically, "and remember she's still a bear. If the cage starts to break open, we run."

Oh, Brother! snorted and waggled his ears.

"You two are pessimists," Tucker said, regarding first Harry and then the mule critically. "Now let's get to work."

Oh, Brother! was rigged out in his harness, except for the bridle, which Tucker put on him only when they were using the buckboard. Today, in place of the bridle, the mule was wearing his hat with a new bobwhite feather in its band.

Tucker pulled a folded tarpaulin off the mule's back. "We'll begin by draping this over the trap. Once she can't see us, she'll feel better."

Sure enough, once the tarp was covering the cage and secured by ropes, the young bear stopped bawling and throwing herself into the wire.

"Is she feeling safer?" Sarah asked, tying the last knot.

"Yes," Tucker said. "Now then, Oh, Brother!, come around here."

The mule, showing no enthusiasm for getting any closer to the trap, backed up to the front of the cage, turning his head to watch Tucker as he did so. Tucker had drilled holes in the front of the skids and run a length of iron pipe through them.

"I'll get the chain," Harry said and lifted it down from the hames on Oh, Brother!'s harness.

When the two ends were wrapped around the bar and secured to the two hooks on the skids, Tucker and Sarah pulled the center of the chain forward and attached it to the evener on the traces.

"That looks right," Tucker said, satisfied with the arrangement. "Now we'll see if it works. Oh, Brother!, ease into it now, steady."

With Sanchez running back and forth between Oh, Brother! and the cage, the mule stepped forward to take up the slack in the chain, and feeling the weight of the cage, leaned into his collar and breast strap. The skids clung for a moment to the wet ground into which they has sunk slightly from the weight of the bear, then slid smoothly forward. Oh, Brother!, led by Sanchez, walked off without apparent effort.

"How does he do it?" Sarah demanded as they set off behind the cage.

"He's a powerful animal," Harry said.

"That's right," Tucker added, "and he knows to a pound what he can pull and what he can't. If that skid had weighed more than he could handle, he would have leaned into his collar, felt the weight, and stopped pulling. Mules are smart, and Oh, Brother! is way above the average."

Sarah glanced quizzically at her father. Harry raised his eyebrows but nodded.

"Now, how do we get the bear into the run without losing a lot of blood?" Harry asked when Oh, Brother! had pulled the cage to a stop in front of the run.

"With a good plan and some luck," Tucker said, obviously enjoying himself. "The drop door is at the back of the cage. What we'll do is turn the trap with Oh, Brother!'s help and position its door square with the open door to the run. Then, when the bear's in the run, Oh, Brother! will pull the cage away from the door, we'll close the run door, and Bob's your uncle." He concluded the explanation by throwing up his arms and breaking into a broad but toothless grin. Sanchez wagged his tail and barked in support.

"How do we get the bear to leave the cage?" Sarah asked.

"And who closes the run door once the cage has been pulled away?" Harry inquired innocently.

"O, ye of little faith!" Tucker cried, shaking his head.

"Is that where the luck comes in?" Sarah asked with a laugh.

"Your father's daughter," Tucker replied. "Come on, let's get started."

As it turned out, once the bear had the chance, she shot out of the cage into the run like a rocket, and Harry slammed shut the run door without being mauled because the bear had found a very large tin bowl at the back of the cage filled with scrambled eggs, hamburger, and cooked red kidney beans.

"Well, if that don't beat two sides and a biscuit, as Hodges would say," Harry observed, unable to keep his face straight.

Sarah clapped her hands and gave Tucker a kiss on the cheek, which led the old farmer to say he planned to take up trapping bears as a regular occupation.

22

Harry and Sarah got back to the house in time to see a taxi turning out of the yard.

"Oh, shit," Sarah said with a groan.

Harry was still enjoying his memory of the bear sitting with the bowl in her lap, shoveling the food into her mouth while Sanchez stood with his nose pressed enviously against the fence, watching the captive feast.

"Somebody made a mistake is all," he said.

"Catastrophe is more like it," Sarah snapped. "I'm thinking seriously of trading places with the bear."

Harry was about to make a joke when a tall, dark haired woman wearing a flowered dress and sunglasses stepped off the lanai and onto the grass and paused, hands on hips, to watch them approach.

"Is that . . . ?" Harry asked in a choked whisper.

"It is," Sarah replied grimly.

The years had thinned Jennifer's face and put some silver in her hair, which she still wore long, but she moved with the same swift grace Harry remembered, and her voice, as he knew from their phone conversation, was as rich and sharp edged as ever.

"Don't be alarmed, Harry," she said stiffly, ignoring Sarah. "As soon as Sarah packs her bags we will both be leaving."

Harry stamped down hard on his anger and glanced at Sarah, deciding to give her room to react as she chose. Despite the anger, it passed through his mind that, browned by sun, dressed in dungarees, sneakers, a torn T-shirt, and one of his aged hats she no longer looked like the unhappy, black suited woman he had picked up at the airport.

"You've had a long trip for nothing, Mother," Sarah said in an icy voice. "And to keep it from being any longer, I'll get my pocket book and drive you back to the airport."

She started for the house, but Harry said, "Wait, Sarah. Let's all slow down."

Jennifer looked as if she'd been slapped hard, and Sarah was tight fisted with what Harry assumed was rage. He was so startled by the exchange he had just witnessed that his own anger had evaporated.

"Sarah," Jennifer began, recovering her voice, "don't be foolish. . . ."

"Foolish! My God, Mother, look at yourself. If anyone's behaving like an idiot, you are."

Jennifer whirled on Harry and shouted, "Are you proud of what you've done? Are you?"

"On second thought, Harry," Sarah responded, "let her walk back to the airport. I'm going to take a shower."

She strode into the house, slamming two doors behind her.

"I suggest you and I go inside," Harry said quietly. "I'll make us some coffee. You must be tired. Maybe you'd like something to eat."

Jennifer, her face red with emotion and the heat, started to say something and suddenly stopped, her shoulders slumping. She finally nodded.

Remembering his limitations, Harry skipped the coffee and gave her a glass of iced tea with some mint leaves in it.

"It's practically a weed here," he told her for something to say.

She was sitting at the kitchen table, staring at the wall and looking as if she might be going to be sick. At the sound of his voice, she started as if surprised to find him there.

"What's going on here, Harry?" she asked in a tired voice.

"I don't understand all of it, and most of it you'll have to hear from Sarah," he said sitting down beside her. "But we have reason to be proud of her."

"*We!*" Jennifer snorted, recovering some of her ire. "She's destroying her life."

"How?"

"She may lose her husband for starters."

"From what she's told me, it might not be much of loss."

"How could you possibly know what's best for her?" she demanded with a sharp, dismissive gesture.

"I think what's best for Sarah is something for her to decide."

"Ridiculous!" Jennifer responded, but Harry thought the delivery lacked her usual conviction.

"What do you think of the Hammock?" Harry asked.

"The what?"

"Where we are is called a hammock. This one is Bartram's Hammock, named after John Bartram, an eighteenth century naturalist. I don't think he ever reached this part of Florida, but that creek out there is called Puc Puggy Creek. Puc Puggy is what the Indians called Bartram."

Jennifer stared at Harry as if he was a zoo exhibit. "You have grown more bizarre with the years, Harry," she said. "I have no idea why you're asking me such a question."

"Neither do I, Jennifer, but it's better than arguing."

Sarah, showered and dressed in shorts and a halter, her damp hair pulled back and tied with an elastic band, came into the kitchen, her purse slung over one shoulder.

"Are you ready to leave, Mother?" she demanded.

"No," Jennifer said, smiling calmly at her daughter. "Your father hasn't finished explaining to me what a hammock is.

Until today I thought it was something you slung between two trees to lie in on a summer afternoon."

At eight o'clock that evening while Harry was in the kitchen, turning on the dishwasher after he and Sarah had cleared away the remains of supper, a car turned into Harry's yard. He went onto the lanai and saw Cora standing beside her open door, apparently not sure what to do next.

"Come in," he said, holding open the screen door.

She hurried across the lawn and said, "Hi," as she passed him.

"You're lost, right?" Harry asked, following her onto the lanai.

"You could say that. Where's Sarah?"

"Upstairs. Why?"

"I want to talk about her."

A lot had happened to and around Harry since leaving Tucker and his bear earlier in the day, and he wasn't quite as sharp as he wanted to be.

"Could I sit down?" she asked. "I'm not feeling any too steady."

Harry got them into two chairs.

"What's that racket?" she demanded uneasily.

"Mostly frogs, crickets, and locusts. It's like that every night."

"Jesus," she said.

"Cora, are you in some kind of trouble?"

"Maybe."

"And it involves Sarah?"

He had not turned on the lanai light and couldn't see Cora all that clearly, but what he could see of her and the smell of her perfume made his heart race as if he was an adolescent.

"Harry, I'm really sorry. I acted like a shit."

"I don't . . ."

"Oh, it's true. I know it is," Cora said, interrupting and putting a hand on his knee.

He put his hand on hers and said, "What exactly did you do?"

There was a moment's pause, and then she said, "Harry, are you drunk?"

"No."

"And you haven't had a stroke?"

"Cora!"

"All right. I was very wrong to try to ignore your connection to Sarah. I've come to apologize and, if you'll let me, to try to make it up to both of you. I want to get her know her better. . . ."

Harry stood up, pulled Cora to her feet, and kissed her.

"You don't have to apologize for anything," he said when they came up for air. "I should be apologizing to you."

They were kissing again when Jennifer came to the door and switched on the lanai light saying, "Harry, I thought I heard voices. . . . Oh!"

"Ah, Jennifer," Harry said much too loudly. "I'd like to have you meet Cora."

He still had Cora so tightly clasped in his arms that she was having trouble breathing, but she struggled to tip her head back and smile at the woman in the door.

"Cora," Harry said in the same excessively exuberant voice, "this is Sarah's mother."

"What are you going to do about this?" Sarah demanded.

She was at the stove frying bacon and making scrambled eggs. Harry was pouring juice and rustling the Wheat 'n Bran cereal box suggestively. He assumed she was talking about her mother.

"I'm not eating that stuff this morning," she continued, "and stop trying to avoid the question."

Harry gave up on the cereal and put two plates on the counter beside her.

"Toast?" he asked.

"Two pieces and butter. Answer the question."

"Nothing," he said.

"Harry!"

He hadn't seen her this upset since she got off the plane. "I mean it. The fact Jennifer came all this way means she's seriously concerned about you."

"She's *concerned* about getting her own way."

"Possibly, but the two things aren't mutually exclusive, especially if she thinks what she wants is best for you."

"Are you expecting to die soon?" Sarah demanded harshly.

"No."

"Then stop talking as if you thought God was listening. We're talking about Jennifer here. Remember?"

Harry watched her stacking the eggs and the bacon onto the plates as if she was shoveling coal.

"She caught Cora and me kissing on the lanai last night."

"Oh, my God, Harry!" Sara exclaimed, her face lighting up in a grin. "Tell me!"

"Not funny," Harry said, carrying the plates to the table. "Jennifer was angry, demanded to know who *this woman* was, and did I make a practice of doing this sort of thing with you in the house. Cora ran. I tried to stop her, but she was beyond listening to me."

"How bad is it?"

"I think it's pretty bad."

"I'm sorry, Harry. Jennifer just sucks the life out of everything. I can't stand it anymore. I've got very serious decisions to make," she said in a choked voice. "I can't make them with her in the house. One of us is going to have to go."

23

Harry was working at his desk, waiting for Jennifer to come downstairs and dreading the encounter, when Jim Snyder called. Sarah had already left for the beach.

"I think we've got some movement," Jim said. "I'm sending Hodges to have another talk with the people at Fielding's Crab and Bait Company. My asking you to meet him there is a little unusual, but I don't want him going out there alone, and I haven't got a deputy to send with him. As for the rest, what is usual about this case? Could you be in Punta Rassa in an hour?"

"You've saved my life. I'll be there."

He scribbled Jennifer a note and left.

Harry found the Crab and Bait operation at the end of a twisting dirt track lined with Australian pines. The company consisted of a weathered rectangular shack leaning on the end of a ramshackle pier with a dozen boats of various sizes berthed along its sides. The pier itself was stacked head high with a double line of crab pots.

Despite the rundown appearance of the building and the pier, the gas and diesel pumps at the shore end appeared to be doing a steady business. Waiting for Hodges to arrive, Harry had seen half a dozen boats fill up. Hodges arrived on foot, complaining that he'd gotten lost twice, despite having been here before.

"Let's go in," he said, tugging half-heartedly at his belt and blowing out his red cheeks, "I'm glad you're here. You armed?"

Harry said he was.

"Good. The people I had to deal with last time I was here didn't exactly roll out the welcome mat."

A clatter of cracked bells announced their arrival. Harry peered into the dimness of the inside of the shack and tried not to breathe the stench of rotting shellfish. Harry heard the voice before he saw the speaker.

"What do you want?" a scruffy looking man in torn shorts, a filthy A-shirt, and an untrimmed gray beard demanded sourly, appearing from the shadow of a pile of wooden crates.

"Where's your boss?" Hodges asked.

"Who wants to know?"

Hodges moved very quickly for a fat man. He grabbed the man by his belt and slammed him against the crates, his feet six inches off the floor.

"I do. Is the message getting through?"

"Okay. Christ, take it easy."

Hodges set the man down on his heels hard. "Get him," he said.

The man went off rubbing the back of his head.

"I didn't hear you say please and thank you," Harry observed, easing the CZ back into his shoulder holster.

Hodges chuckled. "The Captain don't approve of that approach, but sometimes it gets results. I had quite a lot of lip from him the last time I was here."

"I understand you laid hands on one of my men," a very large man with a bald head and eyes a little too close together said, swaggering into the room and coming toward Harry and Hodges, his thick arms bowed threateningly. "I don't like that."

Another scowling man about the same size, dressed in yellow waterproof overalls and boots, followed the speaker.

"Which leg do you want me to shoot you in, Devereau?" Hodges asked in a conversational tone.

Devereau stopped so quickly the man behind him blundered into him, causing a certain amount of swearing. Harry already had his CZ in hand, held behind his back.

"I'll have your badge. . . ." Devereau blustered when he stopped swearing at his backup.

"Send that clown back to his crab traps," Hodges said. "Then find a place where we can talk."

"What's going on here?" Devereau demanded when he had taken Harry and Hodges into an office on the front corner of the building and grumbled his way into his desk chair.

"You're going to answer some questions. This time your memory is going to be a lot better than the last time we talked," Hodges said, placing a tape recorder on Devereau's desk.

"I don't have to answer anything," Devereau said, thrusting out his big chin.

"Here it is. You talk to us, or I arrest you on a charge of impeding the police in their investigations of a capital crime. In addition, the ADA may decide to add a charge of attempted homicide and being an accomplice in a murder, and the last I heard, Old Sparky is still working."

Devereau pulled in his chin and leaned back in the chair. He cleared his throat and looked out the dirty window at the view of a dry docked sailboat with a broken mast and a stove bow.

"What do you want to know?" he asked in a voice stripped of belligerence.

"Who owns this business?"

"Freeland Enterprises."

"Owned by?"

"Rafe Hubble."

"That's better," Hodges said. "Who rented the boat that Brock here shot up after being fired on?"

"Do you know what you're asking?"

"Here or in Avola?"

"Shit. It was Tinker Drew, but I didn't have nothing to do with no shooting." He paused. "And if I'm found floating in the bay because of this, it's your fault."

"What does he look like?" Harry asked.

"Big, heavy black beard."

"That's him," Harry said to Hodges.

Hodges nodded. "Where do we find him?" he asked Devereau.

"The last I knew, he was living in Birdland."

"Do you and Drew belong to the property rights group Derwood Jones is running out of the Hook?"

"I suppose there's no use denying it."

"Who's bankrolling them? It sure as hell isn't Derwood Jones."

Devereau hunched his shoulders and shook his head. "You'll have to find that out for yourself."

One question too far, Harry thought.

Apparently, Hodges agreed. He looked at his watch, said the time and the date, and shut off the recorder. Then he said, "You're in trouble up to your hip pockets, Devereau. Arrests are going to be made. If you're smart, you won't wait until the handcuffs are on you to begin cooperating."

"I didn't do nothing wrong!" Devereau protested, pushing onto his feet.

"Keep saying that and you'll be doing ten to fifteen even without the Fields killing."

24

As Harry knew from listening to Jim and Frank Hodges' laments, the Tequesta County Sheriff's Department was short of money and men. Even with Devereau's testimony to spur them on, no one from the C.I.D. unit was going to Birdland for at least a week. Harry decided he wasn't going to wait. The Drew lead was too good to risk losing. After leaving Hodges, he drove to Birdland.

It was possible that the appeal of Birdland was substantially increased by what, or more accurately, who was waiting for him at home. But he resolutely put Jennifer and her list of grievances out of his mind.

Getting to Birdland meant driving east on the north bank of the Okalatchee along narrow, twisting county roads that wound their spindly way through half a dozen hamlets and less organized gatherings of shacks and trailers with chickens, goats, and the occasional cow in a weed-choked pasture. Harry drove the entire dusty, sun-scalded distance without seeing a human being.

The town announced itself with tilted sign that read, "Birdland pop. 1257." When Harry saw the paint-peeled grocery store with its aged gas pumps and annex of farm supplies sheds, he thought they must have been counting all the people who had ever lived in the place. Three unsmiling men in dungarees and western style straw hats were sitting on a bench on the store's porch. Harry greeted them when he stepped onto the porch, but he was met with a slit-eyed silence.

Birdland, Harry said to himself as he went into the store, population twelve hundred fifty-four and three horses' asses.

The thin, grim-faced man behind the counter did nothing to change Harry's assessment of the community.

"What do you want?" he asked in the sour drawl that when Harry had first heard it made him want to shoot the speaker and put him out of his misery.

Now it seemed to him a natural part of the Florida backwoods, like hookworm and wild hogs.

"I'm looking for Tinker Drew," he replied. "Can you tell me where he lives?"

"Maybe," the man said, resting his big hands on the counter top.

"I'm not the law, if that's a factor influencing your memory."

Two of the men who had been sitting on the porch came into the store and made a poor job of pretending to look at the canned goods. Harry ignored them.

"What do you want with him?"

"I'm not from a collection agency either," Harry said.

"I suppose that's a Yankee joke," the man replied

"No, I'm just trying to do some business with Tinker Drew."

The man apparently overcame his understandable dislike and distrust of Harry. "I ain't seen Drew for a while. He's gone a lot, but when he's to home, he's out on Turkey Trace."

"Where would that be?"

"Where it's always been."

The two canned food inspectors laughed. Harry grinned. "How do I get there?"

He could see the man was tempted to keep the hilarity going.

"Keep on the way you are. In about two miles you'll see a dirt track on your left. Take it. When the road runs out, you'll be at Drew's place."

Just before he reached the door, one of the men said, "Make sure Drew hears you coming. If he ain't in sight when you get out of that Land Rover, you shout his name real loud."

"All right," Harry replied, deciding he wasn't being ragged. "Much obliged."

Harry sounded his horn when he saw the clearing at the end of the road. There was no car or truck in front of the low, dark cabin, and although, as far as Harry could tell at a glance, the place was well cared for, it had an abandoned look. After turning off the engine, he put his head out the window and shouted, "Mr. Drew, my name's Harry Brock. I'd like to talk with you."

Harry counted slowly to thirty, and when there was still no answer, he got slowly out of the Rover and called again. Still nothing. He took his time studying the cabin and the surrounding woods, thick with slash pine, saw palmetto, and stands of stopper shrub where one of the pines had gone down and let the sun in. Off to his right he caught a glint of water. The river, he thought.

He started to call a third time and changed his mind. The place was deserted. Stepping away from the Rover, he decided to take a look at the landing. A boat tied up there might tell him Drew was only away from home temporarily although if no one at the store had seen him for the past few days, it was likely he was gone. Harry thought that if he lived in Birdland, he'd stop at the store at least once a day just to reassure himself he wasn't the last man left on earth.

The thought made him smile. Where would he be without Tucker? The path he had found was wide and the bushes cut back neatly. He was beginning to think well of Drew when several things happened, seemingly all at once. He was yanked around, his left side flared with pain as if someone had struck him with a white-hot iron, and the slam of a rifle blasted his ears. The blow from the slug had knocked the wind out of him, but as he was falling, he saw the shooter, who had been behind him, and pulled the CZ.

He hit the ground, losing what little air he had managed to pull into his lungs, fired, and missed. By now, pain and lack of breath were making things wriggle like a fish in a riffle. Getting both hands on his gun, he fired again, but he was too late. The shooter had vanished around a corner of the path.

Harry tried to get up and failed. Then he apparently passed out because the next thing he saw was the sky instead of the path and found that he was sprawled on his back. When the world stopped spinning, he struggled onto his knees and raised his pistol. The pain caused by the effort made his sight dim again, but the man was gone. With his left arm pressed against his side, he hitched himself back to the Rover, the pain in his side growing worse with every step.

Harry staggered through the screen door, dripping blood on the floor.

"I see you found Drew," the storekeeper said, reaching for the phone.

"And you're sure it was Drew?" Jim said, striding along beside him as a long legged volunteer pushed Harry in a wheelchair towards the hospital entrance.

"It had to be Drew, a big man with a heavy black beard. There can't be two such bad shots."

Jim laughed. "How is the side feeling?"

"It's not too bad if I don't turn or laugh."

"Your clothes look as if you'd bled about a quart and a half," Jim told him as the volunteer unceremoniously dumped Harry on the sidewalk.

"You have a nice day," the man said as Harry struggled to find his balance.

"Well, the Lord has to love all kinds," Jim said, grabbing Harry by the arm and making him holler. "Sorry. Can you stand here while I get the cruiser?"

"I think so. It was that last shot that did it. I know how Dr. Jekyll felt."

"He one of the people who worked on you?"

"No. Maybe you ought to get the car."

Harry slept most of the way to the Hammock. When Jim drove into Harry's yard, he was startled to see a tall, dark haired woman he did not know fling open the lanai door and stride across the lawn toward the car. He scrambled out of the cruiser.

"Is that Harry Brock you've got in there?" she demanded loudly.

Jim got himself between the woman and Harry and said, "Who are you? Is there anyone else in the house?"

He did not like the situation and drew his revolver, watching the lanai as he spoke. The gun got her attention and she stopped.

"My name is Jennifer Wilkes, not that it's any of your business. I asked you a question, but you needn't answer. I can see it is Harry. Is he drunk?"

"Turn around," Jim said. He had not really listened to her answer or her question. His mind was on that dark lanai. "You're going to walk in front of me. We're going onto the lanai. Then we're going to see who else is in the house."

"How dare you. . . ."

"It's okay, Jim," Harry called, inching himself out of the car.

"Let me handle this, Harry," Jim responded. "You're not in any condition. . . ."

"I was right. He is drunk," Jennifer said.

"She's Sarah's mother," Harry shouted, making it onto his feet.

Jim slid his gun back into its holster and raised his hat. "I guess I ought to have seen that," he said to Jennifer, his ears getting red. "I'm pleased to meet you. I'm Jim Snyder."

Jennifer ignored the proffered hand and glared past him toward Harry. "Have you been in an accident?" she demanded.

"He's been shot, Ma'am," Jim told her, "but he'll be all right. There's no need for concern."

With her hands on her hips, Jennifer watched Harry making a slow progress toward her and Jim. Then with a sigh, she pushed past Jim and got her hand under Harry's arm and began steering him toward the house.

"Not too fast," he gasped.

"My God, man," she said, ignoring his protest, "are you totally incapable of learning?"

As they passed Jim, Harry winked at him. Jennifer ignored the policeman and launched herself on a list of Harry's other deficiencies.

"Lord of Hosts!" Jim breathed, eyes wide, as Jennifer, pulling Harry with her, disappeared into the house.

Sarah came home to find Harry propped up on the lanai swing, a drink in his hand and the sounds and smells of cooking emerging from the kitchen.

"What happened to you?" she demanded.

Harry told her.

"And what's going on in there?" she asked when he had finished.

"Jennifer's cooking dinner," he said and tried to stop himself from laughing, failed, and groaned at the cost.

"You look awful," Sarah said. "Are you sure you're all right?"

"I will be," Harry assured her when he could breathe again. "Why not help your mother? It would give you a chance to talk."

"You're out of your mind," Sarah said in a stage whisper.

Harry only smiled, and after some fiddling with her bags,

Sarah went.

Some time passed and Sarah reappeared. "We're ready to eat," she said. "Let me help you up."

"No!" Harry protested. "I got all the help from Jennifer I'm ever going to need. Just steady me once I'm upright."

"What's all this domestic shit about, Harry?" Sarah whispered once he was on his feet and shuffling toward the door. "I'm not taken in, and I hope you're not."

The little family ate and talked together without a food fight breaking out, and when the meal was over, Jennifer folded her napkin and said to Sarah, "This man beside me, struggling to put his fork in his mouth, just spent his day doing things that got him shot. He's been doing this for more than thirty years, which to me says he doesn't have the judgment of a brain-dead cat. Any advice he's given you, aside from how to shoot people, is less valid than what you'd get from a pack of Tarot cards. I'm going home the day after tomorrow. I want you to go with me."

Harry was careful not to make any visible response to Jennifer's speech, but he thought it was above average in content and delivery. He had forgotten how good she was at a verbal skinning. Sarah pushed forward in her chair and stared at her mother as if she had fallen among thieves. For a moment Harry thought she might make a run for the stairs, but then she settled back and shook her head.

"Unless Harry throws me out, I'm staying."

"You can't be serious," her mother protested.

"But I am. Harry, acting the part of the honest broker in this melodrama, has not made it clear to you that I am very seriously considering divorcing David."

Jennifer, her face flushed, began to speak, but Sarah interrupted her.

"I don't love David. I don't think he loves me. He has not called me since he came home and found me gone, and I haven't called him. What does that tell you?"

"That you're both idiots."

"Were you an idiot to leave Harry?"

"Absolutely not, but there is no comparison between your father and David."

"You're right. Harry is twice the man David will ever be."

Jennifer tried again to protest, but Sarah stood up.

"I don't want to hear it, and until you've left, I'll be staying with Colleen."

"I was hoping you'd help me pick up the Rover in the morning," Harry said.

"What time?"

"Is eight too early?"

"I'll be here."

25

Harry drove Jennifer to the airport. When they reached the security checkpoint, she broke a long and, at least for Harry, very uncomfortable silence.

"My life would have been very much simpler if Justin Stone had killed you, Harry," she said in a firm voice.

Harry regarded the grim, stiff-faced woman in front of him and suddenly lost all inclination to continue the conversation.

"Have a safe trip, Jennifer," he said and walked away as fast as he could, but his speed was compromised because the movement of his left hip pulled the wound in his side.

But the pain in his side was less of a burden to him than the pain in his heart.

That afternoon Jim called.

"Bad news," he said. "We've found Tinker Drew in a cabin south of Birdland. It looks as if he used it as a bolt hole. He's dead. He knew and was not afraid of whoever killed him. He was shot in the back of the head with a small caliber gun, probably a twenty-two."

"Professional job?"

"Probably, but it could have been done by anyone."

"Especially someone who didn't want him talking to the police."

"We'll do some looking, but I don't think there's much chance of finding whoever did it."

"Thanks, Jim. I'm going to talk to some people."

"Are you up to driving?"

"I'm okay."

"Is Jennifer still there?" Jim asked with a failed effort at casual inquiry.

"No. She left this morning." Harry could almost see Jim struggling for something appropriate to say. "Thanks for asking, but it's really just as well she's gone."

"I'm sorry," Jim replied quickly and with obvious relief, "but I believe I saw the other day why you would say that."

Harry, beginning to see some humor in the situation, hung up the phone, grateful for the reprieve.

"You know, Harry," Sarah said, coming down the stairs after putting her things away, "before my mother came, I had doubts as to whether I had the right to decide for myself what to do with my life. Now I don't."

"Then it's true," Harry said, giving her a hug. "Every cloud does have a silver lining."

Sarah laughed, and he managed a smile.

Like Millard, Rafe Hubble was something over six feet, heavy shouldered, and dark. His eyes had the same intensity as his father's, but Harry could not find in them the fixity of purpose Millard Hubble's gaze projected. "I hear somebody's been using you for target practice," Hubble said with a wolfish grin.

Harry's left arm was still in a sling, and he walked into Hubble's office with a hitch in his step that indicated pain. Hubble had gripped Harry's hand and jerked the injured man toward him, making Harry flinch.

"You're lucky Tinker Drew was such a poor shot," Hubble continued with a laugh, waving Harry toward a chair.

"Was?" Harry asked, masking both his pain and his anger.

"Sure. He's dead. Didn't you know that?"

"I guess I heard something. How did you find out?"

Hubble sprawled in a chair, regarding Harry with open contempt. "There's not much happens in Tequesta, Lee, and Charlotte Counties I don't know about," he said, grinning, "most times before it happens."

"How do you manage that?" Harry inquired with enough insolence to make Hubble push himself up in his chair and lose his grin.

"What do you want, Brock?" he demanded.

"Some help, if you've got a few minutes to spare," Harry answered, dropping the edge from his voice and sounding like someone asking a favor.

"What kind of help?"

"I'm sure you know that the state biologist Joyce Fields was murdered a while ago while she was working on the Okalatchee. Colleen McGraw and I were shot at on the river, and Joshua Bates and his wife Crystal were murdered in their sleep."

"So?" Hubble demanded with another scowl.

"As you said before, and I believe it, there's not much that happens on and around the Okalatchee that you don't know about. Do you see any connections among the three events? I've been trying for weeks to hook them together with no luck at all."

Harry had guessed right. There was enough flattery in the question to make Hubble rise to the fly.

"You're working for a trash outfit, Brock," Hubble said, thrusting out his jaw.

"You mean the Stoneman Douglas Alliance."

"Damned right. That McGraw and the rest of them have been poking in where they're not wanted. And you're not doing yourself any good getting mixed up in it."

"I'm beginning to see your point," Harry said, pointing to his sling. "But are you saying Colleen and I were shot at and the other three people killed because of being connected with the Alliance?"

Hubble shook his head as if he was explaining something obvious to a child. "There's a lot of people mad as hell with the Alliance," he said. "The Alliance is messing with their livelihood."

"How do you figure that?"

"Christ, Brock, you're not too swift. Who are these assholes on the Alliance Board of Directors? Who is Fields, for that matter?"

"Well, Fields was a very highly regarded scientist. . . ."

"She was an outsider, Brock, bringing in her goddamned *science* as an excuse to tell people what to do. And as for that pansy cousin of mine, he was on some kind of dumb crusade he didn't know shit about. As for you, Brock, my guess is that if you get killed, you'd be collateral damage."

"Did you know Tinker Drew?" Harry asked, still pretending innocence.

"Sure," Hubble said, pushing back from the desk and kicking out his feet.

"Then you'd probably know Derwood Jones."

"Him too."

Hubble was grinning now as if he was enjoying this talk with the village idiot.

"He's heading up some kind of property rights group. I think Drew might have belonged to it."

"River Watch," Hubble said.

"What?"

"The name of the group is the River Watch. Three quarters of the men on the river belong to it."

"What's their purpose?" Harry asked, pretending surprise.

"They intend to keep the EPA and the rest of the state and federal agencies from ruining their lives," Hubble said, his voice rising.

"And the Alliance?"

"Shut them up and the government groups will leave them alone."

"Do you think people like Drew and Jones are leaders?"

"Drew was a fuck-up and paid the price. Jones is a little hotheaded, but he's a good man. He kicks ass." Obviously stirred up, Hubble glared belligerently at Harry. "The Alliance is going to find out just how good at it he is."

"Must take a lot of money to put together an organization that big and keep it rolling," Harry said, shaking his head. "Where's it all coming from?"

"That's beauty of the thing, Brock," Hubble sneered, "you're never going to find out."

On his way home, Harry called Jim and told him about his meeting with Rafe Hubble.

"If he had half his father's brains, he'd be dangerous. He's involved with the River Watch and thinks he didn't tell me he was. He knows who killed Drew and even told me why he was killed."

"Who did it?" Jim asked.

"It was probably Jones. Drew was probably sent to kill Colleen and me and made such a mess of it that when I showed up in Birdland, someone decided to kill him before the police could get hold of him."

"Then it sounds as if Rafe Hubble knows who killed Fields and, possibly, Crystal and Josh Bates," Jim said.

"I think so. He all but told me that Derwood Jones was going to increase his attacks on the Alliance," Harry responded.

"And we're going to have to just wait until it happens, because, based on what we know, we can't intervene," Jim lamented.

"I'm going to keep pushing," Harry said.

With Jennifer gone and Sarah settled again in her routine, Harry was able to think about Cora. In the days since she had fled from him, hurt and angry, he had not called her and she had not called him. He was all too aware of Sarah's comment to her mother that if two people are apart and don't call one another, it tells you all you need to know about their relationship. But he wasn't ready to give up, not, at least, without talking to her, and he did not think he was being frivolous in giving half a day to trying to heal a breach that was giving him a lot of pain.

So the morning after he talked with Rafe Hubble, Harry drove into Avola and with a high level of self-doubt walked for the first time into the Spice Island Gallery on Palace Avenue. Cora's gallery consisted of two rooms, the first and larger was filled with Florida paintings, and the walls were alight with soft greens and vivid oranges and reds. Cora was standing with a customer in front of a large painting of a white gate smothered in red hibiscus and a glimpse beyond of a thalo green ocean under a cerulean sky. She was, Harry gathered, talking about the artist and some of her recent shows.

When the man finally shook his head, Cora pointed him toward another painting. Turning away, she saw Harry. She was dressed in a buttercup yellow blouse and beige skirt. He thought she had never looked lovelier. After hesitating for a moment, she walked toward him with an expression as uneasy as his own.

"If this is a bad time, Cora," he began in a rush, "just say so, and I'll go. I didn't want to do this on the phone and. . . ." He had run out of words and was appalled at having said something completely different from what he had planned. His heart was in his throat.

"Just a moment," she said, "I'll tell Holly I'm leaving," and walked across the room to speak to a small woman in a green dress who looked to Harry like Little Orphan Annie.

Cora returned and asked him to follow her. The gallery backed onto a small, paved square with a fountain, bougainvilleas in planters and benches on three sides, shaded by Dahoon hollies. The square was deserted.

"Do you want to sit down?" Cora asked.

"Yes," Harry said, thinking that she did not look as though she was up to walking.

"I can't blame you," she said, plunging in as soon as they were seated and making an obvious effort to master whatever was distressing her. "I understand, so let's not make this any more painful than it has to be."

Harry's heart sank. "I understand, or maybe I don't, but it doesn't matter," he blurted, desperation dragging his tongue behind it, "but I was hoping we could . . ."

"What's the point?" she flared, folding her hands in her lap so tightly her knuckles turned white. "You've made up your mind. I don't want to make a bigger fool of myself than I already have."

She paused, her breath catching in her throat. Harry stared at her, worried that something had gone wrong with his mind. He did not understand anything she had just said. But he was too rattled to stop talking.

"I was hoping you would let me try to get us past this thing, and that together. . . ."

"Oh, I see, you want me to help you get rid of me!" She jumped up. "Well, Harry Brock, you can go. . . ."

In that moment Harry woke and was on his feet and had her in his arms although the way she was struggling it was nip and tuck if he could hold her long enough to say what he wanted to say.

"I'm trying to apologize, Cora," he shouted, bringing an

elderly man crossing the park to a sudden stop. "I don't want to leave you."

"Take your hands off her, Sir!" the old man said, flourishing his cane and starting toward them.

"You idiot!" Cora cried. "Oh, not you," she said to the old man who had paused at her outburst, his mouth open in astonishment. "It's all right. It's all right," she said, beginning to laugh. "It's just that this man ought not to be let out without supervision."

The man grinned, doffed his hat to Cora, and went on his way. Cora, now free from Harry's embrace suddenly threw her arms around him and squeezed. He yelled in pain.

"What is it?" she demanded.

"I've been shot," he said, dropping onto the bench with a groan, clutching his side.

"If you don't stop playing the fool," Cora exploded, "I *will* leave you."

"Today's the first day I've had my arm out of the sling," he gasped. "Honest to God, I really was shot."

When that was all straightened out, Cora said, wiping her eyes and kissing him, "We're going to my place for lunch."

"I'm glad you and Cora are okay again," Sarah said.

She and Harry were leaning together on the Hammock bridge railing watching the afterglow staining the huge thunderheads in the eastern sky a dozen shades of rose and saffron. Beneath them, the dark waters of the Creek picked up the colors.

"So am I," he replied. "What about you? Is Colleen giving you any help with your problems?"

"I don't talk about myself all that much," Sarah said in a voice that made Harry put his arm around her shoulders, "but, yes, she's a help."

"I'm glad to hear it. Does she talk to you about Jim?"

Sarah nodded. Harry decided he'd gone as far as he should and asked, "Are they talking any more frankly with one another?"

"I don't think so," Sarah replied. "Neither of them seems to know where to begin."

"I think Jim would find it very hard to tell Colleen how he really felt, especially if he thought she might feel he was putting pressure on her."

"It's amazing how reluctant people are to open up to other people," Sara said.

"Your mother and I had plenty of fights, but we never really talked about what we both knew were serious problems between us."

"Why not?"

"I think we were both too afraid of our own feelings. I know I was afraid that if I began talking about mine to Jennifer they would explode and destroy whatever was left of our marriage."

Sarah laughed. "I guess that's what Jennifer's did all by themselves."

They were quiet for a while. Harry was about to ask if she and David had discussed their problems when Sarah anticipated him.

"Things got to the point with David that I no longer trusted him with my feelings. But there's no point in going there."

She stopped talking and stared down at the dark water. Harry waited, wishing he could take away her pain.

"Is Colleen in more or less danger now than she was when the rattler turned up in her mail box?" she asked, changing the subject.

"I think she's in more danger," Harry answered, wishing she had gone on talking about herself and David but deciding she should choose her own time to do that.

"Are you going to tell her?"

"I'm going to suggest she take some steps to make it difficult for anyone wanting to harm her to actually do it. But, no, I don't see any point in frightening her."

The sky was losing its colors, and the wind, as if taking its cue from the sun, began to sink.

"Ouch," Sarah said, slapping her arm. "That was a mosquito. I've been reading some nasty stuff about West Nile fever. Is it a risk here?"

"Not so far, but there's no point in being bitten."

By the time they reached the house, there was a new moon in the sky.

"It's supposed to be bad luck to see a new moon for the first time through glass," Sarah said as they were crossing the lawn.

"Then we're safe for at least a month."

"Harry, I didn't say much to you about your being shot, but it's not because I didn't care."

He followed her onto the lanai. "I know that, Sarah. You said enough."

"No, I didn't Harry. I didn't because I couldn't stand thinking about someone's trying to kill you. Harry, if anything were to happen to you. . . ."

For the first time since they had been together, she burst into tears and threw herself against him. "Harry," she said between sobs, "don't leave me."

26

The shock of Sarah's fear did more to focus Harry's mind on the risks he was facing on this case than all the pain of being shot had done. He was not accustomed to having anyone tell him that his going on living was important to them, except, possibly, his dentist and his insurance agent. He did not find the new awareness disturbing, but it did make the possibility that he might be killed a lot more real. And he thought perhaps Jennifer's assessment of his judgment might have been reasonably accurate.

Harry thought about this on his way to talk to Sue Ellen Burns in Avola. He did not look forward to the interview. The carnage in Crystal Bates' bedroom was still very fresh in his mind, and while he was sure Jim Snyder had not allowed Sue Ellen into the room, it was almost certain Anna had told her aunt what she had found. Talking with her about the murders was bound to be painful for both of them.

Sue Ellen lived in a large stucco house in the Banyan Road section of Avola. The community had been built out for twenty years, and although the existing houses were solid and attractive and their landscaping beautifully maintained, Harry suspected the area was ripe for redevelopment. McMansions were springing up all over Avola's west side, and Harry thought Banyan Road would be next.

"I've been expecting you for some time," Sue Ellen said, taking Harry into a bright, quietly furnished living room.

She was a handsome woman in her forties with light red hair and dark eyes. In her high cheekbones and aquiline nose, Harry could see the Hubble ancestry.

"To be honest, I've been putting it off," he replied, declining her offer of coffee. "I'm sure you haven't been looking forward to this visit."

"If it helps to find Crystal and Josh's killer, I'll be satisfied."

"I'll tell you up front, you may find my questions disturbing."

She gave him a brief smile. "Ask them."

"Do you know of any reason why anyone would want your sister and brother-in-law dead?"

"No."

"Were they having any kind of trouble—financial, marital, anything at all?"

Burns leaned back in her blue wing chair and crossed her legs, smoothed her skirt over her knee while she thought, then lifted her head and said, "As far as I know, neither Josh nor Crystal was having an affair—and I think I would have known. Crystal and I were very close. But I can think of two things that might have been a source of controversy, not that I think the issues are linked to their deaths."

"Okay," Harry responded.

"Family quarrels can be nasty," she said.

Harry thought of Jennifer and nodded.

She took a deep breath. "When our father died, Uncle Millard began pressuring Crystal, Alfreda, and me to sell him our shares in Blue Skies." She paused and then asked, "How much do you know about the business?"

"Not a lot, but I know your father and your uncle had some problems and agreed to put the running of the company in the hands of Adelaide Slocum. I think you and your sisters have seats on the Board and divide fifty percent of the voting rights among you. Does Anna have her mother's votes?"

"Yes. I'm going to tell you something that is painful for me to say, but it goes to the point I was making. Alfreda and I agreed she should take Anna because Anna's being here with me would make her too easily accessible to Uncle Millard and Cousin Rafe's influence."

"Then the pressure for all of you to sell has continued."

"Yes, it has, and in the last year it has grown a lot worse. Uncle Millard's urgings are tolerable, if unwanted, but Rafe's are downright unpleasant and verging on threat."

"Physical threats?"

"I regret to say it, but my cousin is a bully. In the past year Rafe kept after Crystal to the point that Josh threatened to sue him for harassment."

"Why Crystal and not you or Alfreda?"

"Oh, we had our share, but I think he was harder on Crystal because she had begun showing up at Board meetings and demanding to examine the company's books. Alfreda and I warned her she was asking for trouble."

"Who will vote Anna's shares?"

"Probably either Alfreda or I, but Millard is contesting that, and the courts may have to decide what's to be done."

"Is Millard proposing he should be her guardian?"

"Yes. It's preposterous, but once lawyers and a judge get their hands on an issue, anything can happen. He has nothing to lose by trying."

"If one of you were to sell your shares to your uncle, what would the consequences be?" Harry asked.

"He would hold two-thirds of the shares and control the company. But if you're suggesting . . ." she said bridling.

"That your uncle murdered Josh and Crystal to gain controlling interest in Blue Skies Realty? No, I'm just trying to understand the situation. You said there were two issues. What's the second?"

The lie had fallen trippingly from his tongue, but to Harry's relief Sue Ellen appeared to be mollified and replied quickly, "Josh's connection with the Stoneman Douglas Alliance."

"How did you feel about that?"

She did not hesitate. "Ambivalent. I admired his commitment, but it put Crystal in a very difficult position."

"How?"

"Isn't it obvious? We live on the revenues generated by Blue Skies. Restricting development and limiting expansion of existing investments reduces Blue Skies capacity to make money. Opposing increased state and federal interference in the ways we do business is one of the few things Millard and I agree on."

"Did Crystal share your views?"

She stiffened her back. "No. Crystal could be difficult."

"How upset were your uncle and your cousin with Josh over his involvement with the Stoneman Douglas Alliance?"

"They didn't like it." Burns glanced at her watch and stood up, and Harry quickly followed. "I'm on the Banyan Community Association Board. I have a meeting in twenty minutes."

"Thank you for your time. You've been helpful."

At the door he paused. "If you think of anything more, please give me a call."

Harry drove away thinking that Sue Ellen Burns may have told him more than she intended and had ended the interview to prevent herself from making any more mistakes. It was also a matter of speculation why raising the issue of Joshua's relationship with the Stoneman Douglas Alliance had upset her.

"She's afraid of something or hiding something," Harry told Jim Snyder.

"What?" Jim asked.

"Old Millard," Hodges said, leaning forward in his chair and making his belt creak.

The three men were sitting in Jim's office. Harry had decided not to get too far ahead of his support and had driven from Burn's house to the Sheriff's station. Also, he was fishing for any information they might be withholding.

"Now what does that mean?" Snyder demanded.

Frank's Delphic comments always irritated Jim.

"Whatever she's afraid of or hiding has to do with Millard Hubble," Hodges responded.

Jim rubbed a big hand over his face and groaned. "Frank, have you been holding back evidence that Millard Hubble murdered his niece and her husband?"

"No," Hodges began and was cut off.

"Then don't start up!" Jim's ears were getting red.

"Frank's not that far off the mark." Harry turned to Hodges. "Hubble and that renegade son Rafe ought to be looked at. If Millard can persuade the courts to give him control of Anna's votes, he will dominate Blue Skies. People have killed for less."

Harry sat back and looked at Jim.

"You two have been smoking some really bad stuff," Jim said. "You don't have a smidgen of evidence. There's nothing even to establish probability, never mind motive, means, and opportunity."

"Not yet there isn't," Harry agreed, "but from talking with Sue Ellen Burns, I think you ought to be looking at Millard and Rafe Hubble."

Jim glanced from Hodges to Harry and his long face grew longer. "Don't even think about it. Those two are tied to every business and civic organization in Tequesta County, not to mention Lee County, and every one of those same organizations is a big contributor to Sheriff Fisher's reelection campaign."

"I'm thinking the pair of them want to do something they know they can't do without more votes. And that means it's probably crooked, otherwise Crystal and her sisters would have gone along with whatever it is," Harry said.

"Didn't you hear anything I said?" Jim said loudly.

"No," Harry said. "How can we get a look at their books?"

"Maybe we could sic the IRS on them," Hodges suggested, "and sneak a look at their books over one of the investigator's shoulders."

"In which federal prison do intend to spend your declining years?" Jim asked, scowling at his Sergeant.

"Maybe somebody else could tell us what we want to know," Harry said.

"Who?" Hodges asked.

"Adelaide Slocum."

Jim laughed. "You'd get more information talking to an alligator."

"What if you called on her quietly, asked her if Millard had been trying to get the Board to do something his nieces had refused to go along with? Then before she answered with her mandatory NO, you could bring her up to date on the penalties for withholding information from the police in a murder investigation? Nothing heavy, all smiles and warm handshakes but the implications clear?"

Jim shook his head. "Too risky. I'd need a lot of backup, which I don't have, to steer that close to threatening her."

"What if I do it?" Harry asked.

"As long as I don't know about it."

"As soon as you're out the door, she's going to call old Millard, and then he'll be on the horn to his son," Hodges said gloomily.

"Good," Harry said, levering himself out of his chair. "Millard's sitting up there, happy as a cat full of song bird. Maybe if I can shake his tree, something will fall out."

"Make sure it's not your carcass," Jim answered.

27

Driving toward the Hammock, Harry found himself thinking again about Colleen. He had told Sarah he thought she was in some degree of danger, but talking with Sue Ellen Burns about the Bates' murders had heightened his concern. He called her. She was at the university.

"Come out for lunch. Maybe Arlen and Elaine can join us. Cora's got clients. You can bring us up to date."

"About twelve-thirty," Harry replied.

The university cafeteria was plastic everything in alarming shades of mustard and gaslight green.

"The Reuben is edible," Colleen said.

The four were standing in line, reading the plastic menu board. Harry thought Colleen was looking much more rested than the last time he saw her. And in her navy suit and white blouse, with horn rimmed glasses hanging on her chest from a black cord, she looked, he thought with a smile, nothing like the booted naturalist he had first met, dipping fish out of the Okalatchee.

"But your lifetime limit is two," Arlen observed from his considerable height.

"What happens with the third?" Harry asked, already deciding to order it.

"The heart clogs and stops."

"And there's no wine to keep the sludge moving," Elaine said in a disappointed voice. "If God had intended me to be abstinent, I would have been born a hen."

"No more talk about death," Colleen said with a shudder. "There's been too much of it already."

When they were seated, Harry asked Colleen, "What's new in your life?"

"Good news," she said. "No snakes in my mail box. No threatening letters. No vicious correspondence, and the St. John's River Coalition Program Chairman e-mailed me to say the Coalition has decided to take a formal vote on whether or not to throw in their lot with us."

"Why now?" Elaine asked.

"I've no idea," Colleen answered, tackling her sandwich.

Harry's was still steaming on his plate.

"Tinker Drew's dead," he remarked, "but he couldn't have been responsible for all the unpleasantness you've been experiencing."

He kept his voice neutral, but her news chilled him. It probably meant that someone had decided she wasn't going to respond to harassment.

"Does it mean they, whoever they are, have backed off?" Arlen asked Harry.

Harry shook his head. "It's likely to be something more sinister than that."

"Like what?" Colleen asked, her eyes widening.

"I'm afraid Harry thinks you're in more danger than you were when you were being harassed," Arlen rumbled, concern creasing his heavy face.

"Harry?"

"Arlen's right," he said, feeling the bad news was his fault. "I don't want to frighten you, but I think you should start taking precautions."

"Precautions?" she asked quietly.

"Yes," he said encouragingly, "just simple things. Keep your car in the garage. Keep the garage locked. Don't take walks alone after dark. When the sun sets, draw your shades. And above all else, if you see or hear anything that frightens you, call nine-one-one."

"I did what I said I'd do," she said defiantly. "I bought a gun, and I've been taking lessons."

"Colleen!" Arlen said in a shocked voice.

"Don't lecture me, Arlen," she told him, grim-faced. "I'm done being a victim."

"Do you have a license to carry it?" Elaine asked, apparently pleased by Colleen's decision.

"I have a permit."

"Are you carrying it in your purse?" Harry demanded.

"Yes."

"Don't. What is it?"

"A Smith and Wesson thirty-eight."

"Just right. Wear it in a back holster."

"Wait! Wait!" Arlen bellowed, bringing conversation in the room to a stop. "Why are you encouraging her?" he demanded, lowering his voice to a hoarse whisper, which carried like the pronouncement of Poe's raven.

"I don't need encouraging, Arlen," Colleen shot back, her temper flaring.

"How did you get the permit?" Harry asked.

Colleen turned a little pink, but she answered firmly, "Captain Snyder got it for me."

Arlen groaned. "A conspiracy of idiots."

"I reject that!" Colleen shot back. "I have a right to protect myself, Arlen, and I've been taught how to use this gun by professionals. At twenty-five yards, I'm inside the eight ring four out of five shots and inside the ten ring two of the five. So don't burden me with any more of this 'little lady' crap."

Elaine shot her fist into the air and cheered, silencing the room a second time. Arlen screwed up his face and rumbled something incoherent.

"I'm impressed," Harry told her. "Arlen, she's talking about scoring a bull's-eye target. The innermost circle is the one point five inch X-ring, the next, the ten ring, and the next, the eight ring. She is shooting really well."

"And don't forget, Arlen," Colleen put in spiritedly, "I'm on the river most weekends, often on my own."

"You shouldn't be," Arlen insisted, shaking his big head.

Harry thought she might be pushing things, but he knew that in her place he'd do the same.

"I want to change the subject," he said, making a quick check to see that they had stopped being the center of attention. No one was paying any attention to them, so he quickly summarized his suspicions concerning Millard and Rafe Hubble, both regarding Joyce Fields' death and the killing of Crystal and Joshua Bates.

"There isn't a shred of real evidence linking them to the crimes," Harry concluded, "but I think that if we had access to Blue Skies' finances, we'd be able to establish motive."

"How do we do it?" Colleen asked.

"Not easily."

Arlen looked at Elaine. "Could we help? It would be little shady, but I think we could at least find out Blue Skies' credit standing if that would help."

"Sure we can," Elaine said gamely.

"It would be a start," Harry said, brightening. "Something is pressuring the Hubbles to get free from whatever restraints the three cousins have been exerting."

"Maybe Millard and Rafe just want more control of the business," Colleen said.

"Maybe," Arlen said, "but it's been my experience on boards that when executives get antsy about not having enough control, it's because they're up to something that they don't want other people to know about."

"See if you can find out what it is," Harry said, pushing back his chair. Then to Colleen, he said, "Don't forget. Buy that holster."

When Harry got home, he had a message on his phone from the Avola Community Hospital, giving him a number to call.

"A Sarah Wilkes was admitted to the hospital at eleven this morning," a woman speaking slowly with a heavy island accent told him. "She gave us your number. Are you her father?"

Harry's heart was pounding, and he had to struggle to keep from shouting. "Yes. How badly is she hurt?"

"I don't know, but you can see her if you come in."

Harry ran out of the house and almost jumped the Rover over the bridge getting onto the county road.

"I'm in better shape than the rental car," Sarah croaked when he reached her.

"Are you in pain?" He pulled a chair up to the bed and kissed her on the forehead.

"I don't really know. I'm full of juice," she answered with a cracked laugh.

She was propped up on pillows. Her neck was in a brace, her left arm in a sling, and a nasty looking, three-colored bruise streaked the right side of her face.

"You didn't miscarry. The nurse said there's no risk of it, and there's no other internal damage," Harry said in a rush, "but you were knocked around pretty badly."

"Sounds right. Not that I remember much of it."

"What do you remember?"

She frowned slightly as if she was having trouble mustering her thoughts, and then she said, "One minute I was driving along the county road about two miles from the Hammock when I suddenly had a very large, white pickup beside me, trying to climb into my lap."

She stopped talking and seemed to forget what she'd been doing.

"Sarah," he said softly.

"What? Oh, two seconds later, I was climbing a guard rail and rolling down a bank." Her voice faded again then recovered. "I guess I was knocked out because when I came to, I was hanging upside down in my seatbelt and two of the EMS team were breaking out the windshield to reach me. Neither of them was driving a white pickup."

She paused again, and then just before she drifted into sleep, she said, "Oh yes, my hair was floating in the water."

Still riding an emotional roller coaster, Harry left her sleeping and drove to Jim Snyder's office, his guilt riding him with spurs. On the way he called Cora.

"How are you feeling?" she asked after being told Sarah was out of danger.

"Responsible, angry, anxious, and relieved in that order," he answered.

"Do you want to come over?" she asked.

"Yes, but I've got to talk with Jim. Tonight, I'll sit with Sarah if she's awake."

"Unless you don't want me there, I'll join you."

"I want you there."

"Okay." She paused and said, "Harry, I think I'm frightened that you might be next."

"Don't be. Colleen is a much more likely target."

28

Jim wasn't convinced.

"Somebody was sending you a warning," the lawman said, unfolding his long frame from his chair and striding restlessly around the room, his face drawn down in gloom. "You had better start being very careful."

"Carry some serious fire power," Hodges advised. "I'm thinking of that Mossberg five hundred twelve gauge of yours, loaded with double 00 buckshot."

"And I'd think seriously of getting Sarah out of Avola," Jim added.

He was not given to Chicken Little responses, and Harry felt vindicated. "My thoughts exactly."

"But if she's anything like her father, she won't budge," Hodges added with a laugh.

Jim's frown deepened to a scowl. "Frank, it's not funny."

"He could be right," Harry said. "I watched her and her mother square off and didn't see much give on either side."

"It could be that having made their point, whoever did it will hold back for a while to see what you do," Jim said, perching on the corner of his desk.

Harry got up to leave. "The problem is, I'm not going to know what they'll do next or when they'll do it."

Sarah spent the night in the hospital, and Harry and Cora picked her up a little after noon and took her home. Cora was not happy with her dismissal and let several doctors know about it.

"I'm really all right," Sarah insisted, grasping Cora's hand as she was being wheeled out of the hospital.

"You're black and blue over half your body, and you hung upside down with your head in icy water, God knows how long, *and* you're pregnant! You should be under observation," Cora said loudly, emptying the corridor in front of them.

Harry thought it would be a good time just to walk quietly with the elderly, bald volunteer who was pushing the wheelchair, but it was clear his wishes were not being consulted.

By the time they reached the Hammock, Sarah was in excellent spirits, and Cora was reconciled to her being out of the hospital. As Harry drove under the big live oak at the front corner of the lawn, a gray fox, followed by three cubs, trotted around the end of the lanai, crossed in front of them, and disappeared into the woods.

Harry turned to Sarah and said with a laugh "Bonnie and her young ones welcoming you home."

"That animal has a name?" Cora asked from the back seat.

"Bonnie and her mate Clyde. They're gray foxes. Tucker named them years ago," Harry answered. "That was my first look at this year's cubs. Bonnie is introducing them to the neighbors."

"Named after the notorious bank robbers?" Sarah asked with a grin.

Cora and Harry were inching her out of the Rover.

"That's right. They've been robbing his henhouse for years."

"Fur-bearing bandits," Cora said with a bright laugh.

Two days later, Cora left, finally convinced Sarah really was all right, and once she was gone, Harry tried to convince Sarah that she should leave the Hammock. The effort was a failure.

"If you tell me you don't want me here, Harry," she said, her voice shaky, "I'll go. If you don't, I'm staying."

"What did you say?" Cora asked him when he stopped by the gallery to tell her.

"That I wanted her to stay."

"And then you told her that wasn't the point."

"I didn't get to say anything more, because she said, 'Then I'm staying. Period.' "

Cora laughed. "Are you surprised?"

"No."

"Neither am I. Like father like daughter."

Sarah recovered quickly. Her youth, Harry thought somewhat enviously. To Harry's chagrin, within a week she had rented another car and was back on the road. Cora's gentle tease that Sarah's stubbornness came from him didn't ease his mind. He was still worried about her safety but admitted that if he wasn't going to tell her to go, he would have to live with it.

And Jim was probably right. For a while at least, he could reasonably assume that she would be safe. As for the police, they had no success in locating a white pickup with scars and red paint smears on the rider's side of the vehicle.

He picked up the investigation by calling again on Adelaide Slocum.

"This isn't a pleasure, Harry."

The secretary had closed the door behind him, and he was left facing Slocum across her desk. In her purple skirt and jacket she looked even more imposing than usual. Harry was impressed but not intimidated.

"I can understand that," he said, "but times are bad and getting worse."

"Sit down," she said, coming around the desk and pulling up

a chair to face him. "I was sorry to hear about your daughter's accident."

"Thanks," he replied coldly, "but it wasn't an accident. Someone intended to hurt her and threaten me. I don't like it."

"No, but you don't think . . ."

"I do," he interrupted. "Someone is killing people, Adelaide. Whoever drove Sarah off the road left her hanging upside down in a wrecked car in a ditch with water in it and gasoline leaking out of the tank into that water. If there had been one spark, she would have been incinerated. If the water had been a few inches deeper, she would have drowned."

Slocum's face went white and stiff, whether from anger or shock, Harry couldn't tell.

"Why are you here?"

"I'm doing you a favor. You can talk to me, or you can wait a few days and talk with Jim Snyder."

"Are you threatening me?"

"Maybe. I've been putting together a lot of information about what went on between Millard and Rafe Hubble and Crystal and Joshua Bates before they were murdered. Did you know that Anna Bates' aunts sent her to Tampa in order to isolate her as much as possible from Millard and Rafe? Do you know that Fielding's Crab and Bait Company is owned by Freeland Property Development Company, which is managed by Rafe Hubble and owned by his father?"

"I know Rafe was pushing Crystal to sell her shares, but what does Fielding's Crab and Bait have to do with anything? Rafe owns a bunch of property," Slocum said, looking both puzzled and troubled as if she had missed something.

"I don't think Rafe Hubble owns anything. Tinker Drew, the man who shot at Colleen and me, hired the boat he was using from Fielding. They never reported it missing, and Drew, having failed in a second attempt to kill me, was, shortly afterwards, shot and killed."

Slocum rose slowly from her chair. "If you're going to make unsubstantiated allegations, I'm going to . . ."

"Sit down, Adelaide. I'm doing you a favor. You could be hearing this after the ADA has begun forming a grand jury, by which time you could have become an accessory to a number of crimes including murder, intimidation, and suppression of evidence."

Adelaide Slocum was a very quick study. She sat down, looking ill. "What do you want from me?"

"Let's begin with an easy question. What is Millard Hubble trying to accomplish regarding the Stoneman Douglas Alliance?"

"How will answering the question protect me?"

"It won't, but if anything about the way Millard or his son is operating inside Blue Skies has made you suspect wrongdoing, now is the time to talk to Jim Snyder. If this investigation exonerates the Hubbles, everything you have told the Captain will disappear. If it implicates them, you will have become a cooperative witness with nothing to hide."

He sat back and waited while Slocum pondered her options.

"What does answering *your* questions get me?" she asked finally.

Harry took a chance. "Two things: anonymity until charges are filed against the Hubbles and the satisfaction of helping to stop the killing. Unless I'm mistaken, Millard and Rafe Hubble are implicated in four murders. More may follow."

She nodded. "Maybe I'm not all that surprised. I'll tell you what I can."

"Start with what Millard and Rafe want from the Alliance?"

"Nothing. They want to destroy it."

"Who's helping them?"

"They're getting a lot of cooperation from the SFDA."

"That would be the South Florida Development Association?"

"Yes." She shifted uncomfortably. "There's another group," she added with obvious reluctance.

Harry thought he knew why. "Is it the River Watch?"

"How did you know about them?"

"I don't know much about them. I know Derwood Jones is their leader. Who else is involved?"

"Farmers, fishermen, private property advocates, anti-government activists from the rural areas along the river."

"Why are the farmers involved?" he asked.

Slocum frowned. "They're afraid that their water allocation will be reduced or they'll be charged for some of it. They're worried that run-off from their fields, which contains pesticides, herbicides, phosphates, and nitrogen, will be controlled—anything that might interfere with their doing what they want to do with their land."

"The fishermen?"

"They want unrestricted right to fish and no limits on their take."

"Are they all stupid?"

"Probably not, but they are in denial about why their stocks have declined so dramatically in the past twenty years."

Harry nodded. "They blame the Oceanographic Commission, sports fishermen, everybody but themselves and won't listen to what science is telling them."

"That's right," Slocum agreed, "but remember, their parents brought them up on stories about fish once being so thick along this coast you could walk across the Okalatchee on their backs."

"What does Millard Hubble want?"

"That's easy. He wants unrestricted access to land on the river and no restrictions on development. He owns thousands of acres on the Okalatchee and desperately wants the building to start."

Harry leaned back in his chair and asked, "What do you think about all this?"

She had her answer ready. "I'm concerned, no, worried, that Millard and Rafe have set something going they can't control."

"How deeply are they involved in this fight with the Alliance?"

"I don't know, Harry. I've been telling myself I didn't want to know."

"And what does that tell you?" Harry asked quietly. "And where does it leave you?"

29

When the interview was over and Harry was driving back to the Hammock, his head still ringing from what Slocum had told him, Arlen Gott called.

"None of this is official, but you can believe every word of it," Gott said while Harry was pulling off the road. "Elaine and I serve on boards with all of our informants, many of whom shake someone's hand and ships sail or don't, depending."

"But if asked officially, they'll deny ever having talked with you," Harry responded, vaguely irritated by Gott's reference to his captains of industry.

"Exactly. Here's what we learned. Blue Skies is seriously overextended with Three Rivers Bank and Trust and a couple of Atlanta banks. The Hubbles borrowed to buy land bordering the Okalatchee River. The investments looked sound when the land was purchased, but now when they need to begin developing the land, to bring in the money to meet their creditors, they're stymied."

"Why?"

"They can't get permits that a year ago the County Commissioners' would have issued with their usual rubber stamp for development requests."

Harry assumed he knew the answer but asked anyway. "What's changed?"

"Believe it or not, it was what Joyce Fields and Colleen McGraw have been doing. Fields' work, particularly the stuff she was churning out on sick fish in the river—*Pfiesteria* something was the really bad news—and the growing threat from pollution to the manatees, caught the attention of the state and federal agencies. Colleen's public meeting brought it to the attention of the media, and suddenly everybody wants to know what's happening to the river."

"Fields was killed as part of an attempt to stop that information from being published."

"It looks that way. I also learned that the South Florida Development Association had managed to get a tame scientist into her department, but it was too late. She had already done too much damage. The cats, so to speak, were out of the bag."

"Bob Walker," Harry said as if the name had a bad taste.

"That's the one," Arlen replied, "and that's what we got. I hope it helps."

"It does," Harry answered gratefully. "It goes with some other things I've learned."

"Just one more thing, Harry," Arlen said, his voice taking on some edge. "Keep Cora out of this. I don't want her hurt."

"Neither do I, Arlen, and you can sail for China on it."

Once he was on the Hammock, he found a message on his house phone from Colleen.

"I've got some great news," she said enthusiastically when he reached her. "The St. John's River Coalition has voted to declare solidarity with the Stoneman Douglas Alliance on the Okalatchee reclamation and control project. This is huge, Harry!"

Harry grinned as much because of her excitement as her news although having the Coalition on board would mean a tremendous influx of money and political leverage.

"Congratulations," he said. "What happens first?"

"I get the word out to our members and all the media. Then

I get with them to plan a blitz in the legislature. I can't tell you what a boost to morale this is going to be."

They talked for a while longer, and when Harry put down the phone, he was as worried as he was pleased. The Coalition's support meant an enormous increase in resources and political clout for the Alliance. Unfortunately, it also meant that those opposing the Alliance were going to be stressed even more than they were now.

A little later he called Jim but got a deputy who was covering for the receptionist.

"The Captain's in Miami," she snapped, and when he asked for Hodges, she sighed as if overburdened with clowns, "the Sergeant's with the Captain. Try tomorrow," and hung up.

"Wild hairs in Paradise," he muttered as Sarah drove into the yard. A moment later she came into the kitchen with Cora.

"We're having lunch with Tucker. You're invited," Sarah told him, dropping her bag onto a chair.

"Is this a conspiracy?" Harry asked Cora, who, like Sarah, was dressed in sandals and shorts.

"To get your mind off final things for a while," she told him, kissing his cheek, "and to satisfy myself that when it comes to this Tucker person, the truth isn't in either of you."

"Care to make a bet?" Sarah asked with a straight face.

"Talk about conspiracies!" Cora replied.

On the way to Tucker's farm, Harry told them Colleen's news, leaving out his concerns. But after expressing her delight in having the Coalition with them, Cora, who encountered nature mostly from behind glass from twenty floors up, was soon absorbed in the Hammock and agog by the time they met a very large dog and an even bigger mule, coming along the sand track towards them.

"Why aren't those animals on a leash?" Cora demanded, getting behind Harry and peeking at them over his shoulder.

"It's Sanchez and Oh, Brother!," Sarah said happily, hurrying forward to greet them.

"Be careful!" Cora called after her. "Why is that horse wearing a hat?"

"That's a mule," Harry said quickly. "For God's sake don't call him a horse. He'll never forgive you. And don't make any jokes about his hat."

By then Harry and Cora had reached Sarah, who immediately introduced Cora to Sanchez and Oh, Brother! Sanchez grinned at her.

"Does he bite?" Cora asked anxiously.

"No, he's smiling at you."

Oh, Brother! lowered his head and pushed his nose into her chest and snorted softly.

"Oh, my," she said and laughed nervously.

Just as she tentatively reached out to stroke his forehead, Sanchez, following up on his grin, boosted her with his nose.

"Ahhhh!" she yelled, trying to crouch, throwing herself forward onto Oh, Brother!'s nose.

Sarah gave a shout of laughter, "Congratulations! You've been made an Honorary Dog."

By the time they were untangled, Cora, blushing profusely, said, "I never saw myself as a beauty, but I didn't expect to be mistaken for a dog."

"You weren't," Sarah said warmly, bending over to cradle Sanchez's head in her arms and scratch behind his ears. "He thinks he's a person, which he may be. And so is this one," she added, straightening up to lay her face against Oh, Brother!'s glossy shoulder and stroke his neck.

"Why are they out here?" Cora asked.

"They came to meet us," Harry said, starting them on their way.

"How did they know we were coming?"

"Jungle drums," Sarah answered.

Cora, growing brave, rubbed Oh, Brother!'s nose and said it was unfair to gang up on her.

"This is only a mild introduction," Harry told her.

Tucker was working on his hives. He came toward his visitors, surrounded by a cloud of bees that made both Sarah and Cora gasp and draw back.

Sanchez and Oh, Brother! fell back with them. Harry, accustomed to Tucker and his bees, only made sure he stood still until the cloud dissipated.

"Harry's talked a lot about you," Tucker said to Cora, sweeping off his straw hat, "and you're even lovelier than I was led to expect."

"And she's an Honorary Dog," Sarah added.

"Then you are indeed favored," Tucker said with a beatific smile. "Come along, let me show you around."

He offered Cora his arm, and talking earnestly but often interrupting themselves to laugh, they went off towards the orchard with everyone else straggling behind.

"I think I'm jealous," Sarah said to Harry.

"Don't be," Harry said, half seriously, "he's got more than enough love to go around."

They ended the farm part of their tour at the pumpkin patch, where Cora made the old man's day by being astounded by the size of the plants.

"They're fabulous!" she cried. "They're not silk are they?"

"If you knew how much care they are, you wouldn't have to ask," Tucker said when the laughter subsided. "They are very real indeed. If I'm lucky, come September, I'll take one of them to the fair."

After they had discussed the nurture of giant pumpkins for a few more minutes, Tucker threw up his hands and said, "I've saved the best for the last. Let's all go see Althea."

"The bear," Harry whispered to Cora.

Sarah had claimed Tucker's arm and the two of them led the parade toward the cage.

Althea, looking to Harry to be at least twice her old size, was sitting with her back against the side of her cage with a large, blue enamel basin in her lap, scooping food into her mouth. She looked up and gave a blat of alarm, dumped the basin out of her lap, and ran behind the doghouse at the back of the cage but left her spacious rear end conspicuously in sight, there not being room enough behind the kennel for all of her.

"She's still a bit shy," Tucker said.

At the sound of his voice Althea popped her head up above the roof of the kennel, ears erect.

"Come out here," Tucker said cheerfully. "They're all friends."

The head disappeared, but Sanchez and Oh, Brother! had gone around the cage and were pressing their noses against the wire where the bear was hiding.

"What are they doing?" Cora asked.

"Having a talk with her," Tucker said. "She'll be out in a minute."

Cora looked at Sarah, who shrugged, and then at Harry, who just nodded. The expression on Cora's face had him grinning with delight.

"If all of you are playing some kind of trick on me . . ." Cora began, only to be interrupted by Althea's backing out of her hiding place and with her claws clattering on the cement, coming in a shuffling run, head swinging, to the front of the cage.

"There we are," Tucker said encouragingly to her. "Stand up so we can get a look at you."

When she reached the wire, she rose onto her hind legs, planted her front paws on the wire and regarded her visitors with obvious interest.

"Hello, girl," Sarah said. "Uncle Tucker had better put you on a diet."

The bear dropped onto all fours and began scouring the floor of her pen for the scraps of food she had spilled when running to hide.

"Althea's a little too focused on eating," Tucker admitted, "but she was starved for so long, having plenty to eat is part of her therapy."

"What are you treating her for?" Harry asked for Cora's benefit.

"Anxiety and mild depression," Tucker said with a straight face. "I provide the food. Sanchez and Oh, Brother! do most of the counseling although I sometimes take a hand."

Harry put his arm around Cora, whose face was a study in doubt and uncertainty, and told her, "It takes a little while, but you'll get used to it."

"Why should she be anxious and depressed?" Cora asked.

"She was separated too soon from her mother," Tucker replied. "Let's go inside and have some raspberry punch."

On the way to the house, Tucker explained to Cora that Althea's mother had probably been shot or killed crossing a road, and Althea had been left to fend for herself before she had learned how to do it properly.

"By the time she showed up here, she was skin and bones."

Tucker added sugar cookies and scones and a pot of strawberry jam to the table, and conversation gradually shifted away from the bear to the Stoneman Douglas Alliance and its troubles. Harry gave a sketchy summary of where his work had taken him, leaving out entirely his suspicions about the Hubbles and his most recent conversation with Adelaide Slocum.

"What have you found out about Millard Hubble and that rapscallion son of his?" Tucker asked when Harry finished speaking.

Harry winced. It was just about impossible to fool Tucker.

"I wouldn't trust either of them as far as I could throw Althea," Cora said firmly, spreading jam on a scone. "And I couldn't even pick her up."

"The police haven't any idea who ran me off the road," Sarah put in, "although there's no real evidence it was part of any conspiracy. The idiot might have been drunk."

"It's safer to assume it was personal and intentional," Cora said quickly.

Tucker nodded. "I want you to keep on assuming the worst," Tucker said, reaching across the table to pat her hand. "Now, Harry, if you'd rather not answer my question, just say so."

"There isn't much to tell," Harry responded, shaving the truth.

Tucker nodded and began talking about a swarm of wild honeybees that moved into one of his outlying hives that had been unoccupied and what a problem it was proving to be because he didn't want a wild queen invading one of his Carniolan hives.

When the conversation ended, and Harry and the others were leaving, Tucker pulled him aside and said, "I'm hearing that Derwood Jones and his bunch are planning something that they hope will put an end to the Alliance's interference along the Okalatchee. I don't have anything specific, but the people I've talked to are concerned."

"Any names or dates?"

"No, but it might be time for you to go back to the Hook."

30

On the way home Sarah fell silent. Cora noticed it first.

"My head's a little light," she said. "I think that punch had a stick in it. How are you feeling, Sarah?"

"I'm okay," Sarah answered, as if she had come back from somewhere else.

They were passing under a stand of slash pines, and the drone of wind in their branches was suddenly drowned by a crescendo of harsh buzzing. Cora looked up in alarm.

"It's locusts," Harry told her. "It's their mating season."

"I always feel like this when I leave Tucker's farm," Sarah said, stopping in the shade to look back down the dusty, white road.

Harry thought she sounded on the edge of tears, but Cora responded to Sarah's comment before he could think what to say.

"How *do* you feel?"

"When I'm at Tucker's, I feel as if everything's manageable, but after I've left . . ."

"The world comes rushing back," Cora said, finishing her thought. "Is there anything in particular that comes up?"

Both she and Harry moved closer to Sarah, and Harry put his arm around her shoulders.

"David," she said in a dull voice, "and being pregnant."

Harry and Cora exchanged a glance.

"Would talking about it help?" Cora asked lightly.

"Yes, but let's walk," Sarah answered with a forced laugh. "If I don't keep moving, I'm afraid I'll run back there and never leave."

"Tucker would like that," Harry said, releasing her.

They set off with Sarah in the middle.

"It's getting harder and harder for me to think about what I'm going to do," Sarah said as they went forward, surrounded by the buzzing, chirping, shrilling fiddlers of the swamp.

"Because it's too painful?" Cora asked.

"Oh, no," Sarah replied. "It doesn't seem real."

"David's real enough," Harry said, alarmed that the strain had become too much for Sarah to bear.

"Ignore your father," Cora said, shooting Harry a warning look. "He's missed the point again. Go on with what you were saying."

"I think that in some way I've moved beyond my marriage. I seem to be in some other place now. But, of course, I know it's still there."

"And you don't want to go back to it," Cora said in an encouraging voice, "because you might not be able to get free again?"

"Yes, that's it," Sarah agreed with a relieved smile. "I couldn't seem to say it. How did you guess?"

"I've been there, love. But you don't have to be afraid. Just keep moving forward."

"It's not easy."

"No," Cora agreed. "It never is. And as for being pregnant, you've still got time to decide whether or not to stay that way."

"Amen," Harry said, and both women looked at him as if surprised to find him still with them.

The next day Jim called Harry.

"I want to talk to you, but by the looks of things, I'm going to be out of the office all day again. The paperwork will be falling out the door, but I've got a burglary and homicide to cope with, and we're so shorthanded I can't leave it to someone else. And Frank is up in North Avola managing a five car fracas."

He paused and Harry thought that Jim must be very stressed to have said all that without taking a breath.

"Where are you?" he asked. "If you don't mind my being in your crime scene, we could talk while you supervise. I've got some things you ought to hear."

"Great," Jim said and gave him the address.

The day had broken in flames, and the sea breeze had not risen with the huge, fiery sun, leaving Avola to cook in its furnace. Walking from the Rover to the Edwards & Nielson Brokerage building across a macadam pavement already soft, Harry said a short prayer of thanks that he lived on the Hammock where the midday temperature under the canopy of trees was always at least ten degrees cooler than in downtown Avola.

Harry found Jim on the second floor in a suite of offices that had been ransacked. Files had been ripped open and their contents strewn everywhere. Half a dozen detectives were working and talking loudly in the reception area, moving carefully around the chalked outline on the floor of a person with arms and legs flung wide. A man and a woman in Crime Scene regalia were taking pictures and swearing at the detectives who kept walking in front of them.

"Watchman," Jim said, appearing beside Harry, bent over the outline. The policeman looked tired and frazzled. "Looks like he came through the door and went down. Didn't even draw his gun."

"Lights on?" Harry asked.

"That's what we think."

"Then the guy probably knew whoever he walked in on."

"Possibly. Come on, I'll find us a place to talk."

The firm's copier room doubled as a lounge with a stove, refrigerator, major coffee maker, and a green couch and half a dozen upholstered chairs.

"What have you got?" Jim asked, dropping onto the couch.

"Possibly a motive for Joyce Fields' and the Bates' murders," Harry answered and summarized for Jim the information Arlen Gott and Elaine Potter had given him and what Adelaide Slocum had told him.

"Lord, Lord," Jim said when Harry finished and ran a big hand across his face.

"Why the glum look?" Harry demanded. "It's a major break."

"Maybe," Jim acknowledged, "but the *major* part is major headache." He groaned and raised his head. "That's why Slocum left a message yesterday asking me to call her."

"That's good news," Harry said, trying to revive the policeman's spirits. "She's going to cooperate with you on the investigation of the Hubbles and Blue Skies Realty."

"We're not even investigating Blue Skies." Jim was on his feet, pointing an accusing finger at Harry. "I told you, Blue Skies is out of bounds."

"No more it's not," Harry shot back. "While you and Hodges were entertaining the women on South Beach, someone moved the fence."

Jim sighed deeply, planted his hands on his knees, and glared at Harry, looked away, muttered something about God's mercy, then said, "All right, I'm in. You go back to the Hook. Talk with everyone you can. I'll see Slocum and send Frank with some serious back-up to Fielding's Crab and Bait shack again. If Millard and Rafe Hubble are mixed up with that River Watch outfit, somebody knows what they've been doing."

"It would be a start to find out who killed Tinker Drew," Harry said.

Jim nodded gloomily.

"What is it?" Harry asked. "Are you sick?"

Another big sigh. "No, but I feel as if I was."

"Want to talk about it?"

"It won't do any good, but since you asked, it's Colleen. Actually, it's probably me." He studied his shoes and seemed to have forgotten Harry.

"Are you still worrying about the things that you don't have in common instead of those you do?"

"And what would those be?" Jim demanded, breaking free from his shoes.

"You like each other. You enjoy being with one another. You might even be in love with one another."

Harry felt seriously out of his depth here but determined to keep at it. He did not want Jim through a failure of confidence to ruin what was probably the best romantic relationship he had ever had.

"The thing is, we're stuck," Jim said, "and I can't see any way to get us moving. I don't want to force her anywhere she doesn't want to go."

"And she probably doesn't want to push you, with the result that neither of you is letting the other one know what you're thinking."

"How do you know what she wants?" Jim demanded.

"If she wanted your relationship to grow like a toadstool, what would your response be?"

"You mean aside from dancing in the street?"

"Then you'd better find out what she wants."

"How am I supposed to do that?"

"Ask her. Even better, you could tell her what you want, and let her make up her mind what to do about it, instead of treating her as if she was too fragile to make such a decision."

"You don't have to shout at me."

"Sorry."

"Do you think you got through?" Sarah asked and poured Harry more coffee.

They were having breakfast with the early sun pouring across the table. A mockingbird was singing in the wisteria, and while she was asking her question, a flock of ibis passed over the house with a rush and whistle of wings, headed for the marshes on the Puc Puggy.

"I love that sound," Sarah said, watching them out of sight. "Well, what do you think?"

"Maybe. With Jim it's hard to tell. Has Colleen said anything more to you about their troubles?"

"Only that he seems to be drifting away from her. She's pretty depressed about it."

"Could you have a talk with her and say something like what I said to Jim, if you think it would do any good?"

Sarah sat down with her coffee and said, "Good idea, and I've got a good chance to do it. Friday afternoon I'm going up the river on an overnight with her. She wants to take more run-off water samples along about ten miles of the river up towards Denaud. She asked me to help her. Someone gave her the use of a cabin for Friday and Saturday nights. She's stayed there before and says it's very comfortable and definitely old Florida."

"I don't think that's such a good idea," Harry said, stopping himself from adding, especially in your condition.

She had become increasingly touchy about her condition. And Harry was having more and more trouble keeping his opinions on the subject to himself.

"Why not? Colleen used to do this sort of thing all the time before Joyce Fields took it over. Now, she says, she has to do it again."

Temporarily distracted by Sarah's story, Harry asked where the lab work was going to be done.

"Goodrich Enterprises in Tampa. Colleen says there're very reliable. A lot of the state agencies send their overflow work there, and they do forensic stuff for a lot of law enforcement groups."

"Back to my concerns," Harry said abruptly. "Only the other day, Jim Snyder was urging me to get you out of town. Have you forgotten why?"

"No, and my answer hasn't changed."

Neither, Harry noticed without saying so, had her defiant tone of voice. "But you aren't obliged to be foolhardy, Sarah. I shouldn't have to remind you that Colleen has been the object of a lot of unpleasant attention, and so have you."

"I can't be run off the road in a small boat," Sarah said, recovering her humor.

"Don't try to charm your way past me," Harry told her.

"I wouldn't think of it, but is there really any reason I shouldn't go with Colleen, aside from the non-specific one that I'd be safer at home? And would I actually be safer here? If someone wants to harm me . . ."

She lost her smile, and Harry felt guilty for trying to frighten her. To be absolutely honest, she was probably no safer one place than another. He thought of what Tucker had said about River Watch planning something, but the group couldn't know that Colleen was going to Denaud.

"Has Colleen told anyone about this trip?"

"No."

"Good," Harry said, "but I want to know exactly where the cabin is."

Harry studied the tide tables in the *Banner* and decided to visit Derwood Jones the next afternoon when he thought the man's workday would have ended.

He reached Jones' house just as Fannon was getting off the school bus. The scowling boy had grown up and out since the day Harry had first seen him.

"What the hell are you doing here?" Fannon said loudly, looking at Harry as if he wanted to jump him.

"Hello, Fannon," Harry replied. "How's school going?"

But the boy wasn't having any. "Fuck school," he barked, the squeak in his voice taking away some of the menace in his response.

"I'm looking for your father," Harry responded.

"I'm right here, Brock."

Jones had come out of the house while Harry was talking to Fannon.

"Get in the house," he snapped at his son.

Fannon ran for the door, giving his father a wide berth as he passed him.

"What do you want, Brock?"

The man had changed out of his boots and yellow overalls into dungarees and a white T-shirt that looked as if its seams might split.

"I'd like to talk to you, Derwood, if you have the time."

Harry did not offer to shake hands with Jones, having a good idea what the outcome would be. In fact, he was watching Jones very carefully and backed away when Jones stepped close enough to reach him.

"Scared, Brock?" the big man asked with a mocking grin.

"No. Just careful."

"You should be," Jones told him, losing his grin. "I could snap you like a twig."

"Yes, I believe you could," Harry replied, "but I would still like to talk to you."

"What about?"

"Tinker Drew tried to kill me. Do you know why?"

"You were on his property, nosing around is what I heard."

"No other reason?"

"You damn near blew him out of the water with that automatic of yours."

"How did you know about that?"

"I know a lot of things you don't know, Brock."

"Then you know he was shooting at Colleen McGraw and me, and I fired back to get him off us."

"That's your story."

"All right. What are you and the rest of the members of River Watch hoping to accomplish, aside from making Colleen McGraw's life as miserable as possible?"

Jones' grin came back. "What River Watch is *going to do* is get McGraw and the Alliance off this river."

"What else?"

"Get the state and federal government out of our hair."

"Does your effort include killing people?"

"I ain't killed nobody, but if there's no other way, I'd say yes. And it's justified. The people in River Watch have their whole lives invested in this river. We don't intend to lose this fight."

Harry knew he was hearing what Jones believed to be the truth. "Is the South Florida Development Association bankrolling River Watch?"

Jones' eyes narrowed. "Mind your own fucking business, Brock."

"Tinker Drew tried twice to kill me, Derwood. Someone messed with my daughter. I think it is my business."

"You're looking to have an accident, Brock," Jones said, balling his fists.

Harry might have felt anger or fear, but what he experienced was pity because the huge man in front of him had only his strength to deal with the slow collapse of his life. And Harry suspected that the Hubbles had harnessed his fury and his strength for their own ends.

"This advice is free, Derwood," Harry said. "Get out of River Watch, stop listening to the Hubbles, and leave the Hook."

"Wouldn't that just make your day, Brock. Now get out of here before I twist your head off."

31

On Friday Colleen picked up Sarah and left for Denaud, hauling a fourteen foot white runabout with a Merc twenty-five attached to its stern. Harry had another go at dissuading them, but Colleen interrupted his efforts.

"Save your breath, Harry," she said. "I've been through this with Jim, who's even more of a worrywart than you are. I just don't see the risk."

Sarah, in what Harry decided was blatant denial of what had happened to her, also refused to listen.

"We're going to be fine," Sarah told him. "Take Cora out to dinner and forget about us."

Standing in the morning sun, watching their dust settle, Harry had to admit that he had no real evidence that they were in imminent danger.

Still dissatisfied, Harry had just turned back to the house when his phone rang.

"Harry, something terrible has happened." Cora's voice was shaking.

"Where are you? Are you hurt?"

"I'm at the gallery. No, I'm all right, Holly's with me, but the damage is terrible."

"I'll be right there."

Cora hadn't exaggerated.

"They must have smashed the windows and door and then

turned on the fire hydrant in front of the gallery," Cora told Harry when he arrived, having walked straight into his arms. She had been talking with a small group of people from nearby stores, who had come in to look and commiserate with her.

She and Harry were standing in a drenched room, surrounded by puddled water, glittering shards of broken glass, shattered paintings that had been blasted off the walls by the force of the water, and tiles and soaked wallboard hanging and still dripping from walls and ceiling. Holly was wading around with her dungarees rolled up to her knees, pulling paintings out of the rubble. A few firemen and the Fire Inspector's team were poking through the debris and taking pictures. Harry also recognized two plainclothes officers from the Sheriff's Department, talking on their cell phones.

"The water must have poured in here for a long time to cause this kind of destruction," Harry responded.

"Nearly an hour the firemen told me. A security guard on his rounds finally called it in. Let's go outside," Cora said, "I can't stand looking at it anymore. It's so awful, Harry, who would have, could have done anything so terrible?"

"Someone who wanted to make a point," Harry said grimly as he helped her pick her way through the wreckage to the sidewalk.

"Insurance?" he asked her once they were outside.

"Not a problem," she answered dismissively, "but, my God, the artists' work. Most of it ruined! Who could be so barbaric?"

She was pale and had begun to tremble. "I'm freezing," she said.

"Come over here," Harry said and, taking her hand, led her to one of the benches that were spaced along the sidewalk. "Sit down here in the sun."

He pulled off his jacket and draped it around her shoulders.

"Jacobs and Daniels, the two officers from the Sheriff's office, asked me some questions," she said, snuggling into the jacket. "They didn't seem very interested."

"Jim Snyder will be," Harry said. He stacked her still-cold hands between his and chaffed them, trying to think how he could tell her this probably wasn't a piece of random, drunken destructiveness.

"They said it looked like the work of—I think they said *cranks.*"

She had stopped shaking and begun to regain some color in her face. He released her hands.

"What do you think?" he asked gently, hoping a light might go on.

"I suppose they could be right," she said.

"Possibly, but I doubt it."

She looked quickly at him. "I know what you're going to say."

"What?"

"That whoever shot at you and Colleen and ran Sarah off the road has turned their attention to me," she said in a tense voice.

"Yes."

"What can I do?"

"Leave Avola for a while. They won't follow you."

"That was what you told Sarah, isn't it?"

"Yes, for all the good it did."

"And leave you and Colleen and Sarah to face whoever it is alone?" She stiffened her back. "I don't think so, Harry," she said with sudden conviction.

"All right, but if you're going to stay, there are some things you've got to promise me you'll do and not do."

They talked for a while, and he made some progress, but not as much as he had hoped.

"Enough, Harry!" she said finally, leaning forward and kissing him. "Holly and I have hours of work ahead of us, dealing with insurance brokers and notifying artists of what's happened here. And that's only the beginning."

She stood up and passed him his jacket.

"Can I help?"

"No, but if Sarah's not busy, maybe she could help Holly and me with the phoning. We can do it from the condo."

"She and Colleen are spending a couple of nights up-river," he answered uneasily.

"Oh, Harry," Cora said, "is that a good idea?"

"Well, I'm not very happy about it, but I was outvoted."

Just then Holly came out of the gallery and seeing Cora and Harry, waved excitedly at them.

"Now it begins," Cora said with a sigh. "But we're still on for dinner?"

"If you're up to it."

"I might ask the same of you."

She gave him a wicked smile and put up her face. He kissed her, and she hurried away. Harry watched her go, feeling an inexplicable rush of happiness.

It didn't last long.

Adelaide Slocum called him and said, "Where are you right now?"

"I'm turning onto forty-one at Higgins."

"Can you meet me at the municipal parking garage on Heron Street in ten minutes?"

"Yes. What's going on?"

She had hung up before he finished the question. He found her on the roof deck of the garage, dressed in a red suit, pacing beside her silver M3 BMW convertible with its top down. About as inconspicuous as a fire truck, Harry thought.

"You're being very mysterious," he said.

"I have something to tell you, and I don't trust anybody any more, maybe not even you."

Harry took in the dark smudges under her eyes, and the obvious exhaustion draining her face of color. She had paused beside her car and was gripping her hands so tightly her knuckles were white.

"Let's hear it," he said.

She took a deep breath and seemed to be too stressed to find the words she needed.

"All right," she said at last. "Millard Hubble has been keeping two sets of books. Don't ask me how I found out. I hope no one ever finds out, but Blue Skies is on the verge of collapse. Hubble owes millions, and his credit is exhausted."

She sagged against the side of the car.

"There, I've told you," she said in a fading voice, "and I don't have any idea what I'm going to do about it."

"Yes, you do," Harry said, not liking himself for pressing her this way. "You're going to get yourself a top drawer lawyer, and then you're going to Jim Snyder with your information."

"You know what this means, don't you?" she asked, pushing herself away from the car. "I'll be destroyed. My career will be trash."

"Not necessarily," Harry countered. "It might be a tide that lifts your boat, but whatever happens, you've done the right thing."

"Come and tell me that again when you see me selling lingerie in Burdines," she said bitterly.

She looked so miserable that Harry risked a major rebuff by putting his arms around her. To his surprise, she broke into tears.

"How could I have been so blind, Harry?" she sobbed.

"Probably because you're a woman," he said.

"What!" she shouted, pushing herself up to her full height and glaring at him.

"You're right," Harry said. "You are taller than I am."

She laughed, reached into the car and grabbed a tissue and blew her nose. "Making me laugh doesn't change anything," she said, brushing away the tears. "I'm still an idiot."

"You were suckered, Adelaide. It could have happened to anyone."

She sighed. "Maybe, but I'm not *anyone*. You're right about the lawyer, but I'm not so sure about Snyder."

Harry was relieved to see that she had recovered her edge, but her statement didn't please him.

"You're not an idiot yet, but you will be if you don't talk to the police. The jail house is ringing its bell for you even as we speak."

"That's an exaggeration. I haven't done . . ."

"Adelaide, all this is going to come out. When it does, you are going to be swept up with both Hubbles and who knows who else. Imagine being in the witness box, being asked when you knew the Blue Skies books were cooked and then asked why you didn't tell the investigating officers as soon as you had that information. Try to imagine any answer that would convince a jury you weren't guilty of covering up a crime."

She nodded. "You're right. I just don't—"

"Want to look like an idiot," Harry completed her sentence. "It's better than looking like a co-conspirator, and there's no jail time attached."

"When should I do it?"

"Today looks very good."

"All right," she said. She paused and put a hand on Harry's arm. "It's been a long time since anyone hugged me like that, Harry. Thank you."

32

When Harry picked up Cora for dinner, she tossed a bag into the back of the Rover.

"I want some country air," she said.

"Then it's my place."

"As soon as the check is paid. You will not believe what my day's been like."

The stars of the long, long day had been the police, the fire marshal, the insurance adjustors, surprisingly calm artists, and gawkers, who all wanted to give her advice and tell her about their fire experiences.

"Do you think we'll hear the owls?" Cora asked when the last of the wine was drunk, the bill she had anticipated paid, and she was comfortably collapsed in the Rover on the way to the Hammock.

"I doubt you'll be awake long enough," Harry said.

He was mistaken. They heard the owls several times in the night.

The following morning, Harry took Cora for a walk on the back corner of the Hammock. She said she had come prepared for a hike in the woods and appeared after breakfast with her hair done up in a silk scarf, wearing black dress jeans, a light blue sweatshirt, and a new pair of Asolo hiking boots.

"Can you take off the sweatshirt?" Harry asked.

She colored a little. "Really?" she asked, her smile faltering.

"I mean, if it gets too hot."

"Oh, damn," she said but couldn't keep from laughing. "Yes. I'm wearing an A-shirt and a sports bra. I won't frighten the animals."

Harry grinned, shrugged into a light backpack, and said, "I'm glad this is Florida."

"Why?" she asked as they were going out the door.

"Because after last night I don't think I could climb a hill."

As a goal, Harry had chosen Tucker's outermost bee yard, but what he had in mind was something else. About a quarter of a mile from the yard, at the edge of a grassy clearing in the tangle of trees, half in shade and half in sun, Harry stopped by a clump of saw palmetto and said, "Let's sit down for a few minutes, have some water, and rest."

"I'm all right to keep going," Cora replied, a little out of breath with sweat streaking her face.

"I'd like a break," Harry lied and opened his pack.

When they sat down, they sank into shade, and a breeze blowing towards them from the clearing rustled the palmetto fronds and carried the sweet smell of honeysuckle.

"My God, this is a beautiful place," Cora said with a sigh. "I had no idea."

Harry nodded and let the forest do its work. Cora drank some more water and settled into the silence, broken only by the low hum of the cicadas, warming up for the day's concert. A few minutes passed. Then Harry saw what he had brought her to see. Very gently he touched her arm.

Cora turned her head. He was holding a finger to his lips. With a slow movement of the finger he pointed toward the southwest corner of the clearing. She turned her head and caught her breath. Two white tailed does with two small fawns, their coats still streaked brown and white, had drifted silently into the clearing, followed by a third, older doe. The does began cropping the newest leaves on the stopper bushes while the fawns, their tails flicking with excitement, chased one another around their mothers' legs.

Suddenly, a long, tawny shape exploded across the clearing. Snorting in alarm, the deer flung themselves towards the shelter of the trees, but the third doe was too slow, and the panther struck her down with a slashing blow. She fell, blatting in terror, as the big cat clamped its jaws on her neck. There was a small, sharp crack, followed by a deep growl and the deer was dead.

Cora, who had been frozen in silence, tried to clamber to her feet, but Harry hauled her down and clasped his hand across her mouth.

"Don't move," he whispered in her ear as she struggled. "Don't make a sound."

Cora fell back against him and nodded. He released her. Momentarily distracted by her kill and being well upwind of them, the panther ignored the slight disturbance. A moment later she again grasped the dead deer by the neck and began dragging her into the trees. Cora looked questioningly at Harry, her eyes wide and her face white.

He put his lips against her ear and whispered, "We are going to sit here very quietly."

The cat made quite a bit of noise dragging the deer out of the sight of vultures and to a hiding place that suited her. Harry knew what she was doing and was glad. Better she should work off her excess adrenaline pulling the doe through the brush than dump it on them.

When Harry could no longer hear the cat, he said in a quiet voice, "Now we're going to stand up and slowly walk back the way we came in. You go in front. Talk if you want you, but don't raise your voice or let yourself hurry. Okay, here we go."

"Is he going to attack us?" she asked as they got underway.

"No. That's why we're walking slowly and speaking quietly.

As long as she doesn't think we're trying to take her deer away from her and we don't trigger her chase response by running, we're safe."

He fervently hoped he was right.

"Why do you say *she?*" Cora demanded, glancing over her shoulder angrily.

"Because I know her. I haven't seen her for a while, but Tucker and I had a good look at her a few years ago."

"The poor doe," Cora said in an unsteady voice.

"She wasn't as quick as the others. She may have been old or sick. It's how predation is supposed to work."

"I don't like it," Cora said firmly.

"I hope you're not too upset."

"Does she have babies?" Cora asked.

"The dead deer?"

"Well, I meant the panther, but the deer too."

"I doubt if the deer does. It or they would have been with her. I couldn't tell whether or not the panther is nursing."

"She was spectacular," Cora said after a while.

"Magnificent," Harry agreed.

They made a short detour and stopped at Tucker's on the way home. Sanchez and Oh, Brother! met them on the trail and led them to the house, then went off on their own business.

"When the deer came, it was a perfect idyll," Cora said over the tea and chocolate cake.

They were sitting on Tucker's back stoop. Harry was leaving the panther story to Cora, whose fear had been quickly replaced by excitement and pride.

"Then in an instant everything changed. The cat bounded across the opening almost as if she was flying, and the deer flashed away. Except for one. She hesitated, and the panther leaped on her and broke her neck. I heard it snap. It was terrible but somehow wonderful too. I was terrified at first, but

Harry was so calm, I felt I had to be as well."

"Good for you," Tucker said, full of encouragement, giving her another piece of cake. "You could be in these woods for years without seeing a panther. A good many wardens have never seen one. This was your lucky day."

"As opposed to yesterday," Cora said, losing most of her enthusiasm.

"Mostly stucco, wood, and glass," Tucker said with a gentle smile. "They can all be replaced. Of course, the loss of the artists' work is serious, but the sun will go on rising."

Cora brightened a little. "Those I talked to seemed less upset than I was," she conceded.

"They've moved on," Tucker agreed. "It's like growing a garden. By the time you get it planted, you're already planning the next one. I think artists must feel something like that when they finish a painting or a carving or a turned pot. It's already history."

The three of them argued Tucker's point for a while, and then Cora asked to see Althea. The bear was sitting in the sun, leaning comfortably against the side of her cage with her head turned, apparently watching Oh, Brother! and Sanchez who were standing close to her.

"They look for all the world like three people having a friendly conversation," Cora said admiringly as they approached the cage.

"That's about it," Tucker said, causing Harry to groan.

"A mule, a dog, and a bear can't talk to one another," he protested.

"That was true for a while," Tucker replied. The three humans had stopped at the cage and were looking at the animals, which had ignored their arrival. "Sanchez, who wasn't sure he liked Althea, gave up on trying to talk with her, but Oh, Brother! persevered. That made Sanchez feel left out, so he went to work on her. You're looking at the results."

"What do they talk about?" Cora asked.

"Cora," Harry began, "they're not really talking."

"Ignore him," Tucker said. "He's just showing off because you're here. They don't tell me everything, but Sanchez and Oh, Brother! have put in a lot of time on her being orphaned. They're helping her adjust and trying to grow her up a little. Sanchez still gets irritated. He says she's silly, but Oh, Brother! insists it's her age."

"How does a mule talk to a bear?" Cora said.

As always happened, Harry became interested in what Tucker was saying and forgot to be skeptical. Tucker watched the three animals for a moment longer before turning to Cora.

"I think it's a lot like what would happen if the two of us were in the kitchen, putting together a meal. After we'd been working together for a while, we'd stop bumping into one another, and before you knew it, there'd be a meal on the table."

"Okay," Cora said, and Harry could see that Tucker's answer had satisfied her.

He wasn't so sure, but the mule and the dog had met them coming along the trail, and Althea certainly looked as if she was paying attention to something. Tucker moved away from the cage and beckoned to Cora and Harry to follow him. He had taken them to the hen run before he spoke.

"I didn't want to say this where I might be overheard. I've got two pieces of news," he said sadly, staring gloomily at Longstreet and his hens. "The first is I've got to release Althea. She's strong and healthy. She belongs in the woods."

"We've discussed this," Harry protested. "If you let her out, she'll be nothing but trouble."

"You're right," Tucker agreed. "I've called Guy Bridges, the game warden. He's going to bring in a crew. They'll sedate her and transport her up into Charlotte County somewhere and release her."

"Won't she starve with no one to feed her?" Cora protested.

"Not now," Tucker said. "She should be all right."

"You've done a good job with her," Harry said.

"Well, thank you," Tucker said, pulling off his hat and rubbing his head, his mind obviously on something else. "The word is out again that River Watch is planning some kind of retaliation against the Alliance for having brought in the St. John's River Coalition."

"How seriously are you taking this?" Harry asked.

"I know we've heard rumors of this before, but this time I think it's probably true," the old farmer said.

"Maybe it's already happened," Cora said.

"Your gallery," Tucker responded.

"It could be," Harry said.

"It could be," Tucker put in, "and from what I'm hearing, I think Colleen McGraw is their next target."

"Harry!" Cora cried. "She and Sarah . . ."

"Are out in that cabin," Harry said grimly.

"Where?" Tucker asked with a worried frown.

"On the river, near Denaud," Harry replied. "Colleen's taking water samples up there, and Sarah's helping her. They'll be coming home tomorrow."

"I'm not happy about that," Tucker said in a rare expression of disapproval.

"Neither am I," Cora echoed.

"No one but us knows they're there," Harry said in search of something to feel good about.

"And they're sensible people," Tucker agreed quickly.

Cora glanced at her watch and said, "Harry, I've got to get to Avola. An insurance supervisor is coming this afternoon to look at the gallery, and I should be there."

"Let me know what happens with Althea," Harry said, shaking Tucker's hand.

"I will, and you both keep your eyes open. And, Harry, you might call those two girls and tell them to be very careful."

"He'll do it," Cora said, "but those are two stubborn women."

Tucker dropped a hand on Harry's shoulder and said with a grin, "I can't speak for Colleen, but I know where Sarah got her independent ways."

33

"I'm going to take Tucker's warning seriously," Cora said when Harry dropped her at her condo. "Promise me you will, too."

"Of course. I called Sarah and Colleen, didn't I?" He was dissatisfied with himself for not having insisted they come home.

"Yes," Cora said, pulling her bag out of the Rover, "and you're a grump because Sarah told you not to call again and that they were capable of looking after themselves."

"Colleen's putting too much faith in that popgun she's carrying *and* in her ability to use it."

Harry took her bag from her and walked her to the entrance.

She kissed him and said, "Remember, if you're an adult, and Sarah is, you get to decide what you're going to do with your life. Fathers like you, new at the job, may find it disconcerting."

"I'll try to keep that in mind," Harry responded.

Harry drove home, struggling with his growing uneasiness over Sarah and Colleen. Tucker had said he was sure that River Watch was planning some kind of attack, and when the old man said he was sure about something, he was rarely wrong. Once back on the Hammock, Harry tried to work on a report that was due on an insurance surveillance, but he couldn't stop thinking about Sarah out on that river, unprotected and in the company of a person River Watch might be trying to kill. Furthermore, he was still in the employ of the Alliance and supposed to be protecting Colleen.

"Damn!" he said and jumped up so fast he knocked over his chair.

Breaking the *fatwa* Sarah had issued against his calling her for any reason short of an emergency because she didn't want to be treated like a child, Harry dialed Sarah's number.

After half a dozen rings, during which Harry forgot to breathe, Sarah answered.

"Harry," she said without preliminaries, "I thought we agreed . . ."

"Stop!" he said. "This is an emergency. Where are you?"

"We're about a mile down the river from the cabin, taking fish and water samples. What's wrong, is someone . . ."

"No. Listen to me. I want you and Colleen to stop what you're doing and go back to the cabin."

She started to protest, but he cut her off. "Start back right now. I'm on my way and should reach the cabin in about an hour. Until I get there, don't let anyone in the house."

Harry waited while Sarah told Colleen what he had said.

"Okay," Sarah told him, "but you better have a good reason for this."

"I do. Now get going."

There was a moment's pause, and then she asked in a slightly tremulous voice, "How scared should we be?"

"Not at all, but get back to the cabin as fast as you can. And lock the doors."

Then he called Jim Snyder.

"Colleen and I argued about her going up there, but I lost. I'm glad you're checking on them. Give me a call when you've seen them. I'll be here the rest of the day."

Harry walked the last fifty yards to the cabin along a shaded, grassy track, cut through a thick stand of willows. The drive had increased his concern, and he wanted to race to the cabin, but he controlled his anxiety and went forward slowly, determined to see before being seen, if there was anyone watching. When he finally caught a glimpse of the river, he stepped off the road and approached the cabin through the trees.

In front of him was a grassy stretch of open ground running down to the river. He saw with relief that Colleen's boat was pulled onto the bank. To his right, shaded by two tall sycamores, stood the brown-shingled cabin, perched on five foot flood posts cut from telephone poles.

Colleen's SUV was parked under the carport, and aside from the willows' trailing branches stirring in the light wind and a quail family crossing the clearing between the cabin and the river, all was still. Even the crickets were silent. Keeping back in the trees, Harry walked around the cabin, down to the water, and all the way around the clearing in the reverse direction without finding any tracks or other indications that anyone but Sarah and Colleen had been near the cabin for weeks. Relieved, he returned to the road and called Sarah.

"So, although I still don't have any definite proof that you're being targeted," he said to Colleen, finishing his explanation of why he was there, "I think you may be in significant danger."

The three were seated around the table. Sarah was pouring coffee, and she and Colleen had already let him know they were not pleased to have their work interrupted.

"But it's nice to know you're taking your job of looking after me seriously," Colleen said, adding a wintry smile to faint praise.

"If I'd been doing that properly, you wouldn't be out here," he said. "I want you to gather your things and go home."

"Aside from a couple of fishermen and a few boats crossing to the east coast, we haven't seen anyone since we got here," Sarah protested. "And you said yourself we haven't had any prowlers."

"And you haven't told anyone you're here?" Harry asked Colleen.

"Aside from Jim, no." She hesitated. "Well, I might have mentioned it to Bob Walker. He called just before I left, demanding, for the umpteenth time, I send him any river reports Joyce Fields had given me. When I refused, he got nasty. I hung up."

Harry thought about Walker and concluded he posed no threat. It was unlikely he was connected with River Watch.

Colleen broke into his reflections. "Let's compromise. We've got about two hours of work left to do. You come along and help us get it done—it's mostly bottling samples and recording time and place of taking them. We could finish the work, clean up the cabin, and be out of here before the sun sets."

Harry subtracted the time needed to clean the cabin, trailer the boat, and pack the SUV, and saw that he was giving them at most two extra hours. He thought it a reasonable risk.

"Done," he said.

The place Colleen had chosen to complete her survey was a fifty-yard stretch of water less than a mile downstream from the cabin side of the river. She cut the motor ten or fifteen feet from the shore in about six feet of water and told Sarah, who was in the bow, to drop the anchor.

"This looks good," she said when the anchor caught. The bow swung into the current. "Put in the bait traps," she told Harry. "Sarah, get out the nets."

While Harry dealt with the traps, Colleen opened a large, blue plastic box with a hinged lid and a zippered plastic sleeve filled with small nets with long handles.

She passed Harry two of the nets and then handed him four half pint jars with screw top lids.

"Two for me, two for Sarah," he said, beginning to enjoy himself.

"A quick study," Sarah remarked, her spirits revived.

"We'll gather specimens and water samples," Colleen told Harry. "Sarah knows the drill. I'll make a record of the water temperature and the ambient temperature, the time at each sample site—I figure we can make five stops—the fish and so on that we catch, repeating the same procedures at each stop."

She then began telling Harry what to do with the net and the bottles while making entries in a black waterproof notebook she took from the open box. Harry listened to what she was telling him and at the same time checked out the bank and the surrounding river.

The bank was only a couple of feet high and smothered with willows. Harry decided it was part of the flood plain on which the cabin had been built. When the summer rains came, the river would pour over its banks, and the cabin on its pilings would be an island and a mosquito paradise. But at the moment the river, free of boat traffic, was flowing quietly under the late afternoon sun and mercifully free from the winged affliction.

In five stops, the three, working steadily and well together, filled the remaining bottles with algae, small fish taken in the traps, tiny crabs, and water samples. Colleen recorded the final specimens, put away the bottles, and told Harry to rinse the traps and stow them.

"Aye, aye, Captain," he responded cheerfully.

The two hours had flown, and despite his continuing sense that danger was hovering somewhere near them, he had enjoyed the work. Watching Sarah weighing and measuring the tiny fish he had taken out of the traps and calling out descriptions to Colleen had given him the kind of pleasure that a few months ago he had never expected to have.

"Pull the anchor," Colleen called to Sarah and started the engine. "Thanks, Harry," she added, checking to see that everything was put away. "With your help we did everything I'd hoped we would do."

She was advancing the throttle when the bullet struck her, knocking her off her seat. She hit the blue box, bounced off it, and crashed against the bottom of the boat. Sarah sprang to her feet, screaming Colleen's name.

Harry scrambled forward and pulled her down, covering her with his body as they fell. She continued to call out Colleen's name and struggled to free herself.

"Sarah," Harry said, holding her more tightly. "Stop it! Listen to me!"

He was looking down into her face. It was twisted with fear. Two bullets sizzled over the boat, followed by two reports that echoed hollowly over the water. Harry recognized the sound. It could only have come from a high-powered rifle. He also knew the sides of the boat were giving them no more protection than wet paper. Sarah's eyes focused on his.

"Colleen," she said. "We have to help her."

"We can't. She's dead."

It was brutal, but if they were going to make it out of this alive, she had to be able to think and act.

"Oh, God, Harry!" she cried. "Are you sure?"

"Yes," he said and did not add that half her head was blown away.

"What can we do?"

Colleen had increased the boat's speed very little before being killed, and Harry knew that unless he did something very soon, whoever was hunting them would kill them.

"Can you understand what I'm saying?"

"Yes," she said in a steady voice.

"We're going to get out of this. First, I'm going to get Colleen's gun. While I'm doing that, call this number." He gave it to her and repeated it. "Tell whoever answers who we are, where we are, and what's happening to us."

"Okay."

"Start now."

She was digging her phone out of a pocket as he pushed away from her. Another bullet zipped through the stern of the boat with a ping, followed by the whang of the rifle. Swearing, he slithered over the middle seat, trying not to think about the holes in the boat that told him they were being shot at from the river, and that meant from a boat that had to be bearing down on them at that moment.

He had two agonizing thoughts. Sarah would probably not live to have her child, and that if she died, it was his fault. Then, with a sudden, fierce anger filling the space where the fear had been, he said, "Not as long as I'm drawing breath."

34

Dragging himself across Colleen's body and soaking his shirt with her blood, Harry tugged her revolver from its belt holster, shoved it into a back pocket, and reached up and grasped the handle of the motor. He twisted the throttle and as the boat leaped forward, steered them toward the bank. An instant later a bullet slammed into the engine, killing it.

"I got Jim," Sarah whispered when Harry had crawled back to her.

"Did you tell him about Colleen?"

"I couldn't," she said.

"It's all right."

Nothing here was all right. The chances of Jim reaching them with help before this shoot-out was over was almost nil and a very bad outcome nearly certain, but, by God, he and Sarah were not going down without a fight.

The sound of the approaching boat was now loud in their ears, and Harry thought they might run out of time for what he had planned, but there was nothing to do but try to beat the odds.

"We're going into the water and under the willows," he told Sarah. "Wait until I say, 'Go.' I'll be right behind you."

At that moment the boat slid into the willows, their trailing green leaves dragging over them.

"Go," he said. "Roll over the side and stay as low as you can."

She went in a fusillade of bullets that banged through the boat and sprinkled them and the water with shredded green leaves. Harry followed, expecting to be riddled. He splashed into the water with short-lived relief, knowing what they had to do next was going to be far more dangerous.

The boat had dragged itself to a stop in the branches about five feet from the shore. But the river was chest deep where they were, and they were crouched with only their heads above the water. After a pause, the shooting began again.

"There's at least two of them," he said. "Get ready, I'm going to shove the boat downstream far as I can. Then we're going over the bank. That will be the bad part so go as fast as you can."

"Won't they shoot us?" Sarah asked as she helped him to push the boat.

"The branches will give us some cover."

"God, I hope so," she answered.

The boat slid past them, and she and Harry grasped the branches and dragged themselves toward the shore until the bottom was under their knees. The shooting had slackened, but with some regularity bullets still zipped over their heads or thwacked into the boat, which their push and the current had carried about twenty feet downstream where it had stalled in a tangle of leaves and twigs, its bow sticking out into the river.

"If one of them hits the fuel tank . . ." Harry said between grunts as he struggled to pull them out of the mud and up onto the bank. He did not get to finish the sentence.

There was a terrific bang, and the boat was engulfed in flames.

Harry pulled Sarah back into the water and plunged after her as burning bits and pieces of their gear exploded through the trees and fell hissing into the water. Fortunately for them, the trees over the boat had absorbed most of the blast. Coughing and gasping, Sarah got her head back into the air.

"I'd as soon be shot as drowned," she gasped.

"Up the bank," Harry said.

A few moments later, they were snaking on their bellies through the willow tangle and away from the river. He was just thinking they might safely get to their feet and make a run for it when they encountered water. They were marooned on a spit of dry land. Then he heard the boat roaring toward the shore.

Sarah was halfway to her feet. "Wait," he said, "we can't go in there. We'll be mired. Get down. We'll have to stay here."

Switching direction, they scrambled halfway back to the bank and threw themselves down, lying on their stomachs with their heads raised, peering back at the river. Through the branches they watched flickers of the big white inboard rushing toward them. Harry caught glimpses of a man dressed in camouflage clothing standing in the bow, holding a black assault rifle, his eyes fixed on the shore.

Harry pulled the .38 from his hip pocket, flicked open the cylinder to check that the barrel was clear, closed the gate, slipped off the safety, and passed the gun to Sarah.

"I don't know how to shoot," she said.

"Yes, you do," he told her. "You hold it like this. Here, with both hands. Point it the way you'd point your finger at something, and slowly squeeze the trigger. And keep your eyes open while you're doing it."

Harry looked at her with a swelling heart. She was soaking wet, stained with mud and had every right to be scared out of her wits, but she grasped the gun, settled her hips and elbows into the ground, and said, "I'm ready. When should I shoot?"

"If one of them climbs over that bank, shoot him."

"I'll try," she answered, and Harry prayed it wouldn't happen. But not all prayers are answered.

Whoever was at the wheel advanced the throttle, and the boat lurched ahead. The man standing in the bow dropped into a crouch with only his hat and his eyes visible over the gunwale. The engine was now a roar.

"They're going to come right onto the shore," Harry shouted. "Don't worry. We'll be okay."

He would have liked to believe it. The boat plunged into the willows. The bow crunched against the bank, slid up it a few feet, and stopped. The motor died.

The man squatting in the bow leaped up, shouting, and raked the trees in front of him with a burst of automatic fire that passed about three feet over Harry and Sarah's head. Bits of leaves and twigs rained down on them.

"Go!" a second man shouted, and the shooter dropped a hand onto the gunwale and vaulted to the ground.

For the first time, Harry had a clear look at him. It was Derwood Jones. Jones landed in a crouch, looking for his targets. Harry shot him. He fell forward onto his rifle. At the same moment the second man sprang out of the boat from the other side, crashed through the trees to his left, turned, and opened fire with a second assault rifle.

Sarah screamed. Harry turned and saw a red stain spreading across her right shoulder. Scrambling to his knees, he fired three times into the tangle of leaves and branches from which the man had fired.

He heard a groan, more breaking branches, and then nothing. Harry waited another moment, moving his CZ between the fallen Jones and the place where he had last seen the second man.

No sound. No movement.

He had to go after the second shooter. There was no choice. If he crept back . . . But first he had to see how badly Sarah was hurt. Slipping the CZ into its holster, Harry dropped down beside her.

She was still stretched flat on the ground, still gripping her revolver, but she had dropped her face onto her right arm, and her eyes were squeezed shut.

"Sarah," he said, leaning over her.

"I'm okay," she said between clenched teeth. "It hurts."

"I'm going to pull your shirt away from the wound."

The slug, probably deflected by a branch, had creased her shoulder and ripped its way down her back before plowing into the ground somewhere beyond where she was lying. Working quickly, Harry pulled the torn cloth away from the wound, causing Sarah to gasp.

"It's done. It's a flesh wound, and it's bleeding freely, which, believe it or not, is good."

"Harry," she said in a croak, "get on with it."

"I've got to . . ."

"I know. Go. I'll watch this one. Go."

"Just a minute." He stripped off his shirt and ripped it into strips from which he rigged a very rudimentary bandage. "I'll put these pads on the wound. They'll slow the bleeding. When I get back, I'll do a better job."

"Go," she said, "before he comes back."

"Watch this one," Harry said.

"I know. Go."

He picked up Jones' rifle and followed the second man's boot tracks in the soft earth to the spot where he had stopped to fire on them. Something glinted in the mud and leaves beside the tracks. Harry dropped onto his heels. Empty shell casings. He picked up one and found wet blood on it.

Looking carefully he saw more blood spattered on the fallen leaves. He pushed up and went on following the tracks, which were now closer together and erratic, as if the man who had made them was drunk. The trees were very dense here and the ground wet. Harry dropped onto his heels again to peer under the drooping branches. Less than ten feet in front of him he saw the crumpled body of Rafe Hubble.

Harry stood and moving slowing, holding the rifle in front of him, pushed through the leaves to the fallen man. He put a finger on Hubble's neck. There was no pulse. He rolled him over. The eyes stared sightlessly at Harry. Hubble had been hit twice, one of the slugs, Harry guessed, had ripped through his neck, slicing an artery. Hubble had staggered a dozen steps and died.

"Of all the stupid . . ." he said angrily and stopped himself. There was no point. Rafe was dead, and the damage was done.

With a sigh, Harry went back to Sarah, taking the precaution of calling to her as soon as he had turned away from the dead man.

"Is he dead?" she asked.

"Yes. Get up if you can, and I'll wrap these strips of cloth around you to hold the pads in place. The bleeding has slowed down a lot."

She struggled onto her knees and, gasping, lifted her arms.

"God, that hurts," she said through gritted teeth as Harry wound the strips around her chest to hold the pads on her wound in place.

"You can put the gun down if you want to."

"No," she replied stubbornly and had no sooner said it than she shouted, "Harry!"

He had been bent down behind her, tying off the strips. Looking up he saw Jones, on one knee, half his face black with blood, supporting himself on his right hand, pulling a revolver from inside his shirt. Harry grabbed for his CZ, knowing he was too late. Then Sarah fired the .38.

The barrel of Jones' gun wavered and sagged away from his target. Jones yelled and struggled to pull up the weapon. Harry shot him again. Jones slowly fell forward, groaning as he collapsed, onto his left shoulder.

"He had another gun," Sarah said quietly.

"Yes," Harry answered.

"Is he dead?"

Harry walked over to Jones, lifted the gun out of his limp hand, and turned him onto his back. His eyes flicked open. Harry jumped back. Even badly wounded Jones was dangerous—that incredible physical strength. "He's alive."

"Then I didn't kill him."

"No, but you saved our lives," Harry answered, still watching Jones.

She got to her feet very slowly, wincing with pain.

"Rafe," Jones said in a hoarse whisper, blood trickling from his mouth, "I'm hurt bad."

Harry studied him, and for the second time, in spite of what the man had tried to do to them, felt a rush of pity—the assault rifle, the camouflage clothing, the polished black boots, the dream of control—it was pathetic and such a waste.

"I'm not Rafe," Harry said quietly. "But if you lie quiet, Derwood, I'll do what I can to keep you alive. Can you hear me?"

"Brock?" the man asked in a weak voice, his eyes half shut again.

"That's right. If you try to get up, I'm going to kill you. Do you understand?"

"I can hear you, but I can't see you."

"Just lie still."

He lifted his right arm off the ground a few inches and let it fall. "That's easy," he said, tried to laugh, and lost consciousness.

"Will he live?" Sarah asked.

"He might."

She was still gripping the revolver, her face white and stiff with pain.

"Come on, soldier," Harry said, gently taking the gun out of her hands. "It's time to go home."

But before Harry could lift her into Hubble's boat, the Marine Patrol found them. Jim Snyder was with them.

"Are you all right?" he shouted when he leaped out of the boat and saw Sarah and Harry through the screen of branches.

"Yes," Harry said, moving toward the boat as half a dozen heavily armed men poured onto the bank around him.

"Where are the shooters?"

"Both down," Harry answered, dreading the next question.

"Colleen?" he asked.

Harry shook his head.

"Jim, I'm so sorry," Sarah said, trying to reach him and failing.

"Where is she?" he asked, his face set like stone.

"In her boat. The fuel tank exploded."

"Oh, Lord in Heaven," Jim whispered.

"She was dead before it happened," Harry said.

"Shot?"

"Yes. There was no pain."

Jim nodded, and seemed to gather himself and looked at Jones lying in the dirt. "Is he alive?"

"Just."

"There's another one?"

"Yes, Rafe Hubble. He's dead."

He nodded and looked at Sarah. "How bad is it?" he asked her.

"I'm all right," she told him. "Jim, I don't know what . . ."

"No," Jim said, "there's nothing to say. She's gone. I believe I'll try to find her."

His men found her for him.

35

Derwood Jones lived. Sarah spent three days in the hospital, one to deal with her wound and two more submitting to the pediatrician Esther Benson's evaluation of her condition and listening to her graphic, expletive-laden description of pregnant women who jumped out of boats, engaged in gun fights, and allowed cretins like her father to bandage her wounds.

Harry knew Benson from the days when his wife Katherine had been in her care and had insisted that Sarah see her. The small, dark, and intense Benson did not disappoint him.

"You're all right, and I'm discharging you," she told Sarah when she was satisfied it was safe to turn her loose, "but your system's been seriously rattled. Your blood pressure is higher than I want it, and your heart is jumping around like a horny rabbit."

Sarah did not even smile. Benson pulled her covers over her.

"I want to see you again in a week," she said.

Sarah nodded. Still no smile or even eye contact.

Benson found Harry on a chair in the hall and sat down beside him. "Physically, she should be all right. She's very tired. And something's going on with her I can't reach. Maybe its Colleen McGraw's death. How close were they?"

"In recent weeks they'd become good friends. And there's the issue of her having shot Derwood Jones."

"She mentioned it, but I think she's come to terms with that."

"Did she say anything to you about terminating the pregnancy?"

"No, she didn't, and that's probably where the stress is coming from. Who's she talking to about it?"

"Me and possibly Colleen. She's mentioned it to Cora Wingate, but that's all as far as I know."

"Are you pushing her one way or the other?"

"I'm trying not to, but I've let her know I wish she'd have it."

"Why?"

Harry knew Benson wasn't simply being curious. "I'd like a grandchild, but mostly I think that if she terminates the pregnancy, she'll regret it."

"She's wearing a ring. Does the husband come into this?"

"Sarah's leaving him. He doesn't know she's pregnant."

"Oh, oh. She wants all the way out of the relationship."

"Probably."

Benson got up. "I want to see her next week. Are you all right?"

"I guess so."

"Termination decisions are tough, Harry," she said, dropping a hand on his shoulder, "and they're gray all the way. Take my advice and give her all the space she needs and don't let yourself get too involved. Mostly, she's going to need your support, not your advice."

Harry went back into Sarah's room and found her asleep. He told the duty nurse he would be back in a couple of hours and went to see Jim Snyder. He found Jim in his office, dealing with chain of evidence reports.

"I haven't had a chance to speak with you alone," Harry said, dropping onto a chair.

"I should have never let her go out there. I don't know what I was thinking," Jim said. He sat leaned over the desk, rubbing his forehead with his hand, his voice harsh with self-criticism.

"How could Jones have known she and Sarah were on the river?"

"Someone probably saw them going into the camp and called Jones. There's River Watch people all over that area."

"Yes," Jim said, sighing. "I suppose that was it."

"It wasn't your fault, Jim," Harry said. "You did all you could. I had a go at her and Sarah when they were at the house, but outside of locking them in the barn, there was no way of stopping them."

Jim sighed again and leaned back in the chair. His face was scored with pain and exhaustion. Harry guessed that he hadn't slept.

"I can't believe there wasn't something I could have done," he said, "and I want to go into the hospital and blow Jones' goddamned head off."

That shook Harry. He had never heard Jim swear.

"I believe you," he said quietly. "I had the chance to and wanted to, but I couldn't. If we're going to shoot anybody, I think it ought to be that snake Millard Hubble."

"If Harley Dillard does his job, we should be able to put him in a box," Jim said.

Frank Hodges came in and greeted Harry in what for Hodges was a subdued voice and eyed Jim with obvious concern.

"How's the whole case shaping up?" Harry asked, trying to ease Jim's mind.

"All right, but it's going to bang doors all over Tallahassee."

"Sheriff Fisher doesn't know whether to give us a raise or cut our budget," Hodges added, encouraging Harry with a wink.

Harry nodded. "What else is new?"

"Derwood Jones has finally done something smart," Hodges continued. "When he's awake, he's talking to the ADA about the River Watch and its connection to the Hubbles and the Southwest Florida Development Association."

"You've got a cheering section in Adelaide Slocum," Jim put

in, showing a little interest. "She's really grateful to you for convincing her to split on Millard. She's convinced you've kept her out of jail."

"Glad to hear it," Harry replied. "Has Millard Hubble been arrested?"

"Charged and bail denied," Jim replied.

"What are the charges?"

"Conspiring with Rafe Hubble to kill Joyce Fields and Colleen McGraw, felonious assault on you and Sarah, and the list goes on," Jim said with satisfaction. "Derwood has tied him and Hubble and the Southwest Florida Development Association to the Tinker Drew and the Joyce Fields shooting. He also says the Association discussed and approved the harassment of Colleen McGraw and Cora Wingate."

"How about the shootings?" Harry asked. "Can the members of the Association be linked to them? Is there evidence enough to indict any of them?"

"I think Dillard's got Millard Hubble nailed," Jim said. "How far he can go into the Association remains to be seen."

"What about the Bates' killings?"

Jim shoved out his feet and shook his head, scowling as he did it. "Jones is no use to us there. I suspect that it was a professional job. The only way we are going to be able to get a handle on it is if we can find something in Millard's financial records."

"Anything else?" Harry asked, thinking of Sarah in her hospital bed.

"Yes," Jim answered, brightening a little. "We've run a rake over the Fielding Crab and Bait Company and arrested Bronson Devereau and one or two others. Dillard thinks we're got enough to make a case against Devereau for aiding and abetting in the Joyce Fields murder."

"Good news. Anything in the Hook?"

"I'd like to bring in John Dee Rudd, who runs the Old

Beetle's Boat Dock, but the Captain won't let me," Hodges complained.

"What would the charges be?" Jim demanded impatiently.

"Well, he's got a fuel tank that's leaking and draining into the river," Hodges responded. "That would be a start. And if he didn't know what Jones and the rest of that River Watch bunch was up to, I'll never eat another donut."

Jim managed a bleak smile. "You're way past help, Sergeant," he said.

"I know that," Hodges said, going out the door.

"He's been fussing around me like a mother hen," Jim said when his sergeant was gone.

"Jim, what about coming out to stay with Sarah and me for a while?"

"Thanks," Jim answered, "but it wouldn't do any good. I feel as if I was in a room where everything's familiar but the air's all been sucked out of it. I can do a little work, and maybe that's helping, but I'd make poor company."

"You wouldn't have to do anything. You'd be welcome."

"I know, but I'm either going to be able to handle this, or . . ."

"All right," Harry said, "but the offer stands. Tucker sends his sympathy. So does Cora. We're there if we can help. All of us. If you feel that *or* coming any closer, promise you'll pick up the phone."

"I'll do that."

Once in the Rover, Harry called Cora. She was at the gallery. The renovation had started.

"How's Sarah?" she asked.

Harry gave her a report and said he had been talking to Jim Snyder and was now on his way to the hospital. They were interrupted by Holly.

After Cora answered Holly's question, she asked about Jim.

Then she said, "How about you? And don't say, 'Fine,' because I know better."

"I'm worried about Sarah. She's hardly speaking, doesn't smile. Won't tell me what's weighing on her. Esther Benson hasn't been able to get far with her."

"How much did you tell her about Sarah's problem?"

"All I knew."

"As soon as I've finished here, I'll come over. Will you be staying with her for a while?"

"Unless they throw me out."

"Wait for me."

He was surprised how relieved he was to hear that she was going to be with him, and thinking of Jim only reminded him of the times when like his friend he had faced a world, "With all the air sucked out of it."

Sarah was awake. She was sitting up, propped with pillows, to take as much weight off her wound as possible. She was staring gloomily at the wall when Harry entered the room.

"How's the back?" he asked, pulling a chair up to the bed.

"Sore, and don't try to cheer me up."

"Okay. Is there anyone you want to call?"

"Like David, Jennifer, or Clive? Hi, guys, guess what, I've been shot. Oh, yes, I'm pregnant, which isn't going to last, and, David, I'm leaving you. Bye."

"I'm glad you haven't lost your sense of humor."

"Where's the joke?"

"I want to say something because I'm going to bust if I don't. But I don't want it to add one way or another to what you're going to do. Will you hear me out?"

"Is it about the pregnancy?"

"Yes."

"I thought so. Go ahead."

"If you decide to have the child, you are welcome to live with me for as long as you want. If you don't, ditto. If you decide to go back to Milwaukee and have it, I'll give you as much financial help as I can either to stay home or work, and I'll go on loving you whatever you decide to do."

Her hair needed a wash. Her eyes were rimmed with red, her skin was the color of old putty, and Harry thought her jonnie had all the appeal of a shroud. He wanted very much to put his arms around her, but given the moment, her frame of mind, and the bullet crease down her back, it wasn't remotely feasible. He did pick up her right hand and hold it between both of his.

"I don't know where to begin," she said after a long silence.

"Start with what you're feeling," he said gently.

"Rotten," she said and managed a feeble laugh.

Harry squeezed her hand. "I believe it, but we are alive, which is close to a miracle."

"Colleen's not."

"No."

"And I don't know what to do about that. Or the fact that I shot a man. I actually pointed a gun at a man I didn't know and shot him."

She broke into tears, and Harry eased himself onto the side of the bed and managed to get his right arm part way around her. She leaned her face into his shoulder and wept. After a moment, she gasped, caught her breath and said, "I've got to stop. It hurts too much."

Harry eased her back into the pillows, and she lay for a moment with her eyes closed, tears running down her face, clenching her teeth.

"Do you want the nurse?" Harry asked.

"No," she said. "I'll be all right in a minute."

She began to relax and opened her eyes. "Thanks," she said a moment later, "I actually feel a little better. I haven't been able to cry 'til now. It's a relief. But think what poor Jim's going through."

"Yes, and when you're on your feet we'll try to do something about that. But right now remember that none of this is your fault, and there was nothing you could have done to prevent it. If you had stayed home, Colleen would have gone without you. And they would have killed her."

"I know, but somehow it doesn't help."

"You saved your life and mine, you know. If you hadn't shot him, Derwood would have killed both of us. And you didn't kill him."

He could have added, You're luckier than you know, but he didn't.

"I keep seeing that bloody face rising up in front of me."

"It will fade in time—if that's any consolation."

They were quiet for a moment. Harry thought how close Sarah and he had been to death and the look on Jim's face when he learned Colleen was dead. Despite what he'd told her, there were things you never forgot.

"Harry," she said quietly, "thanks for the support. I know you want me to go through with the pregnancy, and I guess I could." She paused and added her other hand to the pile. "But I can't promise I'll do it."

"That's all right," Harry said. "I mean it. It's all right."

The nurse came in and said to Sarah, "You don't look very good," and took her pulse. Then she glanced at her watch, and said to Harry, "Out." And to Sarah, "It's time you slept."

"I'm not sleepy," Sarah replied.

The nurse took a syringe out of her pocket and said, "You will be."

Harry met Cora just outside the door.

"How is she?" Cora asked.

"Exhausted, I think. The nurse is giving her an injection. I hope it works."

"And what about you?" Cora asked, putting an arm through his as they turned down the corridor.

"I've been better."

"Is it Sarah?" she asked.

"No, no. As far as I know, the wound is clean, and she's in no danger of miscarrying. It's her head that I'm worried about."

"Tell me."

They went off, leaning toward one another, Harry talking earnestly.

Sarah came home, and Cora moved in for a few days to look after her although Sarah protested, but Cora was as stubborn as she was. Elaine Porter and Arlen Gott called to see Sarah. Elaine had been filling in for Colleen until the Alliance Board could meet to choose a president.

"It's a done thing," Arlen insisted. "Elaine will make a great president."

Harry was astonished to see Elaine blush. Cora hugged her and said that Arlen was right. After the two had left, Sarah said, "Was I only one who saw something going on there?"

"I think you're right," Cora agreed.

"Who would have ever guessed?" Harry asked, to the merriment of the two women.

As the days passed, he called Jim as often as he could without becoming a nuisance. For Harry, it had become a waiting game—what would Sarah do? And Sarah's continued silence made guessing very difficult.

Then a morning came when she came down to breakfast and said, "I have a request."

"Let's hear it," Harry said.

"I'm going to take a walk. When I come back, I want us to go to Tucker's and have a family conference."

Cora's face fell. "I should be getting back to town. You won't want . . ."

"Please don't leave," Sarah responded quickly. "I want you with us, and I'm making you an honorary member of the Brock family, and if Harry doesn't make the appointment permanent, he's got sawdust for brains."

"It's the meds," Cora protested.

"Out of the mouths of babes," Harry replied, putting an arm around Cora.

"If it ain't broke . . ." Cora began, but Sarah interrupted her.

"I want to thank both of you for being so patient with me. It can't have been easy. I've been a major pill, but the time's come for me to talk with people I trust and care for."

Harry and Cora exchanged glances.

"Okay," Harry said.

36

"I must be getting psychic in my old age," Tucker said, carrying a double-layered chocolate cake buried in chocolate icing to the table. "I baked this yesterday, thinking it might come in handy."

Harry followed with the ancient brown teapot and mugs on a venerable maple tray. He poured the tea while Cora cut the cake.

"I'm just sitting here," Sarah complained.

"That's what guests of honor get to do," Tucker said complacently, passing around the pieces of the cake Cora was cutting. "There, I guess we're ready. Everybody got a fork?"

"Before we eat this cake and Sarah shares her concerns with us, I want to mention two who are not with us, Colleen and Jim. It is a terrible thing that happened to her, but she is beyond all harm now and it's Jim who's left to suffer."

They sat for a moment sharing the silence. Then Tucker looked around the table with a smile and said, "I want to say how glad I am to have you with me."

"Here, here," Cora said, dropping a hand on Harry's arm.

"I'm glad to be here," Sarah said quietly.

"So am I," Harry added, "and I have my daughter to thank that I am."

"And all's well, and so on," Tucker said quietly. "Now, Sarah, I think we're ready to listen to whatever you want to say."

Sarah put down her fork and took a moment to look at the others.

"Getting shot seems to have cleared my mind," she began, a bit tentatively. "I think I see what has to be done."

She stopped, apparently stuck. Harry reached across the table and grasped her hand. "Go ahead," he said. "It's all right."

"You don't know what I'm going to say," she replied in an unsteady voice.

"It doesn't matter, Sarah. We all love you. Go ahead."

He thought he knew what was coming, and it did matter, but he intended to put on a brave face and weather the news without making things any harder for her than they already were.

"I'm going back to Milwaukee, Harry," she said in a rush. Cora quietly took his hand in hers. "I think it's something I have to do," Sarah continued, letting her gaze move around the circle, "but I want to talk it over with you before I commit to it. If you think I'm making a mistake, please tell me now."

"First," Harry said, forcing himself to smile. "I'm going to miss you, but if you have to do this, you do."

"Why now?" Cora asked.

"Fair question. I'm a married woman. I've got a husband back there and a house I used to call home. I haven't talked to David for weeks. It's time I did."

"Are you planning a reconciliation?" Tucker asked.

The question was bland, but Harry knew Tucker well enough to hear the disapproval in it.

"No," she said decisively. "David and I are finished, but for his sake and mine, I've got to tell him that."

She hesitated.

"And Jennifer?" Harry said.

Sarah smiled. "That's right, Father. You nailed me."

Cora looked puzzled.

"It's really Jennifer who's kept me here. She had me spooked."

"What's changed?" Harry asked.

"Well, if I can get shot, stand up from that, face a man who's trying to kill me, and stop him, I guess I can face my mother."

Everybody stared at her. At that moment, Harry was very proud of her.

"At least I think I can," she added with a perfectly straight face.

Their laughter was scattered by a terrific outbreak of bawling and squealing outside, followed a moment later by Sanchez and Oh, Brother!, who pounded around the corner of the house and came to a sliding halt in front of the kitchen door. Every hair on Sanchez's back was standing on end and Oh, Brother!'s ears were wagging like semaphores.

Harry was out the door first. The dog and the mule were staring over their shoulders in the direction of a racket that sounded like someone banging metal trashcan covers together.

"I've got a bad feeling . . ." Tucker said, stepping off the stoop and trotting away toward the noise, followed by the others.

Harry sprinted ahead then suddenly spun around and ran into Oh, Brother!, who was rapidly overtaking him. The big mule braked, and Harry grabbed his mane to stay on his feet.

"Look out!" he shouted. "It's a bear."

"Just what I was afraid of," Tucker said and kept on at a walk.

Harry followed and so did the rest of the group, making a kind of ragged line with Sanchez at the end.

"Is it Althea?" Harry asked.

"The lady herself," Tucker said with a laugh.

The bear was standing on its hind legs trying to open the door of the cage where she had spent her recovery time. The door was held shut by a padlock, and the bear's patience had run out. Biting at the lock, growling and generally displaying her frustration, she was alternating the bites with right and left hooks to the door that made the cage bang and rattle like a garbage truck.

Oh, Brother! stopped and the two women moved in front of him, but when Cora started forward to get a better view, Oh, Brother! took the collar of her blouse in his teeth, and gently but firmly pulled her back. Sarah thought that was funny, but when she tried the same thing, she found Sanchez pressed against her knees, halting her advance.

"What's this?" she demanded.

"Male protectiveness," Harry said, looking back with a grin.

He and Tucker had stopped about twenty feet from the cage.

"At least they're paying attention to what we're doing, which is refreshing," Cora observed.

"Either I let her in or she wrecks a perfectly good dog run," Tucker said, digging in his pocket for a key as he strode toward the cage.

"Watch yourself. That's a bear pounding on the door," Harry called after him.

Althea greeted Tucker by dropping onto her front legs and shoving her nose into his stomach. Oh, Brother! snorted and took a quick step forward, but when the bear backed off to let Tucker unlock the door, he stopped. Tucker pulled open the run door, and Althea loped past him with a bawl of pleasure, snapped up her battered feeding dish, flopped onto her hind quarters, and dropped the dish onto her lap.

"It's obvious what she wants," Harry said, turning to Cora. "What's this about not paying attention?"

Cora was leaning against Oh, Brother!'s shoulder. She grinned. "Watch it. I've got protection."

"I'm going to help Tucker feed Althea," Sarah said, stepping over Sanchez.

Tucker went off with Sarah. Sanchez and Oh, Brother! trotted over to the cage and stood looking through the wire at the prodigal bear.

"I wonder if they really are talking?" Cora asked, coming to stand beside Harry.

"Maybe. Tucker says they are. I no longer know what I think."

"Harry," Cora said in an altered voice. "What's Sarah going to do about the pregnancy?"

"I was hoping to find that out today, but Althea's arrival has at least postponed the answer. What do you think she's going to do?"

"I can't tell. Her decision to go home may suggest she's decided to go through with it. If she doesn't say, will you ask her?"

"Should I?"

"I don't know. She's been discussing it with you. Perhaps you're entitled to ask."

"And perhaps not."

"Right."

"Thanks, I feel a lot better."

Tucker and Sarah appeared with a wheelbarrow piled with bags. Sarah was carrying a pail of water. Harry and Cora watched them enter the run and set out food and drink for the bear. When that was done, they came out. Tucker left the door open.

"How about the door?" Harry asked.

"She came a long way to reach us. I'm going to leave it to her whether or not she wants to stay," Tucker answered. "Let's go back to the house."

Harry did not find out that day, or the next, whether or not Sarah had decided to end the pregnancy. He was gradually resigning himself to a long wait, but the closer the time came to her leaving, the more difficult he was finding it to be resigned. He couldn't deceive himself; he wanted her to carry it to term. But he had decided that he had said all that he was entitled to say on the subject. But it hurt.

Jim Snyder, thinner than ever, his face pale and lined, stopped by to tell him that Derwood had given up the men in Birdland who had been involved, along with Tinker Drew, in Joyce Fields' death. Once they were in custody they corroborated Derwood's charges that through the Hubbles the SFDA had been funneling money to River Watch.

"That outfit's beginning to look like the family that keeps a vicious dog," Jim said. "The family never does any wrong, but its dog is chewing up the neighbors. Well, we're going to put the stick in, and the State Attorney's Office is going to help us do it."

"What about Adelaide Slocum?" Harry asked.

"So far, she looks clean, but we're still digging through the books."

"I'd like to say I'm satisfied," Harry said, "but the Bates' killings are a bone in my throat."

"We're not giving up. When's Sarah leaving?"

"Tomorrow."

"You okay with that?"

"Half a loaf," Harry answered. "Now tell me how you are."

"It varies. The worst of the pain comes in waves. Talking with you helps, and, if you can believe it, Frank Hodges has been a real comfort. But I won't lie to you, Harry, the days are long and the nights are longer. I miss her."

"Of course you do. You love her, and she loved you."

He put out his hand, and Jim took it.

Harry and Cora drove Sarah to the airport.

"Wish me luck, you two," Sarah said when they reached the gate entrance.

"Freely given along with our love," Cora responded, embracing her warmly.

When she released Sarah, Cora stepped away to give father and daughter some private space.

"You're doing the right thing," Harry said, taking her into his arms, "but I'm going to miss you. And remember, you can come back any time and for as long as you want."

"Thanks, Harry, thank you for everything. I'll write—no, probably I won't, but I'll call."

"That will do it," Harry replied, slowly, reluctantly releasing her.

"I'm not keeping any secrets, Harry, about this pregnancy," she said quietly. "I just haven't made up my mind. I think I'll know more after talking with David."

"And Jennifer," he said.

She shook her head. "No. I'll tell her when I've made up my mind and after I've told you."

"She's not going to like that."

"Probably not, but that's how it's going to be."

"It's your decision," Harry said with conviction, "nobody else's."

"I think I understand now what that means," she replied. "Goodbye, Harry, I miss you already."

With that, she kissed him, waved to Cora, and went through the gate and did not look back. Cora came and took his arm.

"Are you all right?"

"I will be. She's going to talk with David before deciding whether or not to end the pregnancy."

"It doesn't surprise me," she said, paused a moment and asked, "If she decides to terminate it, how hard will it be for you?"

"I think I've finally got it through my head that what she decides to do is the right thing for her to do, and I'm going to be fine with it."

Sarah was no longer in sight.

"Good for you," Cora said, squeezing his arm. Then she turned them toward the exit and added cheerfully, "We're having lunch at my place."

ABOUT THE AUTHOR

Kinley Roby lives in Keswick, Virginia, with his wife, novelist and editor Mary Linn Roby.